THERE IS A SEASON

Richard Corley Massey

© 2015 Richard Corley Massey
All rights reserved.

ISBN: 1515122077
ISBN 13: 9781515122074

TABLE OF CONTENTS

The Importance of Being Earnestine	1 - 8
Voices	9 - 21
An Historical and Fictional Preface to "Gabe"	23 - 24
Gabe	25 - 203
Providence	205 - 226
You Are the Man—2 Samuel 12:7	227 - 243

THE IMPORTANCE OF BEING EARNESTINE

It was Sunday afternoon, and I'd been helping Grandma finish up the dishes after she'd fed the whole family dinner. She was in her seventies then, and fixing a big meal like that was getting to be hard on her; but she seemed to love it, and we did too. Grandma and Momma and I had finished up the dishes, and they had sat down with Daddy and my two lumpy brothers to watch the football game. My brother Gordon Jr., or "Bubba," had started playing football that year, so he and Daddy kept up a running commentary on the game, about which neither one of them knew pee turkey. I had to get out of the house.

    I walked out on the front porch, hoping to find Uncle Earnest, and sure enough, there he was, sitting in that odd little chair, leaning back against the wall, and smoking one of his lopsided cigarettes. The chair had been made by my great-granddaddy when they had lived on the farm, and it looked old. I don't know whether it had ever been varnished or anything, but the wood was dark from being handled by so many hands for so long. The legs had gotten rickety, and somebody had doubled wires around each one and had tightened them by twisting a stick between them. The seat was made of a stiff piece of cowhide with the hair left on it, and it looked like it ought to have been still covering somebody's Jersey cow. But it was Earnest's favorite chair.

His cigarette was lopsided because he'd rolled it himself. It looked just like a joint my boyfriend, Bo, might have made, except that it was a little fatter in the middle, and it didn't smell like grass. It had a sweetish tobacco smell because Uncle Earnest had used Prince Albert, a can of which was in his shirt pocket. I think he would have preferred to have had ready-mades, but his job at the building supply didn't pay that much, and he was trying to help Grandma with the household expenses. Then too, he might have enjoyed rolling his own for the same reason he liked that ancient chair.

There's a story in his living with his mother, but I won't linger on it too long, because I think he'd want to keep it mostly private. Suffice it to say that after a life of living pretty high, Uncle Earnest had fallen on hard times.

"Hey, babe," he said. "Y'all finish all the women's work?"

"It coulda been men's work too if you and Daddy and those other drones had wanted to help."

"Now, honey, don't get all women's libber on me. You know your daddy had football to watch." He turned his head and grinned that wicked, handsome little grin of his.

"I declare," I thought. "If I could find a boy as handsome as my uncle Earnest, I'd marry him in a minute!"

Then he went on. "And you can see I'm terrible busy myself. Hard to keep up with all I got to do."

I sat down in the other chair, stretched my legs out in front of me, and punched his shoulder with my fist. "I can see that, Unc. I wouldn't disturb you for the world."

"That's my girl!" he said, catching my fist in his big hand. "You don't wanna start nothing you can't finish here."

He held my hand for a minute before dropping it, and we both looked out across Grandma's lawn at nothing in particular. Then he said in that softer voice he saved for our conversations, "So, you looking forward to getting back to that cit-a-del of higher education?"

"Yeah. Yeah, I am, Unc. Seems odd to say I missed school, but I really did. I get to take electives this fall for the first time—courses I choose myself. That's gonna be fun."

"Now *that's* what sounds odd," he said. "Calling schoolwork 'fun.' I can see wanting to get back to the parties, but to the schoolwork? I don't know, sis. That must mean you was intended to go to school, like I *wasn't* intended to."

"Grandma says you were the smartest one of her children," I said. "I think you could have gone to any school you wanted."

"Well," he drawled, making his voice sound more country than it really was. "If it was any school I *wanted*, it woulda been no school at all. Never did quite catch the point of it."

I started to say, "The point of it is you coulda *owned* that freaking building supply instead of driving a forklift around in the warehouse!" but I caught myself. There was no reason to hurt his feelings, and besides, it wasn't entirely fair. Daddy said that in Uncle Earnest's prime as a salesman, he had made big money for a lot of years. But, in Daddy's words, "Earnest had Teflon hands—money just never stuck."

So what I said was, "School is just something I *do*, Unc. The same way Bubba plays ball or Bo can take a car apart. 'Snothing to brag about."

He grinned again. The sight of his chipped tooth in that beautiful smile tugged at my heart. He said, "I never heard you bragging. You're just saying we're different. Probably why we're such good friends."

I took a deep breath. "So, friend," I said. "I need some friendly advice."

"It'll cost you."

"I'll pay you whatever it's worth."

"Hell, sis, I'll never get rich that way!"

"Unc, you'll never get rich *any*way, so put it on my tab."

He fished for his tobacco can and papers, and with a paper held between two fingers, he began to tap the can softly to spill tobacco into it. "So?" he said.

"So I'm catching a lot of flak from Bo about going back to school this fall. It feels bad. It feels really, *really* awkward."

"And?"

"And I don't know what to do. Uncle Earnest, Bo's been my boyfriend since tenth grade. We've been through a lot together, and he's stuck by me all the way. I wasn't exactly miss popularity in tenth grade, you know."

"You saying you *owe* him?" The slight rise in his inflection was as much expression as he ever showed.

"Well, yes, I guess that's what I *am* saying. He's given me four years of his life. Sort of."

"Seems to me you all have given them four years to each other. Bo's an OK kid, but you haven't gotten anything from him you didn't give back in spades. He's damn lucky *you* stuck with *him*."

He held the cigarette between a stained thumb and forefinger and scratched the back of his neck as if he was thinking. Then he set the chair down on all four legs and half turned to me.

"Sis, I'll be honest with you. In my opinion, you're gonna be a helluva woman when you get your growth. There's gonna be better men than Bo Wilkens standing in line at your door; and some of those men are gonna know how to play a woman in ways you ain't even *imagined* yet. They're gonna do mind games on you that'll turn you inside out if you don't watch it. And the object of all those mind games will be to get what they want."

"But, Unc!" I protested, "Bo is just a sweet old small-town boy."

"I know that. I'm not trying to scare you off of Bo. I'm just telling you that men naturally want to get their own way, and they don't even know they're doing it. We could set here all day and argue with Bo about how school is good for you and how you'll have a better life and earn more money and this and that. And if we do, when we're through, you might as well have farted in the wind. A man wants what he wants—or *thinks* he does—and he'll tell you anything in the world to get it."

"What do you mean, 'or thinks he does'?"

"Well, sis, that's the odd thing. I've known men—and I'm talking about myself too—who'd tell you they were crazy in love, and if this woman or that one would just love 'em back, they'd be happy forever. Two weeks later, the *same* guy'd be saying to me, 'Earnie, what'll I do? This woman is all over me! How can I get away?'"

"I've read about that," I said. "Men are just afraid to commit."

"Yeah, I've heard that too," he said. "And there's probably something to it. Lord knows I ain't never *committed*. But it's a little deeper than that…I think."

He stopped, knitted his brows, and took a last drag on his cigarette. Then he stuck out his tongue and carefully picked a flake of loose tobacco from it. He tried to flip the tobacco off of his finger, and when that failed, he rubbed it on his pants leg. I waited.

"This is gonna sound strange," he said. "But it's the best I can figure it out. I think men are more romantic than women. What's going on with Bo right now is he's got this picture of a little love nest in his mind. By now he's had time to realize what a prize catch you are, and he's afraid he'll never get to have all that moon-June stuff with you. So he's getting desperate to tie you down before you fly away. But you see what'll happen, don't cha? As soon as you're tied down, so is *he*. And *then* he'll see them ties for the first time."

"And then," I added, "he'll want the moon-June stuff with somebody else! Right?"

"The new girl at the 7-Eleven or his sister-in-law, most likely," said Uncle Earnest. He turned his chair straight again and leaned it back against the wall. We looked across Grandma's lawn at nothing in particular.

Finally I said, "You're right about my flying away. I haven't said anything to Bo, but I think he knows. There's a whole campus full of guys at Newton College, and all I've done with them is a little lightweight flirting. One of my suitemates has already had an affair...with a professor, for Pete's sake."

"*You* don't wanna do that," Uncle Earnest said in his flat voice. "I'd hafta kill him, and it'd create a stir."

"Unc, I'm inexperienced, but I ain't *that* dumb! That girl is so screwed up she can barely stand upright."

"But you see what I mean. That professor—that meal-mouthed son of a bitch—

probably persuaded himself that he absolutely *had* to have that girl, or he'd die. He even persuaded himself he was doing her a favor by saving her from all them uncouth college boys. It's something male hormones do to the brain."

"So you're telling me I can never trust a man—never have a really, truly good, honest relationship."

"No, that's what you've just been telling me," he said.

He let me think about that for a few minutes, and then he said, "Sis, didja get all the advice you need?"

"Got about all I can stand," I told him. "Uncle Earnest, if you aren't married in three years when I graduate, you want to get married to me?"

He stood up and stretched, grunting with the pleasure of it; then he walked over to the end of the porch to spit. "I'll give it some thought," he said. "But we'd probably have to hog-tie your parents. And then you'd go and have some baby with an ear right *here* or something." He then pressed his thumb in the middle of my forehead. "Seems like an awful lot of trouble."

"Humph!" I said. "You just don't know a good thing when you see it. You haven't got the sense God gave a billy goat."

He picked up the flyswatter from the window's ledge and made as if to hit me. "I know a good thing. Always have. I just ain't willing to pay the price to get it. And you need to learn some respect for your elders, snooty little college girl."

I rolled out of my chair and grabbed for the handle of the screen door. Uncle Earnest tried to hold the door shut, but I slipped through and ran into the living room, the flyswatter swishing behind my butt. I ran behind Grandma's chair, causing her to open her eyes, squeal, and hold up both hands. Uncle Earnest tried to swat me around his mother, first on one side of her and then the other.

"Earnest!" Grandma screamed. "Earnest, *will* you grow up?"

"No, ma'am," he answered. "Don't believe I will."

As it turned out, Uncle Earnest never had the chance to see me graduate. During the second semester of my junior year, he was killed when a train hit his car. The car was the same Olds 98 he had driven home to Grandma's when his last sales job had given out. Probably its age and size had made it get stuck on the tracks. Or then again, maybe it was the fact that his blood alcohol level was about 0.20 at the time.

I thought long and hard about coming home for the funeral, but I finally decided I didn't want to. It was probably the first time in twenty years that Uncle Earnest's body was inside a church, and I wasn't sure I could stand the sadness or the comedy of hearing the preacher trying to dodge the obvious. I think I was a little worried too that I might make a fool of myself.

Not having been there, I'll have to depend on Momma's account of "the scene," which is what it's still called in our family. It was an open-casket funeral, and as folks walked into the church, they would go by the casket and remark on the undertaker's handiwork. This woman nobody in the family knew came in "gussied up like a two-dollar streetwalker" (Momma's words) and commenced to cry and wail and carry on over the body, "doing everything but dragging poor Earnest out and hugging him." That was embarrassing enough, and one of the funeral-home employees had barely moved her along to the back of the church when a second woman "not much better than the first one" came in and more or less repeated the scene. Whereupon the first woman ran down the aisle and said, "What the hell are you carrying on about, you stupid heifer? It's *me* he promised to marry."

So far as we know, Uncle Earnest's funeral was the first one ever held in the Methodist church that involved sheriff's deputies and arrests for disturbing the peace.

I'd always planned to change my name from "Earnestine" to "Tina" as soon as I graduated college and moved away. But since Unc died, I've decided to stay who I am.

VOICES

In the end I agreed to lie about it. The three of us made up a story while we were sitting right there in the wardroom of the aircraft carrier.

February 13, 1945. Spotted furthest aft, I'm the last one to launch. I clear the carrier deck, feel the landing gear bump into their wells under the wings, and climb to join up with my wingman, Shark Caldwell. The ship's air controller says, "Flapjack flight, take angels five, vector zero-nine-zero."

Our squadron skipper, Commander Charlie McDowell, answers "roger," and I can see him looking around to be sure the other three of us are in formation. A minute or so later, Charlie calls in again to say, "Paleface, this is Flapjack leader, steady on zero-nine-zero, passing through angels four."

The ship says, "Roger, Flapjack. Your bogey's bearing one-two-zero at eighty miles. Heading three-zero-zero, speed two hundred. Altitude about angels three."

The skipper "rogers" and adds, "We'll let you know when we have 'em in sight. Flapjack out."

Then to us he says, "Flapjack flight, clear your guns and stand by. We'll be on 'em in a couple minutes."

In each of our four aircraft, the pilot flips the arming switch and fires a short burst from his machine guns to be sure everything is in working order.

> "Skipper, you're telling me I've got to lie?"
> "We're not saying anything about what you've got to do, Swede. We're just telling you what we know."
> The air operations officer added, "You're a competent pilot, Lieutenant. We don't want to lose you."

It's a clear day with light winds. Nothing to distract us from what we have to do. You can tell from the whitecaps that there are no waves to speak of—but there's no cloud cover either. Unless we come right out of the sun, the Japs will see us as soon as we see them.

At five thousand feet, the wind whistling in the canopy is cool on my sweaty skin. There's a thick metallic taste in the back of my throat, and I shiver a little. Then I repeat the skipper's pep talk and touch the arming switch again.

"Remember," he shouted to us as we all trotted toward the flight deck. "*They'll* be carrying ordinance—maybe even drop tanks—and they won't be as maneuverable as you. *Their* job is to get to the fleet. They'll try to avoid us if they can. So let's jump the little bastards quick and flame their asses before they know what hit 'em."

About five minutes after we reach altitude, I see Charlie's wingman, Mel, gesturing to us and pointing down. But Shark and I have already seen them. Below us there are six toy airplanes with red circles on their wings, skimming over the wind lines on the water.

> "But you're saying I'm a nut case. That I hear voices, right?"
> "Swede, it's out of our hands. If the flight surgeon decides you can't fly, you'll be grounded. You'll get a free trip home."

There is a Season

The skipper waggles his wings and peels off, making a steep bank to his right to swoop down toward the Zeros. We follow him down, first Mel, then me, and then Shark.

If there is any part of that day I actually *do* forget, it may be part of the next five minutes. In a combat situation I do a lot of things at once and make decisions in the smallest fraction of a second. We all know going in that if we're not focused, we're even more likely to die. So it's possible for me to forget details of some of the stuff I actually see. I do see the Japs splitting up when the skipper and Mel hit their formation. Shark and I concentrate on the bunch of four that are still together, and on our first pass, I nail one of 'em. I know I've hit him because I actually see the bullets punching across one wing and the engine cowling. And at that point I make a damn foolish decision.

Listen, Swede. People in bad trouble sometimes…you know, imagine things. You probably banged your head. Maybe harder than you realized.

I yell into the radio, "Shark! This is Swede. Did you see that? I got the son of a bitch! Keep an eye on me. I'm gonna splash him."

There is no reply, which means that Shark is either otherwise engaged or in some kind of trouble himself. A smart pilot—a pilot flying by the book—breaks off the chase right there, no questions asked. A smart pilot looks around for his wingman. But I cannot make myself do it. I'm so afraid the Jap will get away that I just cannot bear to take my eyes off him.

The Zero banks and tries to climb away from me. A good move. Normally his aircraft would outclimb mine every time. But this time there's a thin trail of smoke coming from his engine, and he is *not* pulling away.

"Gotcha!" I say, easing the nose up to bring my guns to bear.

My finger is just tightening on the trigger, and at first I figure the noise is coming from my own guns. Then I realize that the terrific banging sound is coming from somewhere *behind* me, and at the same time, my own aircraft begins to come apart. The stick almost tears itself out of my hand, and I feel the plane yawing to the left, slipping sideways. As I jerk my head around to see what's going on, another Zero roars by on my right side and closes into formation with his wounded buddy. If he hadn't already shot away half my tail assembly, I would probably dead at this point. As it is, my slide has spoiled his aim, and only a couple of slugs from his second burst find the side of my fuselage. One bullet tears up through the instrument panel and punches a hole in the Plexiglas canopy twelve inches from my face.

That's what I mean about fractions of seconds. Half a second earlier, I was about to score a kill. Now *I'm* the one about to die. If the Jap comes back, he'll finish me in one pass.

"Shark!" I yell. "Anybody! I'm hit! Get this guy off me!"

"But hell, Skipper, he was at three thousand feet. If you could hear me, I know you could hear him!"
"Hmmm," the ops officer said. "We should have been able to..."

Maybe one of them does chase the Zero away, or maybe he just decides to stay with his shot-up friend. It doesn't matter one way or the other to me. For the next two minutes, I'm fighting to stay airborne. I can still hear the banging sound, which means that some part of my tail assembly is hanging by the skin. The stick is still vibrating like crazy, and for a while it looks like I have no rudder control at all.

The good news is that the engine is running, and it sounds OK. No loose oil flying around and no smoke. If I can make the control surfaces work at all, I *might* be able to keep it flying.

The noise and vibration are so bad that it feels like the plane is literally going to shake itself to pieces if I make the slightest move. But that left-hand skid is scaring the hell out of me, so I *have* to do something. As gently as possible, I bank right, pushing hard on the right rudder pedal to begin a slow turn. Whatever is hanging loose back there keeps me from having any left rudder at all. It's also jammed the elevator, and there's no forward or backward movement of the stick, which means I can't point the nose up or push it down. If I let up on the right rudder pedal the least little bit, I'll go back into a hard skid to the left.

For a few seconds, I consider trying to bail out, but if I take my feet off the rudders, I know the aircraft will spin before I can drag myself out. Once a spin starts, the g-force will pin me in the cockpit, and I'll be as good as dead. In the cheery words of one of our emergency manuals, I am "strapped to a bomb."

What to do now? There are not a lot of choices. All my training says that if I can't get back aboard the ship, the next best thing is to ditch in the water. I need to find the fleet and put this wreck in the water close to a destroyer—*if* I can figure out where the fleet is.

The panic has almost wiped my mind clean. For a minute or two, I struggle to get myself oriented. We jumped the Zeros about eighty miles east of the carrier. That means I have to fly west, but the sun is almost directly overhead, and the instrument panel, including the compass, is now totally worthless.

I check my watch. It's 1315. Still almost afraid to move the stick, I begin to turn until the sun is directly in my face. Even without a working altimeter, I can see the turn has cost me some more altitude. The waves definitely look closer than they were a minute ago.

"Mayday, Mayday, Mayday!" I shout into my lip mic. "This is Flapjack Seven-Two-One. Any aircraft this frequency, I need some help!"

After a few seconds I feel sure I hear somebody key a mic. There's static hissing in my earphones but no voice.

I repeat, "Mayday, Mayday, Mayday! This is Flapjack Seven-Two-One, broadcasting in the blind. My rudder controls are shot away, and I have no instrument panel. If you can get a fix on me, how about joining up and leading me back to the ship?"

Again, the sound of the mic and the static. Then silence.

One last time I try, sounding much more in control than I feel. "Paleface, this is Flapjack Seven-Two-One, heading approximately two-seven-zero, airspeed two hundred knots at angels three. Location uncertain, but I'm east of the ship. Losing altitude. Will ditch when I'm in the vicinity of Paleface. Seven-Two-One, out"

"Yeah," the ops officer said. "You probably lay down on the beach and passed out. And when you woke up, you thought you remembered. Couldn't that have happened?"
"It could have," I said. "But it didn't. I didn't pass out, and I didn't imagine anything."

I strain to hear something besides the rattle of my own aircraft, but there is nothing. When I check the position of the sun again, it has drifted to the side of the cockpit. I must have accidentally let up on the right rudder pedal—probably with good reason. My leg is beginning to cramp.

For what seems like many hours, I struggle to keep flying straight and level with the sun in my face. And all the time I'm searching the horizon for some sign of the fleet: a picket destroyer, the familiar white wake of a ship, anything! Meanwhile, I continue to lose altitude. When the elevator jammed, it was set at an angle, leaving me in a shallow dive. Eventually I will simply fly into the water.

When I check my watch again it's 1420. The fuel should be getting low by now. From what I can tell by looking at the waves, I'm probably going to run out of gas and altitude at about the same time. Wiping the sweat from my eyes, it suddenly hits me that I am very, very tired. Almost too tired to hold my head up. And the panic begins to fade into something like resignation.

I've heard all that stuff about your life passing in front of you when you think you're dying. I'm pretty sure by now that I'll probably die, but nothing like that happens to me. At some point I do have a flash of my parents' front door and two officers in dress blues (they always send two), one of whom is saying in a weary voice, "No, ma'am, there are no remains. Your son's aircraft was lost at sea."

"Navy aircraft heading two eighty, this is Victor Nine-Four-Zero on guard frequency. What's your destination?"

The voice booms in my earphones so loudly that I almost jump out of my skin! Then I spin the radio frequency knob to "guard channel" and answer. "Navy Nine-Four-Zero, this is Flapjack Seven-Two-One. Destination's the ship, but my instruments are shot away, and I'm not sure of my location. Where are you?"

"Roger, Seven-Two-One, we're directly overhead and up angels three. You look like you're right on the deck; can you climb?"

"Four-Zero-Zero, that's a negative. My tail assembly is all shot up. Can't climb and can't turn left. Can you tell me if I'm close enough to anything to ditch?"

"Roger, Seven-Two-One, hang on. We'll take a look at the chart."

"Swede," the skipper said. "We heard all your transmissions, but you obviously couldn't hear ours. You flew somewhere close to the right heading after you were shot up, but the task force was moving north. It looks like you missed us by about fifty miles or so."

There's a pause that goes on much too long, and then finally I hear, "Two-One, we don't think you're anywhere near the task force. There *is* an island—we make it to be the Carabao atoll—about six miles west of you. Do you have it in sight?"

"Negative, Four-Zero, I do not have it in sight. Can you stand by long enough to give me directions?"

"That's affirmative, Two-One. Turn right twenty degrees."

"Roger," I say. "Got no compass, but I'm turning right about twenty degrees. Four-Zero, can you call in my position?"

"Affirmative, Two-One. We'll call on this channel. You try the ship's frequency."

"Roger, Four-Zero. I'll try," I say. "But I'm right on the deck. Doubt if I'll get out."

I change back to the carrier's radio frequency and call it. "Paleface, this is Flapjack Seven-Two-One broadcasting in the blind. Have found a buddy and will attempt to ditch on the Carabao atoll. I say again, the Carabao atoll. Would appreciate a lift whenever possible. Flapjack Seven-Two-One, out."

When I change back to guard channel, 940 is on the air. "Two-One," he says. "The atoll is almost directly in front of you. You should see palm trees in a minute or two. There's a nice wide beach and not much surf. If your angle of attack isn't too steep, you might try ditching so you'll be close to the beach."

"Roger," I say. "I've got the trees in sight now. I'll cross the south end of the atoll and cut my engine. If I'm lucky, I can put it in shallow water."

"Roger, Two-One. We're standing by. We'll see you into the water, but we're low on fuel. Can't come down and hang around. We'll send the boat for you as soon as we hit the beach in the Philippines."

"Roger, Nine-Four-Zero," I say. "Thanks for all the little things you do—like saving my ass!"

"All in a day's work, old buddy. Good luck with the ditch. This is Nine-Four-Zero out."

"Skipper, did the PBY pick me up on the Carabao atoll?"
"He did, Swede."
"And was my wrecked aircraft in plain sight, almost on the beach?"
"That's what they said."

I tighten my shoulder harness and dip the right wing to bring me in over the south horn of the atoll. That little dip spills the last of my altitude, and I'm gonna hit the water whether I cut the engine or not. But I chop the throttle and even have time to feather the prop before I plow into the water. The nose hits the water first, and for some reason, it actually bounces up a little rather than digging in and flipping the aircraft on its back. To my amazement, the middle of the fuselage settles nice and easy right back into the surf. As the aircraft begins to sink, I crawl out onto the wing, still wearing my parachute and life raft, step off into shallow water, and wade ashore onto that beautiful white beach. After a step or two, my knees buckle.

From somewhere back in the bush on that tiny island, a breeze is blowing the smell of flowers and dampness in my face. Playing in my head like a broken record is the thought that by all odds, I ought to be dead. I ought to be dead several times over. For a long time I just kneel there, feeling the warm sand through my wet flight suit. The whole scene has the quality of one of those things that happens in a dream when you know you'll wake up any minute. When I think about it today, it still does.

It's late in the second day before the PBY arrives, making a low pass to wave at me and then landing outside the atoll and taxiing right up to the gap in the coral circle. I break out the life raft and paddle out to meet him. I never thought I'd want to hug a swabbie, but when that sailor opens the hatch and reaches out to help me inside, it feels like Momma welcoming me home.

In barely an hour and a half, we're taxiing in through the surf in the Philippines, where the marines are still fighting inland, and we're using an old Jap airstrip by the beach.

I report to the commanding officer of the little base and have my hand shaken. My first priority is a shower and some dry socks. Then, since I haven't eaten in almost three days, the CO invites me to the mess tent to have "what passes for chow in this part of the world." The mess steward even brings a semicool bottle of Coke to wash down my navy Spam. He carries the bottle to my table like it's French champagne. It's a touching gesture, and I really should be more appreciative, but I have other things on my mind.

As soon as I can leave the mess, I hustle myself out to the line shack to ask about Navy 940. The chief behind the desk thumbs through his logbook.

"You sure you got that side number right, Lieutenant?"

"Dead sure," I say.

He looks some more, making a show of putting his pencil point down on each line as he turns the pages. "Nope," he says. "No Nine-Four-Zero from *any* squadron."

"But you'd have *had* to log him in, right?"

"If he'd come aboard here I would have," he says. "What kind of aircraft, and where did he originate in?"

"Chief, we never got around to discussing that," I say. "I was way down on the deck in a very shot-up bird, and he was at three thousand feet. By the time I ditched and got on the beach, he was nowhere in sight."

"Well, Lieutenant, maybe you misunderstood him. Or maybe he landed at the little marine strip up north. He coulda been flying in supplies for the jarheads, but we ain't seen him here."

"If you do," I say, "tell him I owe him a few beers."

"Now, Swede," the skipper said. "Don't get so excited. We aren't arguing with you. We're just trying to suggest the way things might have happened. But I gotta tell you, we've been all the way to ComPacFlt looking for information."

A week or so later, there's a carrier onboard delivery plane flying mail out to the fleet, and I hitch a ride back to the ship. After I crawl out of the COD plane on the flight deck and my squadron mates have finished pounding my back and yelling, I have to go and do my most unfavorite things for the rest of the day—writing reports and getting debriefed. In the course of all that, they tell me the Jap plane that gave me tunnel vision *did* spin in and crash. Shark and the others saw it hit the water, which means that I get credit for the kill. With that news and the fact that I'm alive and back aboard the ship, I'm feeling so high that my feet are barely touching the deck. For a while.

Then just when I figure I can finally go back to the ready room and relax, Charlie McDowell and the air operations officer happen by. The skipper puts his hand on my shoulder in a friendly but very insistent way and says, "Swede, come to the wardroom and have a cup of coffee with us. We need to shoot the breeze for a while."

The ops officer starts it off. "Congratulations on your kill, Lieutenant! Your first one?"

"His second one!" the skipper answers with a touch of pride. "He's a damn good pilot—when he remembers to stay with his wingman…"

"I know, Skipper," I say. "It was a boneheaded thing to do, and I'm sorry. I was just so scared the son of a bitch would get away."

"Apology accepted," he says. "If the brass don't make a stink about it, I won't."

"Speaking of brass," the ops officer says. "We need to ask you about something so we can finish *our* incident report."

"Jesus, Commander!" I say. "I already told you everything I know."

"Well," he says. "Just a couple more questions to get some things straight."

The skipper says, "Swede, we copied all your transmissions on our tower frequency right up to the time you told us about the Carabao atoll. But we also picked up some traffic from you on guard channel. You were talking to somebody you called 'Navy Nine-Four-Zero.' Do you remember that?"

"Remember it? Hell, Skipper. That's the guy saved my ass. Without him, I would have plowed into open ocean in about another two minutes. But wait a minute—he was at three thousand feet. If you could hear me, I *know* you could hear him."

"Hmmm," the ops officer says. "We should have been able to. But the fact is, we didn't. Didn't copy any part of his transmissions." There's this awkward pause while both of them concentrate on their coffee, neither one meeting my eye. Then he continues. "In fact, we don't believe there *were* any transmissions."

"Ya see, Swede," the Skipper says. "It's all kind of weird. We haven't been able to trace any Navy Nine-Four-Zero. Fact is, there *ain't* no squadron uses those side numbers. Not here—not anywhere. And there were no flights by *any* US Navy aircraft in that vicinity on the day you ditched. It's all a great mystery to us. *You got any suggestions?*"

For a while I just sit there with my mouth open. Then I start trying to explain it again on the chance they haven't understood what I said. It takes them another fifteen minutes of repeating the same thing over and over in different ways before I finally give up.

Then I begin to break out in a cold sweat. These are two reasonable, hard-nosed officers. I've known them for a while now, and what's more, I trust them. It's clear to me that they don't just *believe* what they're saying. They damn well *know* it!

What's making me sweat, of course, is what *I* know! And the things the three of us know are not at all the same.

Now if I have to, I can agree I'm crazy. Men occasionally do go crazy in combat, or maybe I started out that way. But I'm still smart enough to know that a crazy man doesn't find the only speck of coral within three hundred miles of him because his imaginary voices tell them where it is—and he certainly doesn't know the name of it!

And I'm also smart enough to know what I've got to do. So in the end I agree to lie. We make up the lie right there in the wardroom. Here's how it goes: When the Jap tore up my plane, I hit my head. Then I was delirious off and on and may have heard voices. At one point I could have even changed to guard channel and talked to the voices. After I ditched, I lay down on the beach and passed out. When I woke up I found the lump on my head and realized what had happened. End of story.

It's neat. It's simple. Nobody has to try to remember a lot of details. And best of all, the squadron doesn't have to deal with breaking in a replacement pilot.

It takes me a while to adjust to the idea that I'll never be able to talk about what may be the most important thing that ever happened to me. But then it occurs to me that if I do insist on talking, I'll spend the rest of my life being looked at like a loony. So I decide that maybe living a lie isn't always such a bad thing.

A week later I'm back on the flight schedule.

But sometimes, even today, when I let my mind go I can still smell the flowers on the Carabao atoll.

AN HISTORICAL AND FICTIONAL PREFACE TO "GABE"

The protagonist of my story, Gabriel Corley, is totally fictional and is not connected in any way to persons living or dead. I have, however, allowed the fictional Gabe to share some dates and circumstances with my actual great-grandfather, whose name was E. C. Sperry. For example, Gabriel and E. C. both enlisted in the Confederate army (Fifteenth South Carolina Volunteers, Company K) at a place called Lightwood Knot Springs, South Carolina. As part of that regiment, they both fought in many major battles, although my great-grandfather Sperry died of wounds suffered around the time of the Second Battle of Fredericksburg (May 1863), so I have assumed that that was where he received his "slight head wound." He died within seventy-two hours of entering the field hospital. So much for the surgeon's written assessment of "slight!" My fictional protagonist, Gabriel, was also wounded, but in my imagination he did survive the war and return to his family farm, somewhere close to Lightwood Knot Springs.

Great-grandfather Sperry left a widow, Frances "Fanny" Sperry, and two children, a boy and a girl. The girl was my grandmother, Amelia Sperry, who married T. B. Corley. Among Amelia's children was my mother, Sarah Mae Corley.

After the war, widow Sperry's son discovered that his father, E. C., had left a family in New Haven, Connecticut, when he had gone south before enlisting in the Confederate army. The Sperry son found a way to communicate with E. C.'s family in New Haven, and a number of letters were exchanged between E. C.'s son and E. C.'s brother. It turns out that the brother had fought in the Fifteenth Connecticut Regiment for the whole war! I'm told it was not unusual to find relatives on both sides of Civil War battles. Such is the nature of fratricide.

I have allowed my protagonist, Gabe, to end the war still in the Fifteenth South Carolina Regiment, which was disbanded after the surrender somewhere near Durham, North Carolina. I have borrowed other factoids, such as names and places, and have given them to my fictional cast, although none of the actions or characters in the story is real.

GABE
CHAPTER ONE

December 1905

My name is Gabriel Sims Corley, and what I know is this: we all look different, and we all think we're different, but we really ain't. Oh, I know what's plain to see: we're young or old, poor or stout, and man or woman—even white or darky. But inside we're really all the same.

I began to find this out the night my cousin, William Duncan, and me decided to run off and join the Confederate army. It was in the year 1862, and I'd turned seventeen that May. My brothers had both joined up, and the fellow who'd been courting my sister had joined too. Maw had said absolutely and finally that I wasn't going, but I was in an awful sweat to get in. My brothers were writing in their letters that the Yankees would run every time they seen a Confederate soldier, especially our cavalry. I was about to die of fear that the war would end, and I'd be the only man or boy in the county who wasn't in a uniform. I thought that if that happened, I'd have to dig a hole and crawl in, for I'd never be able to show my face again.

There was a fellow lived down the road from us, and he had decided he wouldn't go in the army no matter what anybody said. He said he didn't have no fight with nobody, and he didn't want to walk away from his farm and leave it to go down and get his head shot off. Then one day some women who had husbands and sons in the army got together and wrote him a letter. They said that if their men were good enough to fight for their country, this fellow should be too; but if he wouldn't, they'd give him what they'd been sewing for him. And they all signed the letter and mailed it to him with a package had a lady's petticoat with lace around the bottom. He joined up that same week.

Ever since we'd heard there was a recruiter over at Goldville, I'd been riding William pretty hard about running off together to join up. And like he most always did, William tried to talk sense to me.

"Gabe," he said. "I don't hardly see how we could carry it off. As soon as you don't show up for supper on time, your maw will know where you are and send somebody for you."

"I been thinking on this," I told him. "Aunt Carrie is fixing to have a baby any day, and if it ain't come by Friday, Maw'll go over there to stay awhile. If I let on that I'm staying over at your house, and you say you're at our place, won't nobody be any wiser for at least a day, and maybe two. All you got to do is meet me at the hill over at Sugar Creek Ford Friday night. Just bring what you're wearing. We'll be in Goldville by morning."

That was how we came to be running barefoot in the middle of a summer night, splashing across the ford and up the hill to the main road. We ran and walked in spells all night long, almost afraid to look behind us, sure that somebody would come riding up and say, "You boys get on back home!" And maybe wishing they would.

When daylight came we slowed down so's it wouldn't look like we were running away from something, and pretty soon we were on the outskirts of Goldville. We stopped at a springhouse close to the road and threw some water on our faces. Then we put on our shoes and walked into town, not looking right nor left, scared half to death we'd see somebody we knew and have to say what we were doing there.

Looking back, it seems an awful foolish notion to imagine we were going to be big, brave soldiers not even afraid of death itself. We couldn't even walk down the street of a country town for fear of seeing somebody who knew us! But I reckon that's what being seventeen years old is all about.

That army recruiter was easy to find. He'd set up in the shade of a big tree next to the stables. He and his sergeant had a little table and two chairs, and they were dressed in the prettiest uniforms I'd ever seen. A whole crowd of men and boys was standing around, gawking at the horses tied under the same tree, both of them with a saber on one side and a carbine on the other. It never occurred to me to wonder why they didn't take all that gear off them horses so they could be cool. All the uniforms and weapons, you see, were like a storekeeper's sign, except it wasn't like you were going to go in the store and pay for something. They were offering to *give* you all this—and the glory that went with it too.

We stopped then. I was afraid to push through that crowd of strangers. William shuffled back a step or two like maybe he was fixing to walk away. But right then the sergeant called out real loud, "Come on up, gentlemen! We're looking for men like you who ain't afraid to whip some Yankees!"

That was all I needed to hear. I nodded at the table and looked at William. Then I just started pushing my way through. We stopped at the table, and the officer with two bars on his shoulders looked up at us for the first time. I remember he had dark hair, sad eyes, and a mustache that drooped over the corners of his mouth. He said, "You boys aiming to enlist?"

I reckoned William was worse off than me, so I swallowed once and answered for both of us. My voice come out queer, but it didn't break.

"Yes, sir," I said. "Whipping Yankees was exactly what we had in mind." And then, since he didn't answer right away, I said, "We can either one of us shoot a squirrel's eye out as far as we can see it."

He fiddled with the papers for a minute like he was studying 'em real hard, and then he looked up and said, "Well, boys, the Yankees'll shoot back sometimes. Have you thought about that? Have your ma and pa thought about that?"

"My paw's dead," I said. "And Maw wants this thing over as bad as I do. My brothers is already in." All true so far. "We were just waiting for me to be old enough."

He raised an eyebrow and said, "*Are* you old enough?"

"I'll be eighteen next birthday," I said. "And William is a year older'n me."

"That right, William?" he asked.

"Yes, sir," said William, raring back a little. "We don't lie."

The officer lowered his voice and looked William in the eye. "Nobody's accusing you of lying, son. It's just that some folks will leave things out. Then we got to go find some fourteen-year-old in camp somewhere and send him back home to his Momma. If you aim to be soldiers, you got to learn to answer straight and not talk back. Can both you boys sign your name?"

We answered at the same time. "Yes, sir."

"Then sign the papers there, and we'll swear you in."

I was sweating so hard my hand stuck to the papers, and I made at least one inkblot while signing my own name.

When the officer stood up to swear us in, he held on to the little table and pushed up, dragging his stiff right leg. He saw us looking and smiled a little.

"A Yankee minié ball, gentlemen. Now raise your right hands, and say the words after me."

So that's how we came to be in the army. We'd done it, and it couldn't be undone! We were soldiers for the Confederate States of America! All of a sudden, I felt homesick, like I had a pain over my heart, even though we were only a half-day's walk away from home. And a cold feeling crept up in the pit of my stomach when I thought about a lead ball punching through the man's leg. I reckon that was my mind giving me fair warning.

Once we'd signed the papers and had been sworn in, the sergeant took out another paper and commenced to ask us questions. Every now and then, he'd stop and write a note. He was older than the officer, and bigger. Not tall but stocky with blunt hands like a farmer, and there was some dried tobacco juice in the crease beside the corner of his mouth. He smiled a little sometimes. His voice could sound almost friendly; but without his having to say it, you knew he wouldn't put up with any nonsense.

"You boys live hereabouts?" he asked

William answered. "We're from down the road in Lightwood Knot Springs, sir."

"You don't have to call me 'sir,' son. I'm a sergeant. 'Sir' is for officers. If you want to call me something, say 'Sergeant.'"

"Yes, sir, Sergeant."

He smiled and shook his head, but he didn't bother to correct William again. "I'm guessing you're farm boys. Am I right?"

"Yes, Sergeant," I said, proud of my new military knowledge.

"Do much riding?" he asked.

"None to speak of," I said. "We can ride all right, but our folks can't afford to feed horses just for saddle mounts."

"Don't ride to hunt?"

"No, Sergeant."

"But you do hunt?"

"We hunt for meat, Sergeant. Squirrel, rabbits, deer, and such."

"Were you serious about that squirrel's eye?"

It was my turn to smile. "Most of the time," I said.

He made another note and turned to the officer. "Not many gentlemen riding to the hounds around here, sir. I think this pair are riflemen. What do you think—infantry?"

"Infantry," the officer said. "There's already a regiment from this part of the state. I know just where they'll go." He looked up at us. "You boys are free to walk around town, but don't go too far. And be back at one o'clock sharp if you want to go with the sergeant to dinner."

When we got back, the officer had loosened his collar and was leaning back, smoking his after-dinner cigar. The sergeant led William and me and three other fellows down the street to a boardinghouse. The woman sitting at the door of the dining room nodded to the sergeant, and all six of us went in and sat down.

We hadn't had any breakfast, and the smell of the food made my mouth water. The sergeant must have been reading my mind, because he said, "Better eat up, boys. You won't get any supper today."

A girl about my age came in from the kitchen carrying a plate of cornbread and a bowl of greens. As she set them down, she looked us over, and then her eyes came back to me. I was trying not to look in her face, but it was too late. We both realized we'd met before.

I knew I should do like the sergeant had said and stock up, but somehow it seemed like the food just didn't want to go down. I reckon it was tasty, and there was plenty of everything, but the longer I chewed, the bigger it got. It didn't help that the serving girl kept looking at me whenever she moved around the table.

Finally she said, "Don't I know you? I'm Cissy McClain. Where you from? Didn't you come to the spelling bee last year?"

I tried to mumble my name, but William answered for me. "We're from Lightwood Knot Springs. I'm William Duncan, and this's my cousin Gabriel."

"Gabriel Corley!" she said. "Now I remember! You *did* come to the spelling bee. We were both in the semifinals. Don't you remember?"

I nodded.

"What're you all doing in Goldville?" she asked. Then she looked at the sergeant, and her eyes got round. "Oh, I know what you're doing. You're joining up, ain't you?"

"Could be," I said. "But you got no call to announce it to the whole world."

"You should be right proud," Cissy said. "Volunteering to help our cause. I just hope you shoot as well as you spell!"

The sergeant put down his fork for the first time since we had sat down. "He'll shoot better if you feed him more and talk less," he said. "Why don't you get him another glass of buttermilk and bring me some of that pie?"

"Yes, *sir*," she said, smiling a little. She winked at me and whirled back through the door to the kitchen.

William must have sensed what was going on in my head, because he turned to the sergeant and asked, "What time does that train come?"

"Supposed to be here at five," he answered. "But you never can tell. Could be five, could be eight. One thing you'll learn to do in the army is wait."

William nudged me with his elbow and muttered, "Don't worry, cousin. Even if somebody does get word back to home, your maw's not there. Remember? We'll make it right enough." And we did.

When the train finally pulled in that afternoon, we almost ran to get in line. The sergeant was handing the conductor some papers and telling him where we had to get off.

Then at last the train was moving, picking up speed with smoke and cinders blowing in the window and us hanging out like puppies poking their heads out of a basket. And we got real quiet knowing that we'd really done it and that there was no going back. For the first time, I let myself think about Maw and about how she'd find out from the letter I'd left on her pillow. I had to bite my lip real hard to keep from letting a tear run down my face. Neither one of us had ever spent more than a night or two away from our families, nor had we traveled farther than the county seat.

At seventeen I already looked like a man, big and raw boned, but I was more than half boy. I could do anything there was to do on a farm, from butchering a beef to shoeing a horse. I never walked away from a scrap, and I could give a hiding, or take one if I had to, without a whimper. But I would no more have sassed my maw than anything in the world, and I'd said my prayers at her knee every night of my life.

We didn't get much of a train ride that time. They unloaded us in the dark at a stop outside Columbia. We were met by a sergeant and a corporal, and we marched (if you could call it that) to a place they called "Camp Johnson." The sergeant found us some blankets and a place in the great long row of tents. Then he said, "You boys get some sleep tonight. Come the morning, I'm a-gonna work you like plantation niggers!"

I was still too nerved up to sleep, and I needed to use the privy, so I said to William, "You stay here by the door so's I can find this tent again, and when I come back, I'll tell you where the privy is."

When I got back he was pacing up and down, and I could tell he was looking around to get his bearings. We hunkered down outside the tent, and after a minute he said, "Lookie here, Gabe. What do you reckon would happen if a fellow was to just walk out of here? There ain't no guards or nothing."

"William, you can't do that, and you know it. That's desertion. They could shoot you for that."

"Nah, they'd never find me if I didn't want 'em to. Even you couldn't find me if I got off down in the swamp."

"But you got to stay," I said. "Give it a try for a few days. You can make up your mind then as easy as now." I grabbed his arm. "Please, William, you just got to stay with me."

William could be right stubborn when he dug in his heels, and I could tell he wasn't convinced, but he didn't shake off my hand. I pulled him toward the door of the tent, and about that time, somebody inside said, "You boys cut out that goddamned jawing! We're a-trying to sleep in here."

That old sergeant was as good as his word. It was still dark when he commenced to kick at the bottoms of our feet. At the same time, a ways off there was a bugle blowing. I sat up and grinned at William. "Well, cousin," I said. "How you liking it so far?"

He tried to smile, but he couldn't make his mouth behave. He was rubbing his eyes, and I was pretty sure I saw tear tracks running through the dirt on his face.

"Aw, perk up, William!" I said, throwing an arm around his shoulders. "We're gonna get used to this before you know it!"

Nobody had to tell us what to do. We just followed the mob of fellows all going to the same place at the same time. We ran to the privy, ran back to the tents, and tried to get into some kind of straight lines like the others were doing.

Then the sergeant was walking up and down the line, and my, wasn't he a sight! He walked like there was a ramrod up his back, his heels digging into the dirt, his garrison cap set down over his eyes. The three big stripes on his arm were edged in gold. And as he walked, he was setting people's heads straight, yelling at us to keep our eyes to the front and our shoulders back, and putting our hands down straight on the seams of our trousers.

"All right now, boys," he yelled in a voice like a steamboat whistle. "You don't look much like soldiers this morning, but you will by nightfall. I'm Sergeant Crockett; remember that name. I'm gonna be your wet nurse until you move up to the real army. But we got to hurry because if'n we don't, the war'll be over, and there won't be a single Yankee left for us. So pay attention!"

Behind me I heard somebody whispering, so I turned my head a little and cut my eyes to see who it was. Sergeant Crockett slapped his boot with a little stick he had under his arm and yelled at the second row, "No talking in ranks back there." Then right in my ear he said, "And no skylarking! If I need you to look somewhere, I'll tell you."

He stepped back to the front, shifted his tobacco, and spat. "In a real battle, you got to listen to every word. Your job now is to kill enemy soldiers and not to get killed yourself. So if I say "wheel left" or "double-time," you got to listen and do it right *then*—no questions and no waiting! Otherwise some smart Yankee'll have a bayonet in your belly.

"You ain't never done most of the things you'll do from now on, but there's a reason for every one of them. What it boils down to is this: the better soldiers you are, the better chance you got of coming back home alive. Now before you get to the mess hall this fine morning, you're gonna learn four commands—dress right, right face, halt, and forward march."

And march we did! Lord, did we march! By the time we fell into our blankets again that night, we must have gone ten miles or more. I was pleased to see that William had smartened up right considerably during the day. We were taking bullyragging from other recruits everywhere we went, and Sergeant Crockett stayed on us worse than a horsefly drawing blood. But there was something about being with all the other new fellows that made it seem all right. I think William was beginning to feel a little less homesick. Anyway, I was.

All of us wanted so bad to look like real soldiers that for the first week or so we couldn't take the time to think or talk about nothing else. Lots of times we'd stuff our food down at mealtime and then jump up to practice some formation—the whole platoon—before the sergeant even got back. We were that serious, and I was the worst of the lot!

Because we were all wrapped up in becoming soldiers, I don't reckon any of us had much time to think about home and family. Still, at night sometimes, when it got dark and quiet, I thought I could hear William snuffling some. But then, he wasn't no ways the only one.

By the time we'd been in camp for about three weeks, we were beginning to think and act like soldiers. As least *we* thought so. We even took to making fun of the new recruits as they came in by yelling "hay foot, straw foot" when they were trying to learn to march and such—same as people had done to us. We had real rifles then with bayonets, and we practiced with real powder and balls. William and me both caught on quick to that part of it, even though the rifles were heavier and took a bigger charge than what we'd used at home. We could most times put four out of five balls in the bull's-eye, even at the longest distance on the rifle range.

When we started drilling on bayonet practice, though, a funny thing happened to William. He couldn't make himself yell out loud. It was peculiar, and he took a good deal of abuse from Sergeant Crockett about it. The other recruits and me, we all tried to help him as much as you can help somebody holler. But he just wouldn't catch on. He could hold the rifle the way we were taught, and he could run up to the hay bales, but he just couldn't scream and stab the bales the way we were all doing.

I tried to tell him, "William, it's just playacting! It's like swinging on a grapevine over the creek and whooping before we drop in the swimming hole. The noise is just to help us get where we're going. I heard you do it before; I know you can!"

But he just kinda pouted, looking down at the ground. And then he muttered to me so the others couldn't hear him, "It *ain't* playacting, Gabe, and you know it. We're fixing to have to jab some other fellow with that there bayonet. Another fellow who's scared and don't want to be here, just like me."

"William, he *ain't* like you! He's a damn Yankee, and if you don't jab him, he's going to jab you—or me or one of these other fellows here. You're just doing what you got to do to protect your family."

But nothing seemed to work. At last the sergeant just gave up on him and said, "Well, Duncan, if you can't do it, there ain't no use wasting time on it. If you get in a spot where your officers say, 'Fix bayonets,' you go ahead and do it. Then you just get behind the other fellows and hit the first Yankee you come to with the butt of your rifle. But I 'spect that when you see some Yankee charging at you, you'll do what you have to do."

Since everything we did was new and strange, it'd be hard to say what we thought was the strangest thing at the time. Later, after our first few times under fire, I came to believe that Sergeant Crockett's "game" of "weasel in the henhouse" was the thing that helped us the most. It started during the last two weeks in camp and happened, with one change or another, almost every day.

We marched out to the rifle range like always, except there was another sergeant we didn't know and two corporals marching with us. When we got there, Sergeant Crockett sent one of the corporals down to the targets and had him set up an old medicine bottle on top of the target frames.

After he had the first rank load their rifles and kneel, the sergeant said, "Boys, that there bottle is a Yankee sharpshooter, and he's a dead shot. As long as he's alive, some of you'uns are apt to take a bullet in the head. You *got* to get him!"

I smiled and winked at William, who was kneeling in the front rank. "If you don't get it, I will!" I mouthed at him.

Sergeant Crockett said, "Now keep your weapons pointed downrange at all times, and listen for my commands, but *get that damn Yankee.* Cock your pieces and be ready."

All the rifle hammers in the front rank clicked back. William wet his thumb and polished his front sight.

"Ready!" Sergeant Crockett yelled.

Every rifle was snugged into a shoulder.

"Fix bayonets!" the sergeant screamed.

Two rifles fired. The rest wavered around, and then the butts were grounded while the men reached frantically for their bayonets.

"God damn it!" the sergeant yelled. "Let them hammers down! You wanna blow your goddamn hands off?"

Half the bayonets fell to the ground while the men scrambled to lower the hammers to half cock. The corporals and the other sergeant pushed between the men and proceeded to kick the dropped bayonets downrange.

"Ready!" Sergeant Crockett said. "Commence firing!"

There was a ragged volley of gunfire. The bottle did not move.

"You," Sergeant Crockett said to William, starting down the line. "And you and you! You're all dead! Lie down where you are. The rest of you—what're you waiting for? Reload and fire! That Yankee hasn't stopped. He's killing your messmates! Corley, Campbell, McClain, step into the first rank over those dead bodies. Load and fire."

This was *my* chance. That bottle was as good as "dead!" I knelt beside William and rammed a charge and then a wadded ball home. But as I fumbled a cap out of my pouch, Sergeant Crockett slapped my hand with his hat, and the cap went spinning into the dust.

"That Yankee's still shooting!" he yelled. "Now Corley's dead." And he pushed me flat into the dirt with his boot. "Mackey, step up here!"

And so it went, without letup, for the next ten or fifteen minutes. Somebody would be drawing a bead, and one of the "helpers" would fire off a pistol right behind his head. "Think that's loud?"

he'd say to a trembling recruit. "That's nothing compared to an artillery round. Why are you looking at me? Keep firing!"

One of the sergeants would scream, "Fall back. Retreat! Fall back, and set up another line!"

When the line began to stagger back, he'd say, "What're you doing? You aim to leave your dead and wounded lying there? Pick them men up! And keep firing! Keep firing! Nobody told you to stop firing."

It would not surprise anybody to learn that our "Yankee" medicine bottle survived the day without a scratch. We were probably lucky that we hadn't shot each other. But the point was made and would be made over and over again during our final weeks in camp. Shooting at a mark is one thing, and some of us were pretty good at it. Being in a battle is another thing, and we were as innocent as newborns about that.

In all the fuss of trying to learn how to soldier, I pretty much managed not to think about Maw from day to day. Underneath, though, I was still dreading hearing what she had to say. When the envelope with her handwriting on it arrived, I put it in a pocket and left it there until after supper when I could find a place to be alone for a little while. This is what she wrote to me:

> Dear Son,
>
> I can't tell you what a shock it was to return home and find that you had run away in the night like a common criminal. I had hoped that I could trust you to remain at home and share the work of keeping our place going so Charles and Thomas would have a home to return to. I reckon that that was too much to hope for in the midst of this war fever. If you were a little older, perhaps you could see things from my point of view: already a widow, I now face the prospect of being childless as well if God should not see fit to send at least one of you home safe.

So I guess there's nothing to do but commit you to God's care and say that I will always love you and pray for you. I also pray that you will remain a Christian as you have been reared to do and that you will not give in to the temptations of army life. You will have to associate with people of all kinds, and I fear there will be many opportunities for impure thoughts and actions. I can only hope you will be strong, remember your upbringing, and not bring shame on the family.

Write me as often as you can. I will try to keep you informed of things here and also of any news I receive from your brothers. Don't forget to pray.

—Your loving mother

I know that William got a letter from his mother at about the same time, but he never was willing to say more than a word or two about it. Since William would usually talk about most anything with me, I came to believe that Aunt Maybelle must have been real mad with me and blamed me for his running off. I reckon, if truth be told, that she never would forgive me, although I'm sure she tried.

We got our uniforms just two days before we left Camp Johnson. The lieutenant had already met with our platoon to let us know that we'd be replacements in the Fifteenth South Carolina Volunteers, and some ladies' auxiliary had sewn that right on the front of all our garrison caps. They said "SC 15." We even got belt buckles that said "CSA." When we were ready to march to the railroad siding, we dressed in our new uniforms and paraded, proud as could be, for folks who had driven out from Columbia to see us off. There was a band and flags, and some of the folks in buggies were crying. But what *I* noticed most was that it was still June, and by the time I had marched to the station with a bedroll over my shoulder, I had sweat plumb through that new uniform.

Richard Corley Massey

July 2, 1862
Dearest Mother,

    I've been tardy in writing you, for which I now beg your forgiveness. But, as you might guess, we have been tolerable busy for some weeks now. Today we were forced to accept a delay, and although it makes us all impatient, there is no help for it, as the railroad cannot carry all the trains needed in the war effort. As I write this, the cars that are to take us to our regiment, the Fifteenth South Carolina Volunteers, sit on a rail siding somewhere in the state of North Carolina. We've been here since late in the evening of June 30, and I see no sign of our moving soon.

    We've set up camp in the shelter of a grove of trees, and here we entertain ourselves as best we can. Most of us take the opportunity to bathe in a branch a few yards away, and I can still hear splashing from that direction. Me and some others are lounging around under the trees to stay out of the heat.

    From where I sit, I can see William with a group of fellows gathered around one of our friends who plays the banjo. His music and our own singing help to raise our spirits. (William, as always, is fond of singing.) It may surprise you to learn that we have yet to hear a single song that could not be sung at a church supper. We often sing hymns, as they are one thing whose words we all know.

    I hope you will find it in your heart to forgive me for the way we left home. Please tell Aunt Maybelle that it was me persuaded William to run off, and if there is any blame, it should fall on me. William is as well and as happy as one can be in these circumstances. Everyone believes that the war will be short, and there is some doubt that it'll last long enough for us to see any action. I sincerely believe that we shall all be home before long, maybe by Christmas.

We miss you all. When you write again, you can address the letter to our regiment. When we are assigned to companies, I will give you a better address.

Well, enough for now. Please continue to pray for us, as I know you have already been doing.

With love and respect,
Your affectionate son Gabriel
PS—Please be sure that Uncle Foot and the others keep the grass out of the cotton in the bottomland, as it will surely be ruined otherwise. If I am not home before fall, be sure it is ginned and bailed before too much rain falls on it.

CHAPTER TWO

We finally caught up to the Fifteenth after three days of hard marching from the railhead in Virginia. The regiment had sent some men to meet us there, and they did not appear to be in a mood to waste much time. We walked all day with short stops for water and dry rations.

On the first morning in camp, we were finally allowed to cook a hot breakfast. About an hour later, the new recruits were mustered as a group, and Colonel Gist and the company commanders rode up. The colonel had us stand at ease while he made a little speech:

"Men," he said. "I'm proud to see each one of you. It always makes me proud to see another group of patriots willing to defend our cause and our way of life. Make no mistake: what you have resolved to do—to respond when duty calls and to give your lives in defense of honor—is the highest calling a man can have. You enroll yourselves today along with the heroes of all of the ages. And those of us who acquit ourselves honorably will receive the everlasting gratitude of our communities and our loved ones when we march home.

"But I want to be honest with you, men. We all know that some of us will not live to return. Our cause is a noble one, but the gods of war take whom they choose. Therefore, know this: If we should not live to see home and family again, those same homes and families will honor our memories. Because we *will* win this war, and your families *will* live in peace again. If the times grow hard, remember your home and loved ones."

Then one of the company commanders raised a flag and shouted, "Gentlemen, the Confederate States of America! Honor or death! Hip, hip—" And we all near about busted our lungs hollering "hurrah!"

After that, Colonel Gist took off his glove and went down the line, shaking every man's hand and asking his name.

When the company commanders called out our names, we left the big formation and went to stand in front of them. William and I were called into Company K. Then Captain Ford came down our ranks and shook our hands again. When he came to me, I told him my name and where I lived.

"I know Lightwood Knot Springs," he said. "Where's your place?"

"Sir," I said. "We live halfway between the railroad station and Bethel Presbyterian Church."

"I know the road," he said. "I've ridden past your very house. Welcome, Corley."

And for some silly reason, a lump came to my throat.

It was only a few minutes later that we met our platoon sergeant, Sergeant Cureton. He was always the sergeant, but of all the folks we knew in the first part of the war, he was the nearest to family for me.

I was like most folks who ain't never soldiered before; I reckoned that life in the army would be exciting and strange and not like anything I'd ever done. Along about the second week, we were sitting on the ground, plucking chickens for supper with some of the other new fellows, when William looked over at me and said,

"Well, Gabe, all them things we learned from Sergeant Crockett were fine and dandy, but I knew how to do *this here* before I left home." Both of us just burst out laughing. Looking back, I wish to God I'd had the chance to see my cousin laugh a lot more than I did.

For me, growing up in the country, being in a fistfight was like shoveling manure or gelding male calves—it was something you might not especially fancy, but you knew you had to do it more or less regularly. When I was little, I was scared of the school-yard bullies, but my brothers and cousins mostly kept me from getting whipped too bad. As I got older, I fought enough to learn what to do with my hands, but I was always more comfortable wrestling, where I could use my legs more. I almost never picked a fight, and I had to get really hot before I truly wanted to hurt somebody. But once in a while, some other boy at school or even at church would take it into his head that I had done him a wrong (I reckon I had sometimes), and he would pick at me until I couldn't walk around it anymore.

Most of the time it would start off with us swinging at each other until one or the other of us got a bloody nose or was stung enough to really see red and tackle the other fellow. Then we'd roll around on the ground until we got tired. Usually somebody would make us shake hands, and we'd forget the whole thing in a few weeks. I was never really hurt bad, but my pride was. The most I ever hurt was when I came home with my face cut or bruised and Ma gave me a hiding for fighting.

But when somebody I had thought was a friend—somebody I had trusted—goaded me into a fight, it injured my pride. Otherwise, the rules about fighting, like the rules about anything else, were understood by everybody—at least everybody I grew up with.

Marion Little was a private in the Fifteenth, same as me, but he was older. I knew he was different from most of us, but I put it down to him being a city boy. For example, he never went to church service in camp, talked about being homesick, or teased with the rest of us. He almost never guessed about when the war would end or where we'd go next, but I didn't know much else about him. He was another member of the platoon, and in those days I just figured any of us would have died for any other if we had had to. When it came to fighting, he would pick fights about such peculiar things that I never knew what he was doing until it was almost over.

Sergeant Cureton had got in the habit of picking one or two of us to be "in charge" when he had to be away for a spell. It was so offhanded that I never thought it had any meaning at all one way or another. Most of us were so patriotic and dead set on being good soldiers that he could have put a mule in charge and we wouldn't have thought anything about it. He'd just kind of toss it over his shoulder. And then one day, with no warning and no reason I could see, Marion decided he didn't cotton to me being "in charge."

The sergeant had walked away, same as always, that time toward the captain's tent. "You boys strike the tents as soon as you clean up, and be ready to march when I get back. Corley, you're in charge," he had said.

We had finished our pipes and were beginning to put away the breakfast things when I said to nobody in particular, "Well, boys, it sounds like we got our orders. We might as well pull up stakes."

I hadn't really meant it to be an order. I didn't think of myself as being able to order anybody to do anything. I was just saying what everybody already knew: the sergeant expected to find us with the tents packed and our blankets rolled, ready to march.

I had taken a step to begin pulling down our tent when Marion said, "I ain't gonna pull up nothing until I'm damned good and ready, 'Straw Foot!' I don't take orders from no thickheaded farm boy."

Like I said, I was caught flat-footed—but not so much by the words. Anybody in our platoon, or anybody we knew, for that matter, might have said the words, either in a teasing kind of way or even with a little heat if they were tired or hungry or didn't feel good. But Marion's voice was cold and quiet, and there was a kind of hatred in it I don't think I'd heard more'n once or twice in my life. It meant *something*, but for the life of me, I couldn't calculate what.

I stood up straight and looked at him where he was leaning on his elbow by the fire with his pipe in his hand. I remember thinking, "Should I answer him? Am I obliged by being 'in charge' to do something about this?" But I didn't have an answer. I just looked at him and shrugged, and I turned around and began to loosen a tent peg.

Then, in what seemed like less than a second, he was there without a sound, and when I felt him there and turned around, his chest touched my arm. "What you 'low, Straw Foot?" he said, mocking my country way of talking in a voice so cold and so angry that I actually took a step backward. "Won't do no good to back away. I aim to teach you some manners."

The camp had gotten quiet; even some platoons around us had quit their stirring to look in our direction. I was confused and real hurt; it was as if a friend had picked a fight in front of the whole school yard. But there he was, and I had to do something.

The spit in the back of my throat was thick from not knowing what was happening, and my voice come out all muffled. "I ain't got no fight with you, Marion, but I ain't backing away. If you think there's something you got to teach me, then I *'low* as to how you better get to it."

And he did. His first lick caught me on the ear, and the second, on my ribs. He was so fast—faster than I had ever seen him move in all the weeks I'd known him, and so fast that even though I had thought I was ready, I couldn't catch the punches. I circled around him and threw my left fist, catching him on his shoulder—and we were into it. After the first little rush, I began to get his rhythm, and then, little by little, we were trading punches almost even.

In a few minutes his breath began to whistle, and he slowed up some. The taste of blood in my mouth had pulled me out of my thickheadedness. I wasn't fighting anymore to keep from getting hit; I wanted to hurt him. I began deliberately hitting his arms and ribs until his fists dropped and I could get to his face.

I could feel my left eye swelling, and the skin felt tight, as if it were being pulled. But he was tiring faster than I was, and then I was hitting him twice for every blow he landed. He caught his heel on a tent rope and went down. As he scrambled to get up, my left fist caught him flush in the eye, and he went down again. He got up again, but slower, and I hit him three times in the ribs, taking only one lick from him. For the first time I suddenly heard all the men yelling, and at the same time I saw that Marion was about done in. I circled and waited for him to swing. When his shoulder dropped, I hit him in the jaw as hard as I could, and he sprawled out on his back.

I stepped back and looked at him. Trying hard not to let my voice tremble, I said, "That's enough. I don't know what we're fighting about anyway. Let's get these here tents pulled down before sergeant gets back." And I turned around and pushed through the circle of men toward my own tent.

It was William's yelling that probably saved my life. "Gabe!" he said. "He's got a knife!" His voice rose almost to a squeak on the word "knife." I turned around and was beginning to raise a hand when the knife swung up, and I moved my hand to block it. The blade cut all the way through the skin between my thumb and my forefinger, and blood just flew. I stumbled backward, turning my head away and raising both arms. I barely noticed that somebody had moved behind Marion from my right. Then I heard a sound like a meat ax chopping bone, and Marion crumpled up in a heap on the ground, still holding onto that knife. Sergeant Cureton was standing over him, holding the big navy Colt revolver he'd used to lay him out.

It was quiet for a minute to the point where I could hear my own breath, and then Marion gradually sat up, looking all confused and rubbing the knot that was swelling up behind his right ear. William was wrapping his handkerchief around my hand when the sergeant began to talk. His voice was real low, but it carried so you could hear every word.

"Now you listen to me, you worthless scum. I'm not gonna blow your brains out where you sit because you ain't worth the powder and ball—and besides, I'm saving it for a Yankee. And when you get out of the stockade, *if* you ever get out, you're gonna fight Yankees too, whether you like it or not. But I'll tell you this: if you ever think on taking a rifle out of *my* platoon—if I ever even *see* a knife in your goddamn nasty little paw in this camp—I'll personally murder you where you stand." And then, the muzzle of the pistol was in Marion's nose. "You understand me?" And he said it again louder. "You understand?"

Until the military police came, the sergeant made Marion sit where he was on the ground. They led him away in chains, and we heard that he spent six months in the stockade before he went to an engineer battalion to do hard labor.

But curious as it seemed at the time, the person got the real talking-to was me. When I came back from the surgeon, the tents had been folded, and my kit had been packed. As we fell into ranks, the sergeant said he wanted to "have a word of prayer with me."

"Listen"—we were walking then—"I'm sorry you got cut. I knew that man was probably a felon, but it didn't occur to me he'd come out this way. The main thing is that *you* got to learn not to be so damn trusting. An army has all kinds of people in it. Hell, Gabe, the *world* has all kinds of people in it. It ain't like your Sunday school back home. Some people don't fight fair. They fight to get what they want. You can't trust people, and you can't never, *ever* turn your back on 'em. You got to figure *everybody's* got a knife in their boot. Most folks don't, but you got to think as if they do."

He was quiet for a minute, and the only sounds were boots and that clanking rhythm an army makes. Then he went on. "There's people in this army—and every other army—will kill you for a chaw of tobacco. Fact of the matter is, you're probably as like to die in camp as you are in a battle. I know you don't want to think about that, but you got to."

"And another thing. When somebody draws a knife on you, don't put your hands up. Back away, and kick as far as you can. Your legs are longer than your arms, and there's a whole lot less that can bleed on your boot heel than on your bare arms. We'll work on it in camp tonight. Now fall in with the rest of 'em."

And then, as he started to walk away, he said, "I don't want you brooding on this, Gabe. It's just something that happened. You're alive, you ain't hurt bad, and you learned something. That's all there is to it."

But I did brood on it. There was too much in it *not* to brood! I guess I knew there were people like Marion in the world. I had heard my family talk about "no-accounts" in our hometown—people who were dangerous without any real cause. But on that day I'd been face-to-face with one of them—could have died from his pure meanness!

But there was more—and something worse—than that to brood on. When Sergeant Cureton's face had gone all white and he'd pulled the hammer back on his pistol, he hadn't said nothing about Marion killing a "man." Hell, I wouldn't even have minded so much if he'd said "a boy." He had said, "Take a *rifle* out of my platoon." There it was—the plain and simple of it. I was a rifle. I guess I'd known that too, but hearing it spoken out loud had jammed my face in. I was "a rifle," and our platoon was twenty-six rifles, and our battalion was many rifles. If I died, the army lost a rifle. That was more important than "my mother lost a son" or "William lost a cousin."

I would never see the army or the war quite the same way again.

By the middle of August, we were on the march. We were moving across Virginia farm country, across counties with fancy names like "Prince William." The houses were nice, and the livestock, fat, although we saw neither horses nor mules to speak of. By then one army or the other had got 'em, every one.

As a farm boy, I could see that this was land worth fighting for. Every so often we'd pass a place where there had been some skirmish, and there'd be trees and sometimes houses or barns that had been blown to splinters by artillery. Then the singing and joking in the ranks would stop, and we'd all be gawking until it was out of sight again. Now and then our pickets would get into it with Union scouts, and once we got into it with some cavalry; but when we heard a bullet whistle over us, we'd drop behind a tree or fence post, and the old hands would laugh at us.

Pretty soon even we new fellows got to where we could tell how close a rifle shot was, and unless one was close or there was a lot of firing, we'd go on about our business.

I have to say that army food wasn't anything to write home about. At least in this stage of the war, we still got supplies pretty regular, which meant that there were grits and rice and dried beans with salt meat. Most of the time we could buy chickens or eggs and sometimes even fresh meat and greens from the folks lived on the farms. Some soldiers weren't above stealing, but at that point I was never that hungry—not even close.

With our food—and *especially* our cooking—being questionable, most of us would get a bellyache or the runs now and then. So when William took to charging off into the bushes, I just reckoned he was dealing with a case of the runs.

But when he didn't get any rest—or give me any—the better part of one whole night, I commenced to worry. In the morning

I said, "William, this is the worst I ever seen you. We might better talk to the sergeant."

"Ain't nothing he can do," William said. I noticed that he was having trouble walking straight, and his face was a funny gray color.

When I fetched Sergeant Cureton, he must have seen the same thing I did, because he spoke right up.

"Duncan, I want you at the surgeon's wagon right now. I don't want to see you back here until he releases you. That's an order. Corley, you walk him to the surgeon's and see he gets there all right."

William was looking worse by the minute, and we made two stops in the bushes before we got to the surgeon's. The doctor was still having his morning tea, but he came right over when he saw William and me and how he was hanging onto my shoulder. He looked William over, asked a couple of questions, and turned to me.

"He's staying here, Private. Get on back to your unit and tell the company commander he's on sick call until I send him back. You can check on him when we stop tonight."

I gave my best salute and headed back to the platoon at a trot. I still felt worried, but I was a lot less worried once I knew that William would be taken care of. I got there in time to grab a biscuit and fall in for the day's march.

"Sergeant," I said. "The surgeon said I was to report to Captain Byrd…"

"At ease, Corley. I spoke to the captain before you were out of sight. That boy is sick. Probably should have been looked at yesterday or the day before."

"Aw, Sergeant, he'll be all right. He gets to ride in the wagon for a day with me carrying his pack. He'll be right as rain."

"The platoon'll share the pack with you, Corley. He'll be right when the sawbones say he's right."

That's the way I left William, and I regret it to this day. He was my cousin. He had looked after me on the school yard same as my brothers had. We had sat together at the back of the Presbyterian church and had found ways to torment the girls sitting so prim and proper in front of us. We had wrassled and run races and had our bottoms whacked by each other's maw and paw. We had enlisted in the army together.

And that's how I left him: lying on a blanket in a wagon, looking lost and alone, such a far, far piece from the place we both called home.

It was a busy day. The Fifteenth was joining up with other columns of men and supply trains and artillery all day. We marched in the dust we were all kicking up. It was late August and hot; even a blind man could have seen something was happening. At some time after noon, a cheer started back down the line, and then a clot of officers on fine horses trotted by. Somebody said, "That's General Longstreet," and I waved my cap and cheered too, even though I couldn't tell one officer from another. But I did know enough to figure out that if we were joining up with Longstreet, there was likely to be a fight.

We camped that night with more men than I'd ever seen in one place in my life. There were campfires as far as I could see in every direction. "Lord," I thought to myself, "with this many soldiers, I don't see why we can't just march to Washington and get this thing over with right now." But I didn't want to seem like a dumb country boy, so I tried to keep my mouth closed and not to stare.

When supper was on the fire, I asked Sergeant Cureton if I could go and check on William, and he allowed I could. As I went along I asked people where the surgeon was and tried to keep my bearings so I could bring William back with me and not get lost. When I got there I went straight to the doctor I'd talked to in the morning. I saluted real smart and said, "Sir, I'm here to pick up my cousin." He knew I looked familiar, but he questioned me anyway, I figured just to be sure.

"And who would that be, Private?"

"It's William, sir. William Duncan."

"Oh yes," he said, kinda looking away from me. "Duncan. You can have a look and take anything you want to send to the family. But we'll need to bury him tonight. There's likely to be fighting tomorrow."

"No, sir, you don't understand. This here is my cousin William. He wasn't wounded or anything; he just had a bellyache."

Then he finally looked me in the eye. "I'm sorry, son. I thought you knew already. Private Duncan died this afternoon around four o'clock. He was sick with dysentery—real sick—but it surprised us that he died so quick. We did all we could."

That was all he said, and that's how I found out my cousin was dead. Then he just turned around and called to a soldier by the wagon. "Corporal, this man is from Private Duncan's unit. Let him view the body and see he gets any personal effects."

The soldier led me to a wagon that had stretchers laid across it, each one covered with a blanket. There were tags on the men's toes, and he just went down the line till he came to one that said "Duncan." Then he pulled back the blanket and let me see William's face. I reckon it looked like him, but then again, it didn't. The face of the fellow on the stretcher was paler and cleaner than William's had been in some time.

"Are you sure?" I asked him.

He nodded and said, "Yup, it's him all right. I was with him when he died. He wasn't hurting none. They'd given him opium, and he died peaceful. There's a heap of 'em died from this dysentery stuff. Wrong place, wrong time, I reckon. You want his kit or not?"

William's kit was a belt, a knife, and a half-written letter to his maw. I don't know who got his shoes.

I sat up till near dawn, trying to finish that letter and crying to myself. The other fellows in the company brought me supper and even a cup of coffee, but I could hardly swallow, and after a while, they drifted off and let me be.

As near as I can recollect, this is what I wrote to William's maw.

August 28, 1862
Dear Aunt Maybelle,

   I take pen in hand with great sorrow and many tears. I misdoubt that I shall be able to finish this, but I know I must try. My cousin, your dearest child William, died in the service of his country this afternoon. Though he wasn't killed by an enemy bullet, he was a true hero as much as if he had been. Maybe more. The illness that carried him off has taken many other brave soldiers who are here to stand between our homeland and the enemy. He died an honorable death.

   Dear Aunt, how am I ever to return home without our loved one? I fear you may lay some blame for William's death on me, and I confess I feel some. I pray that you will find it in your heart to forgive me for taking him away.

   William was a brave and honorable boy and loved his family above all else. I know he would wish me to tell you that he thought about you often and that he conducted himself as a Christian.

   I do not know how I shall live without his company. Please pray for me.

Your loving nephew,
Gabriel S. Corley
Private, CSA

Sometime in the last hour or two of dark, I fell asleep and dreamed I had been buried alive.

CHAPTER THREE

I don't know how I got through the next morning. Sergeant Cureton sat and made me eat something. When we filled our canteens and were issued ammunition, he and the others took pains to be sure I had everything I was supposed to have. Then we were marching again, and the dust was worse than ever.

Sergeant Cureton fell in beside me. "Gabe," he said. "You calculate you're in any shape to fight? If you can't, I'll leave you with the company's baggage. But I'd sure rather have your rifle pointing toward them Yankees. Tell me the truth, 'cause there'll be other scraps. This ain't no time to be a hero. Can you fight today or not? I need to know *now*."

I thought on that for a spell and said, "I won't lie to you, Sergeant. I'm desperate bad off, but I don't think I could sit still doing nothing when we're going into our first big fight. What if one of our fellows got hurt or killed, and I hadn't done anything to help? I don't think I could stand that."

He clapped me on the shoulder and said, "Then I'll be counting on you." And that was that.

Some time around eleven o'clock in the morning, we stopped for a drink of water and rested in the shade. Then we commenced to hear artillery, more than I had ever heard before, and it was closer too. You could feel the ground shake, and the powder smell took my breath away. A little while later we came through a gap, and when the smoke blew away, we saw a long line of our folks spread out to our left. An officer rode up to Colonel Gist, his horse all lathered, and pointed out through the smoke, but our artillery was still going as fast as they could shoot, and we couldn't see or hear anything.

All of a sudden the bugles began sounding "charge," and all them units we'd been marching with for two days set off at a trot into the smoke. When we could see again, we saw soldiers in blue uniforms all in lines, marching across from our right to our left and directly into the cannon as if they'd never seen us. Our front ranks began firing, and we saw soldiers in blue fall. For a minute or two, the Yankees looked like they didn't know what to do. Some of 'em re-formed their lines and started forward. Some others turned toward us and began to fire back. For the first time I could hear bullets buzzing around us. When I saw the first man fall out in front of me, something stopped up my throat, and for just a minute, I thought real hard about turning tail. Real hard!

Then the Fifteenth was at the front, and we heard Sergeant Cureton bawling out, "Hostiles to the front, boys. Take aim and fire. Mark your man. Don't waste powder."

I have to say, I wasn't no hero that day, and any man was around me says he was is probably lying. I aimed at a line of men in blue and fired. Loaded, ran forward, and fired again. Our colors never fell, so we were able to mostly stay together around the flag. Before we came up on the Yankee lines, they must have realized they were in a bad way, because they broke and ran.

Our fellows let out a cheer and took after them. I saw a Union officer riding up and down the lines, trying to make them hold their ground, but it wasn't no use. We must have chased them half a mile before some of their units began to take cover and fire into us. Then we slowed down and got a whole lot more careful. Still and all, by the time we lost shooting light, we'd chased 'em off the field, and they were still running the next day.

Company K had five men wounded and none killed. The Fifteenth in general was in about the same shape. We heard that General Longstreet had flanked the Yankee army, which must not have known we'd been there. Between our artillery and the surprise of all them fresh troops, we pretty well twisted their tails.

The new fellows like me were so excited we could hardly stop talking long enough to eat and roll out our blankets. I could tell Sergeant Cureton was pleased, but he took the occasion to fuss at us about staying together and minding our marksmanship anyway, just so's we wouldn't get too full of ourselves.

I had wondered how I'd behave when we got in a real fight. I reckon everybody does. We'd heard that some fellows never even fire their rifles, and others get behind something and won't move. A few even try to run away. Judging by the little bit of ammunition I had left, there wasn't any doubt I'd fired my rifle. Whether I'd hit anything was another matter. I hadn't run away, though, and taking all things together, I decided I had been more afraid of being a coward than of being shot by a Yankee.

I sure wished William could have been there to help us chase them Yankees.

They called that battle "Second Manassas" because, I reckon, there had been another one near there before.

I say "they called it" because ordinary soldiers usually didn't have names for battles like the names they put on them later for the history books. Some of them, I remember well—I remember pretty much everything we saw and did. Others, I hardly remember at all. They just kind of run together over the years.

What I do *always* remember is marching until I thought we'd drop, going hungry, and being cold. At Fredericksburg, I like to froze to death, and we crept down at night and stole coats and shoes off the dead Yankees left on the field. When we were at the same place again in the spring of that year, we were overrun, and I saw what it was like to fall back and try to stay alive at the same time.

I remember how it felt to eat supper with a fellow one night and to see him lying dead on the ground the next day, his blood or even his brains running out on the ground. After a while I almost couldn't grieve anymore. I'd just used up all the grieving I'd had; I thought mostly about being able to get a night's sleep and praying I'd see home again.

When folks find out you were a soldier, they almost always get around to asking if you were at Gettysburg. I was, and like everybody else, I knew at the time that it was something big. Still and all, it seemed to me like any other big battle. We were under the command of General Early, same as we had been at Chancellorsville. When we first came into the battle, we had the Yankees running, but then it got late, and we slacked off. By the time it was dark, they had the high ground, and there was a *lot* more of them than anybody had figured.

On the second day, General Lee had us pretty far out on the left side of his line, and although we could hear all the cannons, we never saw General Pickett's famous charge. I'm just as satisfied I didn't. I seen enough men die for one lifetime.

Of course, the most important fight for most soldiers is the one where they get wounded themselves.

The battle when I finally took a bullet was in the spring of the year. I remember that the trees had leafed out to where I could tell one from another, the oaks from the gums and the hickories and such. Sometimes, even now, when I'm passing through the woods in the spring, I'll look up and see those little old leaves, pink and yellowish with the shapes just beginning to show good. And then I'll get a picture in my mind of me lying on the bare ground, roots poking into my back, looking up at those same spring leaves and wondering if I'll bleed to death.

On the second day of the fight, we got to the place they called "wilderness," and believe me, whoever called it "wilderness" had it right! The trees and brambles were so thick that you could be a rifle's length from another fellow and not see the color of his uniform. The guns had set fires in the woods upwind of us, so the whole time we were there, we could smell smoke.

We had come into the heavy woods and were lucky to hear the Federals moving up before they ever knew we were there. We surprised them, and it was hot and heavy for a while. We were so close to each other that you could almost feel the heat from their rifle barrels; we were so close that you'd fire at a man and hear your bullet hit flesh—hear him holler and fall.

When there was finally a lull, I crept out to the end of our line, looking for a place to answer a call of nature, and I almost stumbled down a dry creek bed. You couldn't see it till you were almost in it because the trees growing on its bank were as big as the ones on the flat ground above it. I ain't never mentioned the fact that I was going to relieve myself when I happened on the particular knowledge of the battlefield that won me some honors later that day. But I will say that from a soldier's point of view, there's a whole lot more stumbling into things than most generals want to own up to.

I had just got back on our line after my little walk when the Yankees came at us again. Our line was thin right there, and since we had plenty of cover, Sergeant Cureton yelled for us to fall back to some down timber we'd seen earlier. We scrambled our way back, stumbling, shooting, and running back from tree to tree until we got ourselves settled behind the tree trunks. From there we could take our time and pick off the Yanks every time they showed any hide at all. It was a while before we found out that Sergeant Cureton hadn't got back with us.

Up and down the line, I heard fellows beginning to ask, "You seen the sergeant?" and, "Was he with you?"

Well, he *had* been with me when we'd started back, but I'd lost sight of him in the first minute or two. Then I heard something that just stopped my heart. It was Sergeant Cureton calling from over near the Yankee line. At the same time, several of us tumbled over the logs and commenced to move toward him, but those there Yanks weren't having any of it. We didn't get three feet before we had to scramble back to where we'd been. When it got quiet again, he was still calling.

"Boys, I'm hit pretty bad," he said. "Can't you fetch me a drink? Boys, can you hear me?"

Soldiers who'd been at the front as long as we had were used to hearing men between the lines during a battle. People from both sides would be out there, hurting and thirsty. Sometimes somebody would show a white flag or just go ahead and crawl out there with canteens. For the most part we were inclined to let people from either side do that kind of thing. We'd take water to one of our own or even to a wounded Yankee if we could reach him.

Everybody understood that, I reckon because we would've wanted somebody to do the same for us if we'd been out there. When we realized Sergeant Cureton was too far away for us to reach him, one of our fellows shouted over to the Yankee lines, "Hey, Yanks, can't y'all hear our sergeant? He's right there in front of you! Take care of him!"

Sure enough, in a minute we saw a Yankee soldier, a big old fellow with yellow hair and corporal's stripes on his arm, crawling out to where the sergeant was. When he got to Sergeant Cureton, he stopped and picked up his head, and I thought, "Good, at least he's going to get a drink."

Then the big Yankee called out in some kind of funny voice, "Is dis your zageant? Zee, I take care of him." And he put his revolver to Sergeant Cureton's head and shot him.

It's unnatural to ever get used to seeing young men die, especially when they die violent or in pain. But what I see most often in nightmares is my own sergeant's face when the pistol ball scattered his brains out the side of his head. His eyes had this kinda surprised look, and his mouth was in a perfectly round O. The Yankee, who was just as cool as could be, wiped his hand on some leaves and put his pistol back in its holster.

For a minute we were so dumbfounded that we couldn't even think. Just for that little space of time, we all figured we must have imagined it—that it couldn't possibly be true. But then it sank in, and every rifle on our line must have fired at the same time. Except mine.

My mind did this funny thing it does now and then. It just went away and stood over somewhere, looking at me. I could see my face turning red and hear blood hammering at my ears, and the next thing you know, I was crawling up and down the line yelling like I was touched.

"Stop firing!" I was screaming. "Stop firing! Save your ammunition! Listen to me." I reckon that at last my lunacy must have got the better of theirs. "Down this a-way!" I yelled, pointing toward the dry creek bed. "Come down this a-way, and put them goddamn bayonets on your rifles."

I suspect the Yankees were lying pretty low, considering we'd just put a solid wall of lead over their heads. Whatever the reason, they never heard us all tumbling down that bank; or if they did, they didn't know what it was. I trotted down to the bottom of the draw with the whole platoon behind me, and we crawled back up the bank at the end of the Yankee line, just as quiet as red Indians.

Right then it didn't matter to me whether the rest of our fellows were there or whether I was all alone. I wanted one thing, and I was bound to get it or die. I wanted my bayonet in that Yankee's stomach so I could see his face and watch him die.

They never knew we were there until we were on them. Some of them were so surprised that they didn't know it even then. I jumped over one Yankee soldier didn't even know who we were until the fellow behind me pinned him to the ground with his bayonet. I jumped over that man to get to the big Yankee who'd shot Sergeant Cureton. He looked up and tried to draw his revolver just as I got to him, and for part of a second, we was looking at each other eye to eye. Then I swung the butt of my rifle into his face so hard I could feel bone breaking, and I began stabbing him. I say "began" because I was still stabbing him—or what was left of him—two or three minutes later when they tried to get me to quit.

I think we must have killed most of a platoon: some of them were shot after they tried to surrender, and some were shot in the back when they tried to run away. I ain't proud we done that, but it's so, and I might as well admit it. Come to think of it, I reckon that's about what a war is good for. It takes a crowd of youngsters that start out like I did and turns 'em into the kind of animals will shoot another man in the back while he's running away.

The ones survived, we marched back down the draw as prisoners. The officer at the rear looked real surprised when we came marching in, and he said, "Boys, we ain't seen many prisoners today. Who's in charge of this mess?"

I never said anything, but all the rest pointed to me, so I got to answer the questions.

"You mean to tell me one of these damn Yankees shot a wounded prisoner where you could *see* him?"

"Not one of *these*," I said. "The one *done* it is dead."

"Well, I'm glad to hear it. And whose idea was it to flank them?"

"I reckon it was mine, but we were all in it together."

"But you were leading them?"

"I reckon. If anybody was."

"Well, Private, I want your name and unit. I'm reporting this to regimental headquarters."

I suppose that was all well and good; but what would have pleasured me at the time was some fresh water—and a discharge from the army.

Within an hour we were back on the line. We were low on ammunition and fighting with a unit we'd seen but didn't really know—another part of the Fifteenth. None of us were thinking too straight, but what I did was downright stupid. I'm lucky I didn't die on the spot.

The sergeant in that unit was an older fellow with gray stubble on his face. He mostly seemed tired, but it appeared to me he knew what he was doing, and I liked him right off. We were still fighting in the thickets. I remember the peculiar sound of bullets tearing through the brush around us almost like a rainstorm and the sweet smell of fresh tree sap. Trouble was, we weren't going much of anywhere. The Yankees would push us back a ways, and then we'd counterattack and push them back to where we'd been before. In the meantime, some folks died taking ground we'd already had.

I was beginning to pray for night to come when the sergeant said, "I need for one of you fellows to find our captain and get us some ammunition up here. You there"—he said, pointing at me—"you got long legs. Here, take this note to Captain Boyd. Let him know where we're at, and for God's sake, get us some powder and balls, or we can't hold."

I stuffed the note inside my shirt and commenced to crawl to my left until I couldn't hear any firing in front of me. Then I got up slow and careful-like behind a tree and tried to get my bearings. The sun had moved, and in the woods it was hard to remember just which way the shadows had been earlier in the day. I spent a minute or two debating with myself about the direction I needed to go in. It seemed to me headquarters had been to the north of us the last time I had been there, but we'd been back and forth so often that I couldn't be sure.

"Well," I said to myself. "It don't look like the same direction to me, but that there is north, so I'll go awhile and just see." Trouble was, I'd forgot we were in a thicket, and nobody knew where anybody was. I hadn't gone twenty feet when I barged into a snag, stumbled, and fell right on my face. About the same time there was a rifle shot from directly in front of me.

"Humph," I thought. "I reckon barking my shin mighta saved me from taking a bullet this time." But then when I tried to move, my leg wouldn't behave at all, and when I looked down, it was bent at a peculiar angle. There was a ragged hole in my trousers, and blood was soaking the leaves.

"Great God A'mighty, that wasn't no tree limb!" I thought. "I been shot!"

I dragged myself behind a tree and looked in the direction the shot had come from. I was having some trouble getting my mind around the idea that it had really happened. There wasn't any pain to speak of right then, just a burning and numbness like I'd been kicked by a mule. For a minute I lay there, watching my pants leg getting soaked with blood and wondering what the hell I'd do next.

Then I saw something move, and two or three Yankee soldiers came creeping up, motioning like there might be others behind them. I took a careful bead and dropped the one in front. The others disappeared, and in the quiet I could hear the sound of men scrambling around in the leaves. I had finished reloading and was putting a cap under my hammer when a ball tore through the bark of my tree and scattered splinters into my face. Then another one did the same thing on the other side, and then a third ricocheted off a root.

Since there was only one of me, and these particular Yankees were clearly shooters, I knew it would only be a minute or two till somebody got to where he could get a clear shot at me. And there was not a thing I could do about it. Between shots, I began to pray. Maw wouldn't have wanted me to pass on without letting God know I was coming.

If God saved me—and I ain't saying He didn't—he used that old sergeant. In a minute or two, he come belly flopping up behind me, yelling for the others with him to spread out. Maybe I didn't do anything else useful for my new platoon that day, but I did manage to get myself shot and let 'em know where the enemy was coming from.

CHAPTER FOUR

I don't recollect a lot about the place where they sawed my leg off. I do remember the ride to a big tent and me and two or three others moaning and thrashing. I remember that I held on to the side of the wagon so hard that my nails sank into the wood and dug out splinters. With the other hand I was trying to hold my leg so it didn't bounce with every rut, but it was a losing fight.

I reckon God smiled on me for the time and place where I was wounded (if you can see it that way), for there was still laudanum to put me in a haze for the actual cutting and sawing. I have a vision not connected to anything else of a doctor in a bloody apron standing in front of me and saying, "You're one of the lucky ones, son. We left you a good knee."

Some day or two later, I can't tell how many, there was another ride, longer that time, to a building that used to be a schoolhouse. In my mind, that's the "thirsty ride" because there was one canteen of water for the whole wagonload, and we drank it up long before we got where we were going. When they took me off the wagon that time, the opium had wore off, and I bit mighty nigh through my lip trying not to scream.

After that, the worst of it was changing the bandages. I learned to live in the pain all day and all night, but anything was better than having them unwind the wrappings and pull 'em off the stump. I ain't ashamed to confess that I cried every night when it got dark, and I wished to God I had never left home. From what little I can recollect, about as many of us left that schoolhouse dead as alive—or half-alive the way I was.

The third move was not to a "hospital" like the sawing tent and the schoolhouse had been. As rides go, it wasn't all that bad, except I had got used to the opium, and not having it made me sick and dizzy. When we finally got there, it was like a camp with tents, except there were cots in the tents that we could lie on, and we looked to be far enough from the fighting that we couldn't even hear the artillery anymore.

The first person I saw when the wagon stopped was a big darky who let down the gate and looked over the pitiful sight inside.

"Gentl'mens," he said. "My name Grady. I got yo cots all made up, and if you'll gimme a minute, I get each one of you settled."

"Marse," he said to me. "It do look like you could use a little help. Awright if I lifs you?"

"Well," I said, almost too sorry for myself to speak. "I ain't hopping down by myself, now am I?"

"Naw, suh. Naw, suh, you sho ain't. But you gone feel better by and by. You jus' wait and see if you don't. If you don' mind, I gonna carry you dis time." And he lifted me as if I were a sickly two-year-old. "Now, Marse, I done tol' you my name. What I gonna call *you*?"

"Well, you could call me Private Corley or Gabriel Corley, but folks mostly call me Gabe."

"Gabriel! Thas a Bible name, ain't it, Marse?"

"It's a Bible name. And if you want a laugh, Grady, it's an angel's name. I look like an angel to you?"

"Don't rightly know, Marse, being as how I ain't never seen no angels I know of. You might be de very spit and image of an angel for all I know."

"Uh-huh—might be. But if there's many more look like me, I 'spect none of us'll be wanting to go to heaven."

"Oh no, we all be wanting to go to heaven. Jus' not right now." Then, as he set me down on my cot real gentle-like, he said, "If it suit you, I call you Marse Gabriel."

"That suits me fine. And I'll call you Grady."

"Yassuh. I going to fetch you and these other gentl'mens a nice cold drink right now, and if you need the slop bucket, it right here under yo cot. In the morning, if'n we both have time after breakfast, I maybe shave your whiskers."

"Grady, I ain't made no other appointments for tomorrow, so I reckon a shave would suit me fine."

For those of us who were new in camp, Grady's was the last face we saw at night and the first in the morning. I was still sleeping in little bits and pieces, maybe an hour at a time. As often as not, I'd wake up yelling and sweating with a nightmare. When you consider that I was in a tent with five other fellows doing the same way, you can see nighttime wasn't that much of a treat.

That first morning, they rang a bell in the mess tent, and we could see Grady outside helping other men up the path between the rows of tents. Directly he come back with a stack of tin plates and forks. I still didn't much care to have anything to do with food, but I was sipping on a cup of milk.

"Marse Gabriel," he said. "If'n you could see fit to finish off that biscuit, I'll see can I find you another."

"I'm obliged, Grady," I said, "but I'm still kinda off my feed."

"Yassuh, I do see. But if you'll pardon me, it might be worth yo while jus' to have a bite or two whether you wants it or not. You know, jus' so you don't forgit how to chew and all."

"Well, I reckon I don't want my jaw to lock up on me." I took a bite, more to please him than anything else, and found that I could get it down. I kept gnawing at it until I finished the whole biscuit, which was the most food I'd got around at one time since they'd taken my leg.

When he came back to collect the plates, Grady made over me like I'd done a day's work. "Good for *you*, Marse Gabe. We got to get some strength back in yo arms, 'cause tomorrow you be getting some crutches. Then there won't be no more eatin' in the bedroom like this here!"

Then he looked around the tent and said, "'Spect that goes for the rest of you gentl'mens too. Got to get you all strong enough to get around on your own."

By that time he was two beds up from me. The fellow in the bed, man by the name of Reese, was tall and stringy with the beginning of a black beard, and his right arm had been cut off above the elbow. He'd not said a word that I could hear, neither on the wagon nor since we'd gotten to camp. I reckon he'd been saving up, though, because when Grady started to reach for his plate, the fellow snatched it up and threw it at his face.

"Now you get away from me, you shiftless nigger!" he yelled. "I don't have to listen to nothing comes out of your black mouth. I'll eat when I want, and I'll get up when I want. You jus' get away from me!"

Grady had already halfway turned when he saw the plate coming, and then he took his shirttail and wiped the milk from the side of his head. Then he picked up the plate and cup and knelt to scrape up the food from the dirt floor of the tent. Every one of us in the tent was sitting up, looking at the man, but nobody said a word. Grady moved around the man's bed, almost whispering, "Yassuh, Marse Reese. Jus' as you say."

Later that morning, Grady was back, and when he got around to me, we moved outside the tent to a chair in the sun, and he commenced to lather up my stubbly beard.

"Grady," I said, "I'm sorry our bunkmate was upset this morning. We're all of us about half-touched, but there was no call for him to take on that way."

"Oh, hush, Marse Gabe. It ain't nothing at all. Don't even think about it. He just grieving, and he got cause to grieve. If'n I was a-hurting like him, no telling what I'd be doing."

"Still," I said. "This here has got to be some hard work."

"Uh-huh," he said, beginning to scrape away with his razor. "De war put all of us in some hard spots. Jus' got to pray the good Lawd give us strength to do what we got to do." And then he began to hum while he worked.

Well, I have to say that Reese got better about as fast as any of us, but he never got the first bit easier to live with. If anything, he got worse as he got stronger. When we were all up and around, they parceled us out to other tents, and I was glad to get away from him. Grady never changed either, and most of us got to where we were always glad to see him coming.

I've had considerable time to study on Grady over the years, and I think I got some idea about why remembering him in particular has always been important. I knew pretty quick why I felt close to him then: I was like a baby who feels close to his mother. He did everything for me and somehow made it seem like I was doing him a kindness.

I knew early on that Grady was a better Christian than I am, with a whole lot less reason to be; there was not a drop of pretending in him. When he sang a gospel song, all the while tending to some disgusting chore for a swearing soldier, he wasn't just making soothing noise (although it was soothing). He was praising God.

I hadn't been in camp very long when I discovered that I was going to be doing some work myself. When the stump of my right leg had quit bleeding and had started to heal over pretty good, a fellow came around one day and measured it against the other leg. A week or so later, he was back with a hardwood peg. I could hardly put any weight on it and didn't want to try, but he still spent about half a day fiddling with the padding and showing me how to strap it on.

"I know you ain't keen on this right now," he said, "but believe me, you're gonna want it later on."

It was after he had left that the real work began. At first I hung on to Grady's shoulder, barely letting my stump touch the inside of the wooden socket. I reckon I could have done the same thing using my crutch, but I was still afraid to put any real weight down, and my balance was terrible. After a few days I began to get a little strength back, and Grady would ease away and let me try a step or two on my own. About half the time I'd fall the first time the peg hit the ground. But then, little by little, I got to where I could go two steps and then three. Through all that time, when I sat on the ground banging my fist in the dirt and swearing, Grady was as solemn and as patient as he could be. Then when I was ready, he'd reach a hand down and stand me up like a big brother would do with a hurting child. Somehow he seemed to know just how much to let me do before I was completely wore out.

"Marse Gabe," he'd say, "reckon that's enough for this mawning. Wanna get you back to yo cot now, and we practice some more in the evening. But I do believe you about as quick to learn as anybody I ever seen."

Of course we both had sense enough to know that I wasn't any better or worse than anybody else at learning to walk again. He was saying what I needed to hear to keep me going. But in some odd way, he did mean it. That's why I said he didn't playact. He was the same person all the time, and it was real.

It could have been that he was just naturally kind and strong and able to look past our human faults—able to be an accommodating servant. But the one thing I can't ever forget is that he was doing all this for men who were fighting and killing Union soldiers to keep *him* from having his freedom!

We didn't think about that much. We were told, and told ourselves, that the fight was about "states' rights." But Grady couldn't help thinking about it, and it never made even a little difference in the way he treated us. That's what I can't forget. There was a man born and brought up to believe he wasn't even a real man, and yet he saw us, men who might have owned him and his family, as if we were his brothers.

It took some getting used to the idea that a nigger-slave was, and I reckon still is if he's alive today, a better man that I am. I didn't realize it right then, but as much as anything else—as much as the terror that made me want to vomit before a battle, the sound of exploding shells, the stink of death, or the sound of men dying (and I still have nightmares to this very day)—coming to know in my heart that Grady was my better changed my life. It's like it just turned everything I had always known to be true right on its head. And there ain't no way to get it back like it was.

I left that hospital camp a different person altogether. I was lighter by a lower leg and a foot and wounded in some other ways that ain't as easy to see with your eyes, but I had crossed over the line between boy and man. I had learned that the truest things we think we know aren't always true at all. Grady was, and is, a big part of that change, but he wasn't all of it.

Of course, Grady hadn't always been a hospital orderly. He had started the war as a field hand on the farm where our hospital camp was set up. He and the farm were the property of Mr. and Mrs. Robert Pinckney III of the Virginia Pinckneys.

When I got to where I wanted to get about the camp some, I noticed that Grady would walk to and from the house we could see across the fields and would usually come back with supplies or food, like butter, eggs, or milk, and sometimes even with a wagonload of fodder for the camp animals. When I'd try to use the new wooden leg, his arm around my waist and mine around his shoulders, I'd let my curiosity run on a bit. Truth is, I was desperate homesick for the commonness of a farm—I mean for doing the things that felt like home that I'd seen him doing, like hitching up a mule, pitching fodder, or shelling corn.

I don't believe I ever heard Grady mention so much as the Pinckney family name when we were in the tent or around a crowd. But one day we had a session with my new leg and crutches, just the two of us.

"Grady," I said as if the thought had just crossed my mind. "What did you say your master's name was?"

"Don't know as I said yet, Marse Gabriel, but I belongs to Marse Robert Pinckney. Miz Agnes Pinckney his wife, but she de onliest one at the homeplace now."

"I 'spect Mr. Pinckney is in the army like the rest of us," I said.

"Yassuh, he a colonel. 'Cept he ain't like a real colonel, you know, fighting and such. He work in an office in Richmond, seeing the soldiers get the rations they needs. He always been a right poorlie gentleman. Don't imagine he could be a real soldier."

"Humph," I said, hauling myself up off the ground for about the third time. "*You* might not think he's a real soldier, but most of us in the army think food and blankets is a heap more important than brass buttons!"

"Is dat a fac'?" he said. "Well he a fine gentleman if dere ever was one. I didn't mean no disrespect."

"I know you didn't, Grady. I just wanted you to understand that if it wasn't for folks like Colonel Pinckney, General Lee and the rest of them high mucky-de-mucks couldn't move an inch."

"Don't reckon I ever thought much on dat."

"So is Mrs. Pinckney running the place by herself."

"Yassuh, Miz Agnes in charge until Master get home again. Of course, most of the darkies know what we got to do wifout being told. And if we *ain't* doing, Miz Agnes only got to mention it. Wouldn't nobody on the place say a word again' her, 'cept maybe ol' Mattie in the kitchen, and nobody listen to her sass."

"Does Colonel Pinckney get home often?"

"He don't get home at all, Marse Gabriel. When de war was jus' begun, Miz Agnes used to go down dere for to visit. Dey was even balls and such like, and she and her maid would take the train down so she could be wif Marse Robert. Seem like lately dey won't even let Miz Agnes nor nobody else on a train. But Mattie say Miz Agnes get letters real regular, so I figure dat's how she know to run the place jus' right."

One day when I was getting around well enough to begin to be bored, I was helping out over in the cook tent. About then Grady came up in the wagon with victuals and other supplies the ladies in the town had sent.

As I was helping to unload the wagon, he said to me, "Marse Gabriel, reckon you feel well enough to walk back from the big house if you was to ride over in the wagon wit me?"

It was an idea that I found more than a little agreeable. Cook let on he didn't care one way or the other, so when we were finished unloading the supplies, I hiked myself up onto the bed of the wagon and scooted on my rear up to the seat.

Lord God, you would have thought I was King Solomon himself—I felt that free and right just being in a farm wagon again and bumping across a field!

"Grady," I said as we got closer to the house. "That looks like a tolerable big barn. How much stock the Pinckneys got?"

"I can't say zactly, Marse Gabriel. There's about as many horses and mules as I got fingers and toes if you counts the riding horses and the ones for the carriage. And course, we got milk cows and some fo' meat. Don't nobody count the hogs unless we taking 'em to market."

"That's right smart of a farm! How many acres you calculate they work?"

"Lawd, Marse Gabriel, I ain't got no head for them kinda numbers. Seems I heard one the drivers say somethin' 'bout fifteen hundred acres."

I whistled in surprise. "How many head of darkies, Grady?"

He chuckled. "I don't reckon I ever tried to count. There's nine…no, ten cabins."

Without saying anything, I calculated in my head that that would be forty or forty-five people. "What you raising mainly?" I asked.

"Oh, we raises corn and some wheat, and ever'body got a garden. But the money crop is fine bright-leaf tobacco! Bes' in the country. You see it on yonder side the house when we gets there."

CHAPTER FIVE

I heard her before I saw her, the way I will still sometimes hear that voice in my dreams. Grady and I had put the wagon in the barn and had unhitched the mules, Grady going on all the while about this outbuilding or that animal, as proud as if he owned them himself.

We walked up to the well, which was just behind the porch of the big house. Grady let down the bucket and drew a cold drink. I almost set in to blubbering when I was reminded of the taste of fresh well water from my own yard, but then I was doing that a lot in them days. He dipped the tin dipper for me and then reached for the gourd for himself, and he was about to drain it off when a woman's voice on the porch behind us said, "Well, Grady, have you brought company with us all unprepared?"

We turned around, snatching off our hats, and like he was introducing President Jefferson Davis, Grady said, "Miz Agnes, this here Private Gabriel Corley of the Fifteenth South Carolina Infantry. He over at the camp, and I was just interducing him to the place since he a farm boy hisself."

And I, adding my own stammer, said, "Ma'am, I'm honored to meet you. I never meant to intrude on your home. I was just treating a case of homesickness like Grady said. We'll be on our way back to camp directly." And I stumbled back a step as if I was fixing to go.

It was right then that I began to understand why it was Grady spoke of her the way he did. She was down to where we were standing in one motion, her feet skipping down the steps but barely touching 'em so it seemed as if she were floating down on her skirt. She was tall for a woman, and the top of her head reached my shoulder. And under a little lace cap, that head was covered with curls the color of honey. I didn't notice right then, but I would come to know later that her eyes were light gray with little laugh wrinkles at the corner and the longest eyelashes I'd ever seen.

With both her hands she caught my own left hand, and she said in the warmest voice I will ever hear, "Private Corley, you must never, *ever* think of yourself as intruding on our homeplace. A wounded soldier—no, *any* soldier who has taken up arms for our cause—is at home here, and it would grieve me to the heart to have you think otherwise."

And then, since I was standing like I'd been hit in the head with an ax, she dropped my hand and said in a teasing tone, "For your penance, Grady and I will make you sit on the back steps and talk with us while you finish your water." And I did.

Considering all these words I been writing, I don't reckon you'd be inclined to believe me when I say that I'd never been much of a talker. But it's the gospel truth. In the past, talking—especially in polite company—had been like a chore to me. As I look back on it, I suspect that I heard so much of my own voice *that* afternoon because it was the only way to keep Agnes talking.

She fixed those big gray eyes on me and said, "First you must tell us about South Carolina. I've never been farther than Richmond, and I was a poor student in geography class. What is your home like?"

"Not too different from here, Miz Pinckney. My family lives on a farm like this one, except that we can't raise that fine tobacco like you all do here. And of course, our farm is smaller."

"I have a brother and two sisters," she said. "I'm the third one. My brother is in the army in General Stuart's cavalry. Do you have brothers and sisters?"

"Yes'm, I got two older brothers, both in the army, and one older sister. Her beau is a soldier too. I reckon most everybody is. I'm the youngest of the lot. They all tell me I'm spoiled."

"I'm sure they're just teasing you, Private Corley. I'll bet you're not spoiled at all. Do you write to you mother often? You must, you know; she worries about you every day. What church do you attend?"

"We're Presbyterians, ma'am. Maw was raised Methodist. She says Presbyterians are stiff necked, but she made us learn the catechism all the same."

She laughed then, and if I hadn't already been half in love, I would have been after that laugh. "Oh, Private Corley, we're Episcopal, and I'm sure we *invented* stiff necks. Your mother was quite right to make you memorize the catechism. You didn't like it at the time, but you will remember it all your life. I bet you'll make your own children do the same."

She stopped for a minute and looked as if she was trying to make up her mind to say something. Then she said, "I wonder, would it be too cruel if I asked about your wound?"

"No, ma'am, I don't mind."

"You needn't call me 'ma'am,' Private Corley. It makes me sound so old. I was just wondering if you're still in any pain."

"Yes, ma'am...I mean, yes, it still hurts. It's right peculiar, because sometimes the part that ain't there hurts. I'll reach down to rub my foot and realize it's gone. But compared to what it was, the hurting is so light now I mostly don't notice."

Suddenly, without any warning, there were tears in her eyes, and she pulled a handkerchief from her skirt pocket. It surprised me because I didn't know what I had done. "I'm sorry!" I said, plumb scared to death she'd want to stop talking.

"Don't be silly, Private!" she said, reaching down to touch my arm. "It's my fault entirely. After all, I had to ask. Sometimes I'm just too forward, asking things that are none of my business. My mother and sisters are always warning me about that."

I don't recollect what else we talked about, and it really doesn't matter. When she put that little lace handkerchief back in her pocket, my heart was gone for sure. After a bit (I ain't sure how long, but I do remember that shadows had moved across the steps), I saw Grady looking up at me from the bottom step with a little smile on his face, and it occurred to me that I was talking without her asking any questions.

At last she stood up and shook her skirts as if she was exasperated. "Well, Grady, this is a fine how-d'ye-do, ain't it? You bring company, and I talk his head off, and we don't even have a cup of coffee to offer him." Of course, that didn't signify, since none of us had seen coffee since the first few weeks in the army. "So here's what we must do. You all have to be back in camp this evening, but Sunday noon, if Grady can catch a chicken and Private Corley is still in camp, he'll be ordered to dinner here on pain of court-martial. He'll meet my aunt Sudie, and if I can keep just a little quiet, perhaps he will even be allowed to talk. Goodness, are you going to walk all that way back to camp?"

"Yes, ma'am, I really need the practice, and I reckon Grady will let me lean if I have to."

"Then"—her little warm hands were holding my left hand again—"we'll say good evening, and I hope your walk will not be too taxing."

Noon on Sunday finally came after what seemed to me to be about a month. Grady had let it be known that I was invited to dinner at the big house, and nobody in camp seemed to notice much. The doctors and the rest of them were always so busy that if you weren't about to die or didn't need help desperate bad, they might near wouldn't see you. In fact, nobody seemed to know much what to do with us who were alive and able to get around but not in any shape to fight. So one less mouth to feed at Sunday dinner seemed to suit everybody just fine. Grady helped me shake the dust out of what I had left of a uniform and arranged to make a wagon trip back to the farm at just the right time of day.

I was surprised and flustered when he pulled up to the front door of the house. The big front porch and the rustle of Miz Agnes's and Miz Sudie's Sunday silk skirts reminded me again of what had been in the back of my mind all week: I was an ignorant country boy likely to do most anything in a fine house like this.

Miz Sudie was little, and round like an apple. She walked with a cane that had a silver handle, and she looked stern as a schoolmistress. Both the ladies were dressed for church and still had their gloves and bonnets on when we got there. I don't mind telling you that when they looked down at me from that high porch, I felt like a chicken thief in a court of law.

Miz Agnes was holding her hands in front of her, and she give a little bow and said, "Private Corley, I'd like you to meet my great aunt, Miss Sudie Collins. I've already told her what I know about you."

About then Miz Sudie got to looking even more serious, and she snapped, "Oh, for goodness' sake, Agnes. Let's don't stand on ceremony for once. Gabriel, I am so pleased you could come. You must call me Aunt Sudie. Come up here and shake my hand before Agnes and I take off our bonnets and get some dinner on for you. You look half starved."

Looking back, I'm still surprised when I remember that by the time we were all sitting at the table—just the three of us around a long, shiny table with silver and fine china and white napkins—I had already forgotten to be edgy. Miz Sudie said a right long blessing with a considerable number of "thees" and "thous," but once we got to passing the food, it really felt like I was family.

"Gabriel," Miz Sudie said. "That's spoon bread, and the bowl is hot. Put a pat of butter on it. Do they serve that where you're from—is it North Carolina?"

"No, ma'am, it's South Carolina. I don't recollect seeing anything just like this. I 'spect we'd be more likely to have hominy. But this sure is tasty."

"Well," she said. "You'll have to be sure to ask if you need more of anything. Mattie is not the most accommodating darky in the world, but she's the best cook in the state."

And from what I could tell, Miz Sudie was right on the money. Mattie shuffled back and forth from the kitchen, looking at me like she had serious doubts about inviting poor whites into the dining room, but the food would have brought tears to a grown man's eyes.

I got to enjoying the food so much that I directly forgot what I'd told myself about a thousand times during the week: watch the ladies and do what they do so you don't make country-boy mistakes. But I must have done all right—or at least they were too polite to say otherwise—because we all seemed to enjoy ourselves. It was almost as if they were happy to have something solid and familiar they could do for the cause—to be feeding a real hungry soldier and not just sewing or making bandages or whatnot.

Miz Agnes talked about her brother again; she wondered where he was and when she would get another letter. Her paw was dead like mine, and her maw lived with one of her sisters who hadn't married yet. Miz Sudie quizzed me about my family, how South

Carolina was different from Virginia, and what we raised on our farm. And we all said things we maybe didn't entirely believe about how soon the war would be over and how everybody's sons and brothers would all come home.

After dinner we sat awhile in the parlor, the ladies rocking and sewing and me trying to keep my wooden leg from sticking out all the time. In that fine room, that damn stick of wood seemed to be the size of a singletree and about as awkward.

When Miz Agnes went to help Miz Sudie get ready for her nap, Grady stuck his head around the door to know if he should help me to the outhouse, all real genteel-like.

And then I was back in the parlor again, alone with Miz Agnes.

"Private Corley, I wonder if you'd like to see our stereopticon pictures?

"Well, I can't rightly say, since I don't believe I know what one of them is."

"Oh, then you must see it. It has the most wonderful views of London and Paris."

Of course, she was right about the pictures. Even though I was glad I didn't have to say where I thought Paris might be, the pictures were fine, and the stereopticon thing made it seem as if I were standing right in the same place. But the thing I remember isn't the pictures. It's the scent of Miz Agnes when she held the stereopticon, leaned over me, and showed me how to slide the pictures up and back.

When I'd looked at the whole stack of pictures twice, she clapped her hands and said, "Of course! I know what we'll do. It's probably wicked to do on a Sunday, but we'll play cards."

"Hmmm. Well, Miz Agnes, that might take some doing. Maw has never allowed us to have picture cards. Don't know whether that's Methodist or Presbyterian or just Maw, but she seems to think card playing is of the devil."

"But I'm sure your mother would want you to be polite to your hostess, Private Corley. Since you have taken dinner in this Episcopal home, you must oblige the lady of the house. Besides, I promise the games I know will only corrupt you the tiniest bit. Here, let me show you what the cards are and how to hold them."

Turned out I was even clumsier than I'd thought I was, but Miz Agnes was patient, and by and by, I began to get the hang of it. Course by that time, I'd a been happy to do most anything as long as she stayed in the same room with me; but once I got the gee and haw of it, cards turned out to be right entertaining. And when she was helping me with it and our hands touched, I like to stopped breathing.

It seemed to me that we had just sat down when Grady was at the door, just standing there. When Miz Agnes looked up to say, "Yes, Grady?" he responded in a quiet, indoor kind of voice.

"'Scuse me, Miz Agnes. I don't mean to disturb you'uns, but Marse Gabriel and me needs to be getting back acrost the field. I got some chores, and I reckon they be a-waitin' on me."

I felt a little pang of guilt at the thought of the wounded men waiting for him, but Lord, I sure didn't want to leave that parlor. Of course, I couldn't let on, so I quick pushed myself up from the chair, and Miz Agnes scrambled to hand me my crutch and make like she was steadying me. Our words ran into each other, me trying to speak my manners in a way that would have satisfied Maw if she had overheard and Miz Agnes brushing it off as if it was nothing at all they'd done.

Then we both stopped and just looked at each other for a minute, and she gave a little sigh that like to killed me and said, "Well!" Then she paused, and like the lady of the house, she said, "Private Corley, I do hope we will have occasion to see you again before you return to South Carolina. Please consider our home like your own for whatever small things we can do. I'm sure Grady will be glad to bring us news of your progress, and perhaps you'll be able to find time for another visit. Grady, I do believe the cook has put some things in a basket for you to carry to our brave boys in the camp."

CHAPTER SIX

One night just before dark, I was finishing up with the cook and Grady was in the cook tent when we heard the jangle of cavalry coming from toward the main road. A sergeant and five men trotted up and asked for the officer in charge. When the sergeant swung down from his horse and saluted our surgeon, Major Knight, we all edged in close enough to hear. The news was that a group of deserters was in the area, and they had been raiding farms mostly for food but also for whatever else they could carry off. They had shot a darky at a farm down the road a few miles, and we needed to be careful.

"But surely," the doctor said, "they wouldn't bother a hospital camp!"

"Maybe not," the sergeant said, "but, sir, these here are deserters, and there ain't no way to tell what they'll do. If I were you, I'd take whatever precautions I could. We'll be camped on the main road a half mile that way. If you have any trouble, send somebody for us." And with a quick salute, he mounted up and was gone in the dusk.

The major sank onto a camp chair, unbuttoned his blouse, and ran his fingers through his hair. I noticed again the circles under his eyes and thought to myself, "He looks about done in."

"Well goddamn 'em to hell!" he said. "What next? It ain't enough we're out of medical supplies and trying to nurse a camp full of invalids! Now we got low-life buzzards waiting to pick our carcasses!" And again, he said, "Well goddamn!" Then to no one in particular he said, "I'm medical corp! What am I supposed to do about criminals? I ain't even supposed to carry a gun, and I wouldn't be much good if I did. I'd be more like to shoot my own foot off than anything else!"

I could feel my face starting to flush, and almost before I knew what I was saying, I had spoken up. "Sir, I can still handle a rifle, and it would pleasure *me* right considerable to shoot a deserter. It ain't like they're humans. They're lower than vermin."

A long speech for me, but it made me hot to think of people who'd turn on their own at anytime, but especially in the middle of a war. It brought back the feeling in my belly I had felt for weeks after Marion had taken after me with a knife all those months ago.

The major looked at me with some surprise. He probably hadn't heard that many words from me during all the weeks we'd been in camp together. For a few minutes he stared at me without really looking at me in particular, and then he seemed to grab onto an idea. "What's your name? Corley, is it? How many men in camp do you reckon would feel like you and be able to actually handle a weapon?"

I calculated in my mind quick-like and could name at least six without too much thought. Several of us were missing parts, but we all had at least one good hand. "Major, I can count at least six or seven if we all had something to shoot with."

"Cook," he said. "Catch a horse and go after that sergeant. Tell him we need some weapons: handguns, rifles, carbines—whatever he can spare. If he can send one trooper back with them, we'll form our own militia. Corley, who's the senior line officer in camp who can get around pretty well?"

"Sir, that'd be Lieutenant Powell. He's missing a left arm, but we could pair him with somebody like me who's got two hands and can reload for him. Two of us together can be at least as good as one deserter."

And that's exactly what we did.

Cook came back with two carbines and four pistols and powder and balls for all of them. We organized ourselves under Lieutenant Powell and divided up into shifts: three men would be awake and armed—at least one of them would need to be able to get around on two feet—and three men would sleep. I was already sick to death of the war, but I got to admit that I felt prideful and kind of important to be doing something again.

It had been almost a week, and we had decided that the deserters must have gone another way. I had the midnight-to-sunrise shift along with the lieutenant and a private from North Carolina we called "Cotton-Top" for his light hair; he was a country boy like me. It was a clear night with about a half moon, so there was enough light to see pretty good. The lieutenant and Cotton-Top were walking the sentinel posts, and I was leaning on a wagon with my carbine when we heard a horse coming fast out on the main road. The lieutenant called across to the two of us, and we took cover, both looking around to be sure there wasn't anybody coming from behind us. When the rider turned off the road, we recognized him as one of the cavalry troopers, and the lieutenant stood up and waved his hat. The trooper pulled up and slid from his saddle in one motion, bringing his carbine out of the saddle boot.

"Lieutenant, them deserters is just down the road. They tried to burn a barn at the next farm, probably so's they'd have enough light to rob the house, but we set 'em to running. We think they're headed down the creek bed for that farm over there," he said as he motioned toward the Pinckneys' house. "With them knowing we're on to them, they must be pretty desperate for food. Sergeant and the boys is behind them; he said I was to stay with you until he gets here."

By that time Cotton and I had got over to them, and everybody stood for a minute, all of us looking at the lieutenant. "Well," he said finally. "I reckon we ought to stay between them and the camp, but not too far off. If they do come here, they'll head straight for the cook tent."

But then my own mind was racing. The thought of Miz Agnes alone in that house with the darkies had me just about wild—but not so wild that I wasn't thinking.

I said, "Listen, Lieutenant, what about this here: If the corporal will let me swing up behind him, we can ride across to the big house and be ready if they do try anything there. They almost got to come through the farm to get here. If they do happen to get here first, you fire a couple of shots, and we'll come straight back. Here, Cotton, you take this here carbine and give me that revolver. With the cavalry at their back, they ain't going to linger in any one place for long. I know the folks at the house, and we could roust them up to get ready."

There was some hemmin' and hawin', but we all knew we didn't have much time, so it was agreed. Then, almost as an afterthought, the lieutenant said, "Corley, if we do start firing, you better stay at the house and send the corporal back over here alone. He ain't going to want two people on his mount, and the folks in the house might need you anyway."

We made it across the field as fast as that horse could move, but I like to killed myself jumping down with my crutch and pistol and all. I was up the back steps faster than I had moved even when I had had two good legs, and then I started banging on the door, calling for Miz Agnes and Grady. Grady come stumbling out from a cabin, sleepy eyed and unbuttoned, and I commenced to yell at him before Miz Agnes had even got to the door.

"Grady, is there a gun in the house? There's deserters in the creek bottom, and they might be coming this way."

"Lord a mercy, Marse Gabriel. Yassuh! Yassuh, there's Marse Robert's double gun. And he's got powder and shot fer it."

And then Miz Agnes was there in the doorway in her nightdress and a shawl, her hair in a braid and her eyes wide above the lamp she was carrying.

"Private Corley, what are we to do?"

"Miz Agnes, there's deserters. This here's a corporal from the cavalry that's after them, but they might be coming this way."

"Yes, I heard, but what are we to do?"

"Please, ma'am, give Grady the double gun. He and Cook must stay with you in the house. The other darkies should hide in the fields. The corporal and I will be here in the yard if anything should happen, but it ain't going to."

"Here, Grady," she said, holding the lamp out to him. "Find Mr. Robert's gun in the cabinet quickly, and do as Private Corley has said. I will be in directly." And as Grady brushed past her into the dark house, she grasped my hand and leaned her forehead on my shoulder. "Oh, Gabriel, I know I should be brave, but I'm not. I'm frightened near to death. Will we be all right? Is there to be shooting?"

And just as she had held my hand without thinking, I found myself pulling her to me, wanting desperate bad to hold her away from the danger and to make her fright go away.

"It's all right, Miz Agnes! It's all right. There ain't no way in hell one of them scum will get near your house or you. You just drag yourself some cushions out into the hallway away from windows and doors, and if they do come—which they probably won't—the corporal and me'll make 'em wish they hadn't."

But they did come. The corporal had tied his horse by the front porch so it wouldn't be seen from the creek side of the house. Grady was at a back window, where I had loaded the double gun with buckshot for him, the corporal was behind the smokehouse, and I was at the well.

The deserters didn't seem to much care about being careful. They just walked out of the woods below the barn in a line, one of 'em riding a fine-looking horse they'd stolen from some farm and the rest walking in front of him. In the moonlight they looked like ghosts at first, but then they got real enough. As near as I could make out, there were six or seven of them, they were walking as if they were tired, and every one was armed. The corporal did exactly what I would have done if I'd had a rifle—he took the mounted man first. When the line came abreast the barn, I heard his carbine and saw the rider pitch over backward in a way that let me know he wouldn't be getting up again. The others dropped to one knee or fell behind a fence post and commenced to fire at the smokehouse.

It was a long pistol shot to the barnyard, but when one of the deserters ran up and knelt behind a fence post close to the smokehouse, I rested the .44 on top of the well and fired. He dropped his rifle and fell the other way, grabbing his left shoulder, but in the moonlight I couldn't tell whether I saw blood or not.

Now the others knew the corporal was not alone, and I could hear several balls thump in the dirt around me and ricochet off the stone well casing. If I'd had two good legs, I would have rolled away and crawled to a tree, and I cursed my wooden leg again. There was nothing for it but to lie flat behind the well and hope for the best. Anyway, I wanted to be able to stay where I could protect the back door of the big house.

I had fired a couple more rounds at their rifle flashes and was thinking about reloading when I noticed out of the corner of my eye that one of them was catching the horse. He mounted quick and kicked the horse into a gallop, heading straight for me. I think the corporal got off a shot, but the fellow was riding low, almost behind the horse's neck. I knew I had three, or maybe two, rounds left, and I inched around the well just enough to squeeze off a shot as the man came up on me. In the dark and the rush, I must have hit the horse, because he shied to the left and almost went down, throwing the rider.

But the man was either real determined or real desperate, because he was on his feet and firing at me quick as could be. I got off one more round and saw him hesitate. Had I hit him or not? I aimed again, taking particular care, and dropped the hammer on an empty chamber, which made the loudest "clink" I'd ever heard before or since. I remember thinking, "Well, Gabe, I reckon this is as good a place to end it as any," because he had a bead on me for sure.

I was just waiting for it to happen when a gunshot almost deafened me right behind my head. The deserter seemed to fly backward the way I'd seen men taken by a minié ball fly, his arm flung up and his pistol flying through the air. When I looked around I saw that Grady had crept out of the house and was crouching behind a flower bush at the steps. He'd put a charge of buckshot in the chest of a man maybe thirty feet away.

For a minute or two, I was not able to speak, and the sounds of gunfire between the barn and the smokehouse more or less faded. Then I pulled myself up behind the well and began to reload my own pistol. "Grady," I said. "Under some other circumstances, I s'pose I'd scold you right severe for leaving the house, but I think this time I'll let it go. Can you reload that thing yourself?"

"Yassuh, Marse Gabe," he said, a hint of a sob coming in his voice.

"Then be sure you let the hammer down to half cock on that other barrel, and get back in the house." He did.

If my count was close to right, I figured there couldn't be more than five of the deserters left still on their feet—and more likely, there were four. If they were paying attention, they knew by then that there were three of us. It was possible that one or more of them could get behind us—at least behind me—but if they were watching and thinking straight, they probably wouldn't try again.

Then as I focused on the barn again, I seen a shadow running hard in the field toward the camp. Almost as soon as I caught sight of him, a cavalry trooper rode him down, and I saw a saber swing in the half light. The man went down heavy and didn't move. At the bottom of the barnyard, other riders came out of the dark, and I saw one of the deserters running for the barn door, which he never reached. A carbine shot knocked him off his feet.

And that quick, it was over. Within a few seconds, it seemed, the troopers had two prisoners tied back to back and another lying down, his head propped up on a fence post.

The corporal came running to me, shouting as he ran. "Private, are you all right?" To answer him, I dragged myself upright and plopped my hat on.

"If being terrified don't count, I reckon I'm in fine shape," I said.

"Humph," he said, "I'd say for a man on light duty, you done tolerable well for yourself. I think between us, we made a fair to middling cross fire."

"Yes," I said. "Between us and Grady. Maybe they ought to start issuing double guns, for he sure put it to good use."

When the lanterns were lit, I could see that the sergeant and his troopers had three prisoners alive and that one of them was wounded. (The ball from my pistol had broke his shoulder.) And even though I had been raised a Christian, I have to say it didn't concern me even a little bit to know they'd all be hung or shot. If ever men had planned their own end and earned it, it was them three. I can understand men being too scared to stay on the line or to advance into fire. I can even understand their running away and trying to get back home. But deserting to live like criminals and hurting their own people—that's just unnatural.

They hoisted the wounded man onto a horse and set off for the main road, the other prisoners walking in front of them. The corporal remembered what Lieutenant Powell had said about my staying at the house, and he trotted off to tell him I was all right and would be at the house overnight.

As I figured, Grady had been weeping, but quiet-like, just snuffling. I clumped up the back steps to sit beside him, and without even thinking, I found my arm around his shoulders.

"Grady," I said. "I'm sorry this had to happen. I'm sorry I put you in the way of having to hurt anybody, but there just wasn't any way around it. You know what they did at the other farms, and they could have done as bad, or worse, here. They might a hurt Miz Agnes or burned the house or done God knows what." I didn't even want to think what was in my mind. "More than anybody, I wish that this thing was all over and that nobody ever had to kill anybody again, but it ain't in our hands. And that's just the way you got to think about it—it was taken out of your hands. You also got to remember that you saved my life, and maybe Miz Agnes's too. I sure won't ever forget it. That's about the finest thing a man can do."

And then Miz Agnes, who was trying hard to keep her teeth from chattering, chimed in from the porch. "Grady, it's the bravest thing I ever heard tell of—just the bravest thing in the world! It is! And you just wait till Mr. Robert hears about this. He'll be so proud of you. Why, there's no knowing what he'll do!"

And so we tried to comfort him and ourselves until he finally surrendered his gun to me and walked, head down, toward his cabin and the circle of darkies waiting there.

CHAPTER SEVEN

Against everything I was feeling at that particular moment, I made a stab at being a proper man. "Miz Agnes, you ought to get back to bed and rest if you can. I'll sit on the back porch and just keep an eye out."

"Why, Gabriel," she said, using my first name again. "Do you really believe there's any danger now?"

"No!" I said real quick. "No, they got every last one of them deserters, and even if there was one hiding somewhere, you can bet he's running south now as fast as he can go."

"That was my thought exactly," she said. "And goodness knows I'm much too upset and excited to sleep. Why, I may never sleep again! Please, Gabriel, come up on the porch and be comfortable in a rocking chair while I fetch you a blanket. I'd like to just talk awhile, if you don't mind."

When she got back with the blanket, she came to my chair and stopped for a long minute, looking out at the yard. Then she did the most amazing thing. Ever so softly, she draped the blanket around my shoulders, and bending down, she put both hands on my face and kissed me, first on my cheek and then on my lips. And just as if I had been expecting it and knew exactly what to do, I caught her around the waist and pulled her into my lap, where her face seemed to find a natural resting place in the hollow of my neck.

We should have realized right off that what we were doing was wicked, but as much as it's possible for human beings not to think, I reckon we were doing without thoughts. At first I was almost afraid to move for fear that she had made a mistake and would think better of it. But then she turned her face, all wet with tears, up to mine again, and there was no thinking about mistakes. It was as if we'd been loving each other for years and had just that minute found each other again after a long, long time away.

I suppose the past we remember can look sweeter than it actually was at the time; but all these years later, it *still* seems to me that that was the sweetest night I've ever known or ever will, even though it was stuck right in the middle of the most miserable years any human being ever spent. After an hour in that rocking chair, which left us both cold and stiff, we fumbled our way into Agnes's bed. And with her leading me, all gentle and reassuring, we did what I had barely allowed myself to think of up to then.

As it turned out, she was only two years older than I was at the time, but she was a hundred years older in experience and a woman in her prime. As much as I've loved and enjoyed the favors of my own dear Amelia over the years, I'm not ashamed to say that Agnes Pinckney's beauty when she stood up and pulled her nightdress over her head in the candlelight literally made me feel faint.

I don't think either of us slept more than ten minutes at a stretch that whole night. First light found us clinging to each other for dear life. I guess we'd be there still if the sound of Mattie stirring in the kitchen hadn't forced us to push the quilt off and hunt around on the floor for our clothes, Agnes whispering and giggling as she imagined Mattie's outrage if she were to walk in, and yet not the least bit afraid or worried. When I thought about her carelessness later, it just amazed me, and then it made me swell up with pride to think that she could have loved me that much—that our being together like that could have been more important than anything, even her own reputation!

Before we tiptoed out of her room, me leaning on her shoulder so I could walk quiet, Agnes made me sit down on the edge of the bed and held my face in her hands again.

"Gabriel," she whispered. "I want you to be careful how you think about all this. I know you were reared as a Christian, and I was too. But right this minute, there is no question in my mind at all that God is smiling at us. Maybe under any kind of normal circumstances, we'd be wrong. Maybe if this were a year ago, we would have seen it coming and just stopped being together. But these aren't 'normal circumstances,' and we may never live to see anything normal again. It's possible that in a few weeks or months, one or both of us could be dead. A little while ago, you risked your life to save mine. Tomorrow the army could send you home or, God forbid, back to war. While we have a little time to get to know and love each other, we've got to take every minute we can possibly get and do everything we can possibly do to share our lives. It would be a sin not to. And"—she shook my head back and forth—"you are not to feel guilty or reproach yourself even a little bit. I forbid it. Do you understand me? There simply is no blame, and if there were, it would be on me. I'm the older and more experienced person here, so you must trust me." And again she said, "Do you understand?"

I pondered what she had said for a minute. "Agnes, I don't know whether I can understand much of anything right this minute. I do know that I could no more have kept from loving you than I coulda stopped breathing. What we did tonight is just more of the love I already been feeling. It sure ain't anything different, and it seems about as natural as breathing. If God sees fit to send me out to kill other men, there can't be any shame in us loving each other. When I've had time to think, I reckon I might come to see it differently, but I don't believe I will." And I never have to this very day.

We somehow managed to sneak me down the long hall and off the front porch before Agnes, still in her nightdress, walked back into the kitchen, yawning and stretching as if she had just woke up. Then, cool as you please, I heard her send Mattie onto the back steps to invite me in for breakfast while she went back to her room to bathe and dress.

Of course, you can't really hide much from folks who live in the same house with you, and before many days had passed, I reckoned all the darkies knew about Agnes and me. Grady, who had probably known something longer than anybody, never said a word to me outright, although it was no secret that we understood between us.

I was getting stronger every day then. I s'pose I could have pretended to get better slow, but I was too proud to do that, even though I knew what getting better meant.

Whenever I could find reasons to sneak away across the field, I would go to the house. Sometimes I would make as if I had some errand, like taking Grady something from the barn or asking Agnes for something for the camp, but after a while, it was too much trouble to even pretend. Agnes watched for me and would find some way to sneak me in the house. She even figured out plots to get Mattie out of the house.

In the middle of the day, when all the hands were off in the fields, Agnes and I would meet in the barn. I would hoist myself up into the sweet-smelling hayloft with her, and we would undress each other and spread our clothes out to lie on. We both knew that time was getting short, and a kind of sadness and desperation began creeping in. Still, I wouldn't trade the memory of those weeks for anything in the world.

But it had to come sooner or later. One evening Major Knight was having tea in his tent and shuffling through the paper work he hated so much when he sent for me. I knew it would be something I wouldn't like, and I walked over slow, a big knot growing in my stomach.

"Corley," he said, "sit down. It's my duty to tell you that your fame seems to have finally caught up with you. Regimental headquarters has finally processed a recommendation that you be cited for bravery in leading your platoon in some kind of raid after your sergeant was killed. Am I understanding that correctly?"

"Yes, sir," I said. "I reckon it was something like that. But that was a while back."

"Yes, I know," he said, "but things got brought to a head when I wrote a brief report on your action in protecting the camp, not to mention the local homeowners, from those deserters. Without our little hospital militia, God only knows what might have happened. And that was really your idea, so I thought you ought to get some credit. That cavalry sergeant, by the way, signed my report and seconded my recommendation. Anyway, the upshot of all this is that you've been promoted to sergeant. So congratulations, Sergeant Corley." He stood up to shake my hand.

"Now the rest of it is not so pleasant. Given your history and the nature of your wound, it seems to me they ought to give you a medal and send you home. But things in this war seldom go according to my imagining. They're sending some captain out here to talk to you about extending your enlistment, though I can't believe that they would send you into combat again. In any event, this Captain Rose will be here in a day or two, and you're to make yourself available to talk with him.

"If you take my advice, you'll simply tell him 'no.' There is absolutely no precedent for their forcing a disabled man to fight, and I don't think the army would do it. But of course, you do what seems right to you. I'm just saying you don't have to be any more influenced by Rose than by me.

"Well, that's all I had, unless you have something else to say. No? Then congratulations again, and good night." Then as an afterthought he added, "Oh, Corley! I know you've made some friends among the local folks. You might want to let them know you'll probably be leaving us so they don't have to come and ask me about you."

Yes, I reckoned I would want to do that.

Later that night, me and Agnes sat for a long time on the back porch, rocking and talking. We had more or less stopped trying to sneak around Mattie, although we were never real obvious about making love when it would rub her nose in it. That night she'd gone to her room behind the kitchen long before I'd gotten across the field, and we could have had the run of the house, but neither one of us seemed to have the heart to do anything but sit and talk. Agnes had lectured me strong about not fretting over her, but that night I had to fret some out loud again about what would happen to her when Colonel Pinckney came home. I couldn't very well bear the thought of her being shamed and maybe even sent away because of me—because of us. And like she always did, Agnes listened patiently, her hand on my arm, and then repeated what she'd said before one way or another.

"Gabe, it's sweet of you to worry about me, and I know you can't help it. If I were in your position, I suppose I'd do the same thing. But you'll just have to trust me that I can handle whatever comes along. Robert is a kind and understanding man. Even if he comes to know the full extent of all this, I don't think he would want to shame me—or his family—publicly. If it comes to putting me away—if he feels like he has to—I know my family will take care of me. And if not, I can take care of myself.

"But the fact is, I don't think any of the white folks in the community know about us. Some of them may suspect something, but

I'd be very surprised if it were more than a vague suspicion. The darkies will all know something, of course, because they share everything sooner or later—kind of like a countywide telegraph! But you've seen how they are. They wouldn't want to cause me trouble, and they certainly wouldn't want to hurt Robert."

And so we rocked awhile longer, she in her shawl and me wrapped in a blanket. And then she said, "Gabe, I know it's a strange thought, but you've saved my life in more ways than one. I've been so lonely and so worried about everything, but I've had to bear up and be brave alone because I've been running the place and have had to set an example. And then you came, and suddenly I had a reason to look forward to getting up in the morning. Right from that very first time I saw you standing by the well with Grady, having you close has given me the strangest feeling of comfort. And the closer we've gotten, the stronger I've gotten. I feel like I've gone from being a frightened little girl to being a real grown-up woman. But more than that, I've felt like I can do anything I have to. Having you and yet knowing that I'd have to lose you"—and there, her voice caught—"I don't know. It's like I've had a purpose for being. As if I'd been put here for this specific reason.

"I'll never stop worrying about you and wondering why we were given what we have. Good Lord, I've spent whole nights running over all that in my mind. But when everything's said and done, I just end up being happy for what we've had. And that leads me back to thinking that in the worst things that happen, there's still a kind of rightness. Does all that make any sense to you, Gabe? Oh, I know you must think I'm daft when I try to talk about it, but figuring it out has been a great comfort to me. And I hope it is to you."

At that particular time, I honestly couldn't find much comfort in anything, but I didn't let on, because it sounded as if Agnes had got things arranged in her head in a way that was helping her. I don't remember what I said, if anything, but my feelings were a mixture of little-boy sadness—like I'd just lost everything I'd ever cared about—and some kind of fury. I think that for the first time in my life, I was near to cursing God. I couldn't bear to think that I was going to have to walk away from the dearest person—the dearest times—in my entire life, and there wasn't even a body I could tell! I was mighty near crazy with grieving over it. And maybe that was a good thing, for there were months and years coming when being furious was about the only thing kept me going.

CHAPTER EIGHT

The second day after our all-night talk, Captain Rose finally came. He was mounted, and he wore a uniform like no cavalry I'd ever seen before or have seen since. There was a great feather in his hat, not like an Injun feather but a fluffy one that flew in the breeze when he trotted up. He wore a patch where his left eye used to be. The glove on his left hand only had two fingers, a thumb and a pointer. When he dismounted, you could see his left leg was so stiff that he couldn't walk any better than I did. And he had a mustache almost as big as his hat's feather.

There's a picture in one of the children's school readers of what a pirate was supposed to look like. I reckon that's about as close to describing Captain Rose as I can get—and the men who rode with him didn't look much better. They were every one of them missing something or twisted or limping or dragging a leg. They looked like a mounted version of our hospital camp, except they was sitting on horses rather than cots.

The captain's recruiting talk was about as peculiar as his looks.

I quick walked over (I was using a cane by then and getting around at least as well as he was, on the ground anyway) and saluted him. "Captain, I'm Private—I mean Sergeant—Corley. I expect I'm the one you come to see."

"The very man himself—Corley!" Then he tossed back a salute and pulled off his gloves to shake my hand. "I'm pleased to meet you, and if you're as much of a fighter as I've heard you are, I believe you'll be pleased to meet me. So let's set and talk a spell.

"Corley, I don't want to waste your time or mine. I've read what the regiment has written up on you, so there's no need to go over all that. I know what I need to know. When you make up your mind, you're a man who's not deterred by small matters like enemy fire or losing a leg. You're the kind of man who's too valuable for this army to lose, and I'd like to convince you to fight with my troop." It sounded like a stopping place, and I started to answer, but he never even took a breath.

"Now you don't need to talk for a while here. I know what you might be thinking, and you've got a right to think it. You've already done more than your share, and you've been in the army long enough to know that a smart man never volunteers for anything. By all rights, you should be going home. But my question to you is, what would you do if you did go home? And I think I know the answer. You ain't like some folks who'd tend the garden and be happy. Before you ever got back to South Carolina, you'd be fretting about leaving others to do the work that still has to be done. I mean, of course, driving them infernal Yankees back to where they came from so we can all go home and love our women and raise our children proper. My thinking on the matter—and you may not cotton to my reasoning—is that the more of us who know something about fighting and stay with the army, the sooner we'll all go home. And that thinking will leave the boys and old men at home where they belong to keep things going. The long and short of it is that I'm offering you the chance to join this lot of cripples and get some real work done. To be honest with you, Corley, they fight better and smarter than any group their size in this army or any other. We ain't notably handsome, but we kill a lot of Yankees. So tell me what you think. Do you want to stay in it or not? Because if you do, I'm hoping you'll join us."

There was another pause, and I waited a short minute to be sure he had really stopped. Then I said, "Captain, I s'pose I'm honored, or should be, but I'm not so sure I'm your man. For one thing, I ain't cavalry, and I don't know anything about cavalry tactics. I don't even know if I can set a horse, much less fight from one."

And he replied, "We're not cavalry, Sergeant. We're mounted infantry. The horses move us fast because some of us (like you and me, fer instance) don't move too fast on our own anymore. What we do is plug holes. We can get where we're needed pretty quick, and we know what to do when we get there. If you'll accept my word on it, you can set a horse plenty good enough for this lot."

Then there was another pause—a longer one. It was a cool day, but I was sweating just from the work of thinking. My mind was like a bad team that wanted to pull in different directions at the same time, and no matter how hard I stared at the toes of the captain's boots, I couldn't seem to find the right words. Finally I said, "Captain, could you let me study on it for a little spell? It seems like my decider done quit working, and I need a while to get it started."

He chuckled. "Fair enough, Corley. And while you're trying to get that decider functioning, is there a place to water our horses and unsaddle awhile? What about the barn we can see across the field?"

"Yes, sir. That's the home of Colonel Pinckney, who's stationed in Richmond. The family has been very accommodating, and I'm sure you'd be welcome."

"Have you met them?" he asked. And when I nodded, he added, "Then please be so kind as to ride with us and let them know who we are. Most civilians seem to be frightened just looking at us."

There was an extra horse at the rear of the column, and when Captain Rose motioned to the trooper holding the reins, he immediately rode up and handed them to me. I ain't particularly book smart, but I was smart enough to see right off that it was already agreed on to get me in the saddle one way or t'other. The trooper held my horse's bridle, and I swung up without any trouble—until I looked down for a place to put my peg leg and realized that it wouldn't stay on an uncovered stirrup. And again, as if it had already been thought of, the captain said, "An easy matter to remedy, Corley. We've had lots of experience."

And so we trotted into the yard of Agnes's house; it was the last time I would see it for many years. Grady must have been watching, because he and another darky come from the barn right off and began to draw water for the horses. I nodded to him and walked toward the back porch. When I was halfway up the steps, Mattie came and stood in the door.

"Marse Gabe," she said. "Miz Agnes been feeling sick ever since this mawning. She say to tell you she see you tomorrow if you come."

"But Mattie," I said. "She'll see *me*. If she's sick, I want to speak to her. Maybe there's something I can do."

But she never moved out of the door. Her voice was not unkind; in fact, it was about as kind as Mattie had ever managed to sound toward me. "No, sir, Marse Gabe! She done give me stric' orders. She don't want to see nobody 'tall until she feeling better. You come back tomorrow, and she be glad to see you."

But there was no tomorrow. By nightfall I was many miles away, believing in my heart that I would never see her again and, for the first time in my life, not much caring whether I saw anybody I loved again.

Captain Rose was just as peculiar as he'd looked the first time I'd seen him, but he knew exactly what he wanted to do, and he was better at getting what he wanted than anybody I'd ever seen. He called us his "Myrmidons" after some ragged soldiers from one of the old Greek stories. We'd had those stories in our schoolbooks, but Maw had never wanted us to read them because she'd said they were "heathen." I hadn't read the tale he was talking about, but it had to do with a war over some city in the old days, and the Myrmidons were supposed to be old soldiers like us who had lots of experience in the troop and were all hacked up.

If it pleased him to think that way, it was all right with us. What really mattered was that Captain Rose seemed to know half the officers in the army, and he could always beg for food or a weapon or a horse no matter what outfit we hooked up with. Food was already getting scarce then, and some other troops were beginning to look underfed; but somehow we always seemed to be able to come by a wagonload of this or that. One time it would be tins and tins of biscuits that some cavalry unit had gotten in a raid on a Federal supply depot. Another time it would be a side of beef, even though nobody had seen a cow in months, or we'd somehow come by repeating rifles that he had shamed somebody out of because we were "cripples."

Unlike other infantries, almost all of us enlisted had pistols as well as rifles. A lot of the others even carried cavalry sabers, although I never wanted one because they weren't much use on the ground. I knew how to use a rifle with a bayonet, and I was more comfortable with that than I was with any sword.

The kind of weapons we had might not seem important if you don't understand an infantry war, but it was. When I was still fighting with the Fifteenth South Carolina, we all had muzzle-loading rifles with bayonets, and most of us carried some kind of knife. In a pitched battle, we got one shot and then had to reload while the next man fired his one shot. If there was a charge by the Federal troops, we could get overrun and would either have to fall back or meet them with our own bayonets and sometimes, in the worst of it, even with the butts of the rifles. But in Captain Rose's troop, a lot of us weren't able to fall back because we couldn't run, and none of us would have been a match for an able-bodied man with a bayonet. On the other hand, with breech-loading rifles, revolvers, and even some repeaters, we could stand and just keep firing if we paced ourselves.

If we saw that we were likely be overrun anyway because we were so outnumbered, we'd fall back early to the horses and find another place to stand and fight. Knowing it's either shoot fast and accurate or be overrun and die has a marvelous effect on a man's efficiency.

For the most part, the units we fought with seemed glad to have us, and we did come to believe that sometimes the Federals knew who we were and would avoid our place in the line if they could.

Still, it was a bloody war until the last day of it, and we lost men in almost every skirmish. What I learned over time, and what most of the troop had already known, was not to get too friendly with any one person. I don't mean we didn't take care of one another—we did. We never left wounded or even dead on the field, and by the end we were all friends, those of us that survived. We just didn't get so attached that we'd be all broke up when the man next to us went down.

I studied hard on what I ought to do for almost three weeks before I finally broke down and wrote a letter to Agnes. It was plain I couldn't say anything about what I was feeling, but I was so eaten up with love for her that I could scarcely keep my mind on staying alive.

In a peculiar sort of way, I was probably a better soldier after I came to believe I would never see her again. Sometimes that seemed to make me downright careless about my life. I recollect times in a fight when I'd just pull myself up behind a tree and take aim on a line of Yankees as if I were shooting squirrels and those whizzing sounds around my ears were nothing but mosquitoes. It's like I half wanted to die, or at least I wasn't bothered about it.

I guess God must have a perverse side, because I was wounded at a time when I was an experienced soldier who knew enough to be tolerable careful most of the time. But I was never touched during the times with Captain Rose when I almost threw my life away.

When I finally made up my mind and found pen and paper, here's what I wrote to Agnes:

Dear Mrs. Pinckney,

You may not remember who I am, since you were so kind to many of the wounded in the hospital unit stationed on your farm. But as one of those wounded, I cherish the memory of your kindness given to lonely, homesick men in a time of great distress. So I take pen and paper to express my gratitude and that of the others as well. Surely God will have a special star for your crown and also a special place for all the neighbors who were so kind to us.

I continue to do well and am so far in good health also. I think you did not get to meet the commander of the troop with which I am now serving, but he is a splendid officer and gentleman. I feel honored to be have been given a second chance to serve our cause.

I hope this finds all of you well and that the farm continues to be safe. May God bless you and all your family.

Gratefully,
Sergeant Gabriel Corley
PS—Please forgive my writing, as this pen is bad.

This is the letter that finally reached me months later. I carried it until the paper wore out on the creases and it fell apart.

My Dear Sergeant Corley,

How very kind of you to write. Indeed I do remember you! How could I ever forget the two brave soldiers—one of them already terribly wounded—who defended our home on a dark night? I am delighted to report that I was able to visit with my husband, Colonel Pinckney, in Richmond shortly after the time when you were reassigned. I explained your courageous actions and those of the cavalry troop to him. Colonel Pinckney, like me, is filled with gratitude and would be pleased to shake your hand if the fortunes of this dreadful war ever allow you to return to this area.

Although the hospital camp is now being broken up and the war seems nearer than ever, I am in good health, as are most of the people on the farm. We remain in good spirits in spite of some minor privations because our thoughts are always with our brave soldiers suffering in the field. May God bless and keep you and all your comrades.

I remain always in your debt.
With sincerest gratitude,
Mrs. Agnes Pinckney

In the weeks after I finally got Agnes's letter, Captain Rose began to move us south. In the winter of 1865, we crossed over into North Carolina, and I realized that most likely, I would not see Virginia or the Pinckney's farm again. Until that point I had cherished the notion that I would somehow be able to end the war close enough to visit again "just passing by" on my way home. In fact, I was willing to go as far as need be to arrange a "passing" if I could do it. But we weren't fighting with the Army of Northern Virginia then. Captain Rose explained that the famous general Joe Johnson had come from Tennessee, and all the troops in North Carolina would be under his command.

We had seen General Lee more than once during the years in Virginia, and we had come to believe that as long as he was in command, we would never be whipped, at least not for good. But Lee was defending Richmond then, and we were bound to take on Sherman. I wanted real bad to believe that General Johnson would be able to drive Sherman back, but the soldiers we joined looked mighty thin by that time, in body and in numbers. It wasn't nothing unusual to see an advance, and there'd be so few fellows in each regiment that their flags were right on top of one another. There were fourteen- and fifteen-year-old boys recruited even into the cavalry units, but they was dying like men, and I was proud of them.

At a place called Bentonville in North Carolina, it come to my attention that the remains of my old regiment were fighting up the line, so of course I rode up to see if I could find anybody I knew. We had left home with almost five hundred men. At Bentonville there couldn't have been more than one hundred fifty, and most of them, I didn't know. A lot of them were replacements from other regiments that'd got cut up too bad to even be regiments anymore. Everybody I had been close to through the first years of the war was dead, was hurt too bad to fight, or had slipped off home.

It was on the first day of the battle at Bentonville that we lost Captain Rose. I think he had been like me, taking more and more chances and caring less and less about what happened to him. By then he couldn't fool us any longer about "whipping them infernal Yanks," and he stopped those peculiar speeches that most of us hadn't understood anyway about "Myrmidons" and "coming home carrying our shields or being carried on them." His face had taken on the look of a man already dead, and even his pirate's mustache was growing wild and unwaxed.

It was late in the first day when the general ordered a charge against one side of the Federal line, and we were called to back up the front line. We rushed over and dismounted so we could give fire support to our boys moving up, but Captain Rose never got off his horse. He just wheeled around and trotted out into the front of our infantry, waving his pistol in his good hand.

For a while it looked like his luck was going to hold. The Federals on that side were separated from the big part of their line, and they looked rattled. We were pouring it to them as fast as we could shoot and reload when all of a sudden we heard bugles, and what looked like three or four more regiments came pouring into the Yankee line.

Captain Rose never even looked back. From where we were situated, we could see the bullets begin to hit him then, the Federals moving up and shooting as they went. For all we knew, he was already dead by then, but finally his horse was hit too, and it stumbled, throwing him sprawling on the ground. We never saw him again.

The troop went on fighting as best we could, trying to support our boys as they fell back and then fell back again. There were three of us sergeants, and without anyone saying anything, we seemed to figure out for ourselves how and when to move the men around. At the end of the second day of the battle, it had got quiet, and soldiers on both sides were trying to start fires. Then some captain from General Johnson's headquarters rode into our camp.

When he rode out again, I had been sworn in as a lieutenant with a written commission signed by the general in my rucksack and a set of used lieutenant's bars for my shirt. If General Sherman turned out to be as much of a Turk as I had heard he was, I planned to lose the commission and make myself a private soldier again when the time came.

When the time finally did come for us at a place called Durham Station, it wasn't at all what I had been led to think it would be. As soon as we began to allow ourselves to start thinking about losing—and it wasn't that long before—we began to entertain ourselves by scaring each other with terrible tales.

"We would be considered treasonous rebels and would all be imprisoned for life. We would try to surrender, and Sherman's troops would just keep on shooting us. All our families' houses and land would be taken away and given to the current slaves, and we would be the new slaves." And so on and so on.

CHAPTER NINE

The end was bad enough, and it would get worse and worse for years to come, but it wasn't near as dramatic as all of our imaginings.

We lined up by regiments and were allowed to march to the place where we stacked our rifles. The Federal troops were drawn up in ranks just watching—there was no bullyragging, no hurrahs, just a kind of quiet that was almost sad. When the time came to give up our arms, I dismounted and hobbled over to stack my carbine with the rest. I was taking off my pistol belt when a Yankee sergeant stepped up, saluted, and said, "Lieutenant, that won't be necessary. General Grant has sent orders that officers can keep their side arms."

I almost said, "I ain't no officer," but I caught myself in time. Then he went on.

"But I do believe I'll relieve you of that sorry horse. He looks about all done in."

I considered, for a little minute, starting the war over again just because he would steal a horse from under a peg-legged man!

But then I found myself saying, "Well, fool, I guess he has a right to take about anything he wants. You lost the war!" And I handed him the bridle.

He turned and shouted to a man in the ranks, "Corporal, let's have the lieutenant's saddle and bridle on that bay mare, and be quick about it." Then he said, "I'll want them saddlebags filled with biscuits, and mind you, hold the horse's head for the lieutenant to mount!"

About then, my mouth must have been hanging open for the flies to get in, for his voice got quiet and sounded more humanlike, and he said to me, "Lieutenant, it's over, and thank God you and me are still alive. You rebs whipped us to a standstill. I'm a witness to that! The least we can do is treat you with respect, and by God, I mean to see that we do. Good luck to you, sir." And with that, he saluted me again and slapped the young mare on her rump.

I started to follow the rest of the troops, tears clouding my sight in spite of everything I could do, but something made me rein up. I turned and walked the horse back to where they still stood in ranks and said, "Sergeant, I'd be obliged if you would tell me your name and where you hail from."

"Glad to, Lieutenant! I'm Martin Mueller, that's M-u-e-l-l-e-r, and as soon as this here army will turn me loose, I'll be home again in Marietta, Ohio."

I leaned down from the saddle and held out my hand. He took it, and we clasped hands for a long minute. Then I said, "My name's Gabe Corley, from Lightwood Knot Springs, South Carolina. If there's ever any way to repay you for your kindness, I'll surely find it." Then I kicked the horse and left before every single man in the ranks could see the tears that was fixing to run down my face.

I didn't sleep much that first night. There was a lot to think about. We learned that General Lee had surrendered a few days before we had and that the rumor about President Lincoln being shot was true. I hardly knew what to think about that. Lincoln had been the enemy, but I had never bore him any personal grudge. Killing him didn't seem like much of a way to start off for folks who had already been licked in a war. We didn't have so much as a crooked stick to defend ourselves with, and it appeared to me that if the Federal generals were in a mood for revenge, we were all pretty well cooked.

That was worrisome in a way, but it wasn't where my mind mostly was. The next day, all the South Carolina boys would be getting together to start for home. Some of the Fifteenth was still around, and I knew what I ought to do was find them again and set out for home. But I hadn't quite given up the idea of finding Agnes's homeplace again, if only just to see her face one more time.

When I let my mind run free, I would even think about lunatic things like finding a job in the town where I could be close to the farm and at least catch sight of her in the store or at church. I was so torn up inside that my brain hardly worked at all. But when dawn came, I was in the saddle looking for the other South Carolinians. By midmorning we were several miles to the south, moving slow but steady.

We were lucky that we didn't have that far to go. The railroads were torn up, and Sherman's troops had burned or stole whatever they could on either side of their line of march, so finding food was nigh impossible. Even when folks had saved a few chickens or other animals they could run off into the woods, it didn't seem right for us to go begging when they were hungry themselves. I confess that some of us did pick up a few ears of corn or a turnip when we could—we were that hungry ourselves. An empty belly don't make for Sunday-school manners. We shared what we had, and we almost made two saddlebags of hard Yankee biscuits last till we got to where we split up.

When I began to recognize some landmarks, I found the railroad line and followed it to Goldville. Then I took on down the road that had brought me there the day William and I had enlisted.

Up till then, I hadn't thought that much about going home because I hadn't been set in my mind that I *would* go home. I began to wonder what it would be like. Maw and I hadn't written but one or two letters since I'd left the hospital camp—at least that's all that'd found me. She knew I had been wounded, but I hadn't been able to say to her what I'd said to myself: that I was missing part of a leg. I knew she'd still love me—would always love me—but something in her letters was different from the way I remembered her. It made me uneasy about just walking in on her like I was fixing to do.

Then too, my oldest brother was dead, and I hadn't heard anything much about the second one, Thomas, after he'd been mustered out. I reckoned he'd been wounded pretty bad, but I didn't know how. Why else would they have sent him home? I didn't even know who would be left on the farm, whether all the darkies would have gone away, and whether there was even any way to get in a crop.

I was in this state of wondering about everything at the same time when I crossed the creek and started up the path through the woods toward home. When I saw the house and barn, there was somebody on the front porch. When I was sure I was in sight, I waved my hat. I was surprised he didn't wave back, even if he couldn't tell who I was. After all, a man on his own front porch would usually wave back at any white man or any darky he knew. But whoever this was, he just looked out as if I wasn't there.

When I got closer I said "howdy," but he still didn't answer. By the look of him, I could tell it had to be Thomas, and it made me even uneasier that he didn't seem to see me. "Oh, God! I said, "Please don't let him be blind."

I tied the mare at the barnyard fence without unsaddling her and stumped my way to the porch, speaking again. "Thomas, that you?" But still no answer. I was climbing up the steps when Maw came to the door. We both stopped and just stared for what seemed like a minute or two, and I said, "Maw? It's me. I'm home."

Then she came to me, wiping her hands on the front of her apron, and threw her arms around my neck. We were holding each other, both of us, I think, weeping a little and holding on hard. Finally she pushed back, still holding my arms, and said, "Let me get a look at you—or what's left of you. You can't know how often I've prayed for this very minute—prayed just to see my baby's face and know he's all right, which I see you ain't. Why didn't you at least warn me, Son?"

"I don't know, Maw. It was just too hard for me to say. It took me some long time to say it to myself. I'm sorry, Maw. I mean, I'm glad I'm alive, and I'm glad I'm home, but I'm sorry about the way I left and about coming back a peg leg. I wouldn't want no child of mine doing it. I know it ain't right or fair to you."

"Son, I don't think I want you using those words 'peg leg' again. It's a proud thing to be wounded in the service of your country, and we won't make light of it. I don't mind saying I was more than a little put out with you, running away like that when I wasn't here—and near frantic with worry. But it's all water over the dam. The way things stand right now, I'm just so glad to have you home that I can't hardly stand it." She stopped and hugged me again for a long time before she dried her eyes on her sleeve. As I watched that little gesture, her holding the sleeve to her face, I recognized how old she looked, and it jarred me.

"Well, I reckon I should be pleased you didn't come home without nothing at all." She looked out at the mare with the US brand on her flank and went on. "You seem to have made off with a good Yankee horse at least. Come and speak to Thomas, and then put your animal in the barn. For all we know, Sherman's boys might come back for it."

I looked at Thomas again and said, "I already spoke to you once, Big Brother, but you ain't bothered to speak back. You nursing a grudge?"

Maw was watching me then and looking from Thomas to me and back. After a minute or two had passed, she said, "I was waiting to see if having you here would make any difference. I keep hoping something will wake him up, but so far, nothing has." She stepped to his side and smoothed the hair off his forehead the way you would with a two-year-old. Then she spoke to him. "You're just not there, are you, Brother?"

Then to me she said, "They brought him home a few months after the big fight at Gettysburg, and he ain't changed since the first day I saw him. They told me he was wounded, but this ain't on account of the wound. He walked away from the battle by himself. They said it's a wonder he wasn't killed outright—he just stood up in the middle of all the shooting and walked away. I reckon his mind just decided it was better to go somewhere else. Wherever it went, it's been there ever since.

"The doctor in town said he might come back sometime, and I waited for a long time. I got up every morning and told myself, 'Well, he'll be his old self again today.' But he won't. He won't think or talk, and he won't do anything more than just a little bit. We taught him to feed himself and to go to the outhouse by himself—mostly. I been working on trying to get him to chop wood or even hoe in the garden, but even if he strikes a lick or two, he sets it down if I leave him and just stands and looks the way he is now. I'd give a pretty to know what he's seeing."

"I don't think I want to know," I said. "I was at Gettysburg too, although I never knew Thomas was there. I pray he still ain't seeing that; but if he is, I understand why he doesn't talk. There ain't much I want to say about it myself. I just want to forget it."

I was so tired that I felt like I wanted to go to sleep and never wake up, but Maw and I talked late that night. I had helped Thomas get to bed. He didn't seem contrary in any way. If you pointed him in the direction you wanted him to go in, he would do most of what you told him. He undressed himself with me talking to him all the while, and when I had put the nightshirt over his head, he had lain down by himself. He was snoring within a few minutes, but he slept restless, moving, making noises, and sometimes sitting up in the bed. I found out later that we'd have to leave a lantern burning some nights to get him to lie back down.

I was anxious to know about the farm. Like Agnes, Maw had been running the place by herself ever since I'd left. There was one family of darkies, Uncle Foot and Aunt Rannie's, that had always been on our place. I had grown up working and playing with their children, and of course, after my paw had died, we'd depended on Uncle Foot to help us with things we'd never learned.

In a peculiar sort of way, we all thought of everybody on the place as family, although, of course, everybody understood where the fences were. Even though our house was just a plain old farmhouse, Uncle Foot's family never used the front door, and they always called the adults "Marse" and "Missus."

My parents considered it trashy to abuse anybody, especially their own "servants" (we never used the word "slave"), and we learned early on that Maw and Paw wouldn't tolerate our acting uppity to them—especially to the adults. If Aunt Rannie was working in the house and she told a child, white or black, to do something, we knew we'd better do it, 'cause Maw or Paw would stand right behind her. I'd even heard Uncle Foot argue with Paw sometimes, like maybe about what to plant and when; but what Paw finally said was what we all did.

For me, anyway, that had always seemed to be the way the world was made. You wouldn't discuss it any more than you'd argue about water being wet.

Maw said that when word had came to the community about President Lincoln freeing all the slaves in the Confederate states, it hadn't seemed to make much difference at first. She and Uncle Foot had talked about it, she said, and Uncle Foot had reckoned he didn't know anywhere else to go. Maw'd told him they were free to stay on as long as they wanted. In fact, she wanted them to, but everybody would have to work for their keep. Since everybody, nigger and white, had always worked, there was nothing new about that part of it.

After the Yankees came through South Carolina, Uncle Foot's oldest daughter had taken her children and gone off to be with her husband, who lived down the road. One of the sons had left too, one named "Julius" who was about my age. But from what Maw had heard, he was still in the community.

When it came to doing the actual work of farming, I calculated that I could count for about half a man. I could do something like working a garden or, say, digging post holes; but it was obvious I couldn't do work that needed two good legs like plowing or putting on a new roof. I'd have to make adjustments and relearn different ways to do some things. Others things, I could still do with some help.

If Uncle Foot and his family agreed to stay and share the work, we could at least feed both families and, in a good year, maybe even lay some aside. On the other hand, if all his children decided to leave, we'd be hard put to just survive.

For the first time in my life, I had to think serious about what it meant to have our own darkies around us. We'd always figured they were like children, dependent on us. "Children" is the word all white folks used, and it's true Maw done all the doctoring on the whole place, and Paw had done things like managing the cash money and buying seeds and such. But the fact was, we'd been depending on them at the same time, maybe even more than they depended on us.

Maw and I talked mostly about all these things, and especially about working the farm and about family I hadn't heard from, until finally my eyes began closing in the middle of a sentence, and she packed me off to my own bed.

I woke up when the sun hit my eyes and sat up quick, reaching for my rifle, until I looked around and recognized my own room. By the look of the sun, it was well into the morning, but I'd slept outside without a roof for so long that I didn't wake up indoors until it was right in my eyes. I just stretched awhile and enjoyed the feel of the feather bed and Maw's quilt over me, and then I smelled cooking and put my foot on the floor.

It come over me in a kind of wave that the last time I'd climbed out of this bed, I'd had two feet, and for a minute I stopped and felt how much I hated the cold, hard piece of wood that served me for a foot. My raggedy uniform was gone, and Maw had put some of my old work clothes on the chair. They felt strange on my skin, soft and clean compared to what I'd been wearing, and I liked it. It was another sign that I really had come home.

I shuffled, barefooted and rubbing my eyes, into the kitchen where Maw and Aunt Rannie were waiting for me. Aunt Rannie like to broke my neck hugging me, and then she spent the rest of the morning snuffling into her apron until Maw fussed at her. They had made biscuits with white flour, and there was butter and fat back and cane syrup. I ate like I hadn't seen food in a month. There was still no coffee, of course, and wouldn't be for some time, but they'd parched corn to make a kind of substitute that was all right if you put lots of milk in it.

While I was still eating, Uncle Foot came to the door, and I stood up and shook his hand like he was a white man because that's the way I felt. Maw looked at me peculiar but never said a word.

Then I took my "coffee," and Uncle Foot had a biscuit, and we all four sat on the back porch and had the same conversation that Maw and I had had the night before. Uncle Foot and Aunt Rannie allowed as to how they wouldn't want to go anywhere else even if they knew someplace to go. Aunt Rannie said she'd raised all of us chaps and thought as much of us as she did her own, and she couldn't bear the thought of leaving "my marse Thomas and him the way he is."

Later in the morning Uncle Foot and I, along with his oldest boy, did a kind of inventory. There were still greens in the garden from the last fall, a fair amount of salt pork, and some corn in the crib. We had three mules and one old horse, although they looked awful poor. And then, of course, there was my mare. They'd managed to keep one milk cow and a calf, and there were some hogs running loose in the woods we could maybe round up and pen. If we could finish getting the gardens in and start thinking about some corn and cotton, it wouldn't look too bad.

So far as I knew, there wasn't any money anywhere, so getting seeds and equipment would be a right smart problem. If the stores in town managed to get ahold of things, maybe we could talk them into letting us borrow or even farm on shares. Farmers like us had always done that some years, and this sure wasn't the time for pride.

Maw had said she wanted me to do all the arranging, but if I knew her as well as I thought I did, she'd be right over my shoulder while I was doing it. People expected a man to do the talking for his family, but the land was rightly Maw's until she died, and I (and the boys after me) never went to talk business without asking her along too.

CHAPTER TEN

How we did it, I still don't exactly know, but we managed to hold on to the land through all those years they came to call "Reconstruction." There were four hundred acres in our family since South Carolina was a colony, and we plowed and planted maybe one hundred fifty acres most years. We did borrow against it, sometimes for years in a row, but in our town the bank never wanted to take away family land. They would allow you some slack in making payments as long as they knew you were trying. I mention that because it wasn't true everywhere. There were people who took advantage of our being down and out; some were associated with carpetbaggers, and some of them were just plain greedy. They'd snatch the land as soon as they could and even put folks out of their houses, which helps to explain why some are still so hot about a war that should have been over and done years ago.

That summer passed as quick as the years of the war had been slow. Uncle Foot and I, along with his family, set about finding out how we could run a hand-to-mouth farm. That first year or two, we were never actually starving, but we all looked a mite scrawny sometimes. It seemed like days were never long enough. Lots of the extra tasks that weren't about surviving never got done. Things weren't painted or repaired the way we would have liked. There was almost never an extra penny for candy or store tobacco. Things were patched, and then there were patches put on the patches. And we kept on going. There was a kind of pride in saying, "We ain't dead yet," especially when we saw all our neighbors doing the same thing.

Some of those who had less land or poorer land finally couldn't keep on. Proud people like us, they drifted away from the land or went to work for other people. Direct or indirect, some of them probably gave up and died.

When I was working from dark to dark and falling asleep at the supper table, I didn't have time to do much grieving about Agnes. But if I had a minute where it was quiet and I could think for myself, I still treated myself to pictures in my mind: Agnes skipping down the steps as if she were floating or serving my plate at that first Sunday dinner or lying bare on top of her clothes in the sweet-smelling hay, her skin all damp in that warm loft. Sometimes, just Agnes smiling at me, our eyes seeing nothing else but each other.

I could fall into them memories the way you fall backward into a deep swimming hole, and when I came up again, my eyes would be wet. Maw knew me well enough to see something was going on, but I reckon she figured it was just war memories or something else she shouldn't ask about.

It wasn't like I didn't have the war memories too. During the day I could mostly put them by, but when I was asleep, my mind was fair game, and I'd wake up sweating and yelling. Occasionally Maw would come and wake me when I got too loud, and then she'd sit for a minute on the edge of the bed the way she'd done when I was a shirttail young'un and had had bad dreams.

I grieved for Thomas and for whatever he was suffering behind his eyes that only seemed able to see the things that had drove him daft. But mostly, when my mind was centered on anything besides the work I was doing or on planning, it was centered on memories of Agnes. And when I began to have trouble recalling exactly how her face looked, I grieved that too.

I mention this partly to explain why it was I didn't have time to think about keeping company with women my age in the community. There were still church meetings when I'd be with people my age, and sometimes there would even be a corn husking or all-night singing; but I wasn't much inclined to want to see women in any courting way, nor did it bother me much that I wasn't.

Like every place that had sent men to the war, our county had a shortage of men my age. Most every family had lost someone, or the man who had come back was so stove-up that he wasn't much good as a husband. From time to time, Maw or my older sister would mention this or that woman who'd asked if I was keeping company with anybody. But I never gave them any encouragement.

Then one day during the second fall I was home, Julius and I were snaking logs out of the wood lot to sell for railroad ties, which was one of the few ways we could get cash money, when Amelia Sperry came riding by. She wasn't driving a buggy, and she wasn't even riding sidesaddle. She was riding astride with her pantaloons showing at the top of the stirrups. We stopped and took off our hats, and Amelia rode right over to where I was standing. When Julius saw she meant to talk, he went off a ways and set down with his pipe.

"Morning, Julius," she said. "Morning, Gabe. Gabe, it seems as if I haven't seen you in a spell. If you don't start coming to church more often, the preacher'll be talking about you from the pulpit."

"I reckon you're about right, Amelia. At least that's what Maw says. But to tell the truth, I'm about wore out by the time Sunday morning gets here. Seems like I just want to set on the porch and rock. Anyway, I'm not real sure God would look kindly on a congregation that had me in it. Still, I'm pleased at your being concerned."

"Well, you know, I'm not *that* concerned, Gabe. If you remember, you and I were never exactly the prizewinners in Sunday school. You and William used to sit in the back row and shoot beans at the back of my bonnet."

"And then you'd chase me with a stick in the yard until it was time for church."

"Well I haven't done that in some time now." There was a moment of quiet, and she looked at me and smiled a little smile. Then she asked, "Anybody else chasing you these days, Gabe?"

"Not as I've noticed. As you can see, I'm even less of a prize now than I was then."

"Hmmm, I wouldn't count on that," she said. "I've heard some of the fair maidens hereabouts—and some of the not so fair—mention your name with considerable interest. It might surprise you. Don't take it too seriously, though. I wouldn't want you to grow vain. It's just that us old hens do tend to gather in flocks these days, and people will go on."

"Yes," I said. "I suppose that's the danger in flocks. But knowing you, Amelia, I'm sure I can count on you not to go on. You never were one to cackle much." To my surprise, I found that I was enjoying our conversation. I had forgotten how much I had fancied her in our Sunday-school days, and it was pleasant to be picking at each other again.

We stood for a moment. Then I said, "I reckon we better get back to this here log. They only pay us if we get it to the railroad, you know."

"I imagine that's so," she said. Then, in a more serious tone, she continued. "Gabe, I never caught up to you with that stick. The worst I ever did was sneak a kiss from you, and I might as well have been kissing a mule for all the heat it generated. But I've been thinking we might want to give it another chance sometime. Why don't you consider taking me for a drive Sunday afternoon?"

I studied on that for a minute, enjoyed the feeling it gave me, and found myself catching her stirrup in my hand and saying, "Miss Sperry, I would be honored to call for you at four this Sunday afternoon, if that would be quite convenient."

She fluttered a hand to her breast, looked shyly down at my hand, and said in her best playacting voice, "Why, Mr. Corley, I *am* surprised and delighted. I shall await your arrival with keen anticipation."

I slapped her horse's flank, put on my hat, and whistled to Julius, and Amelia and I parted company. For the moment.

Amelia Sperry had never been what folks call a "raving beauty." She was not as tall as some, and she was not slender like the pictures you see of women with almost no waist at all in the mail-order catalog. But she had thick, dark hair that was beautiful, a laugh that came from way back in her throat, and a quick smile. In fact, there was lots that was quick about her, including her tongue, her temper, and her mind. But what had attracted me early on (and what grew over the years) was something I had trouble identifying in words. I reckon maybe "boldness" comes closest to describing it.

I don't mean she was what boys and men call "easy." Her brothers made it plain that she'd been able to lick most of them in a fair fight when they was younger, and if anybody had made the mistake of being too familiar, I knew that even then, she would have made them pay. The boldness was more about being willing to stand toe to toe with anybody, man or woman, and say what she wanted to say without any kind of coyness. It was the kind of thing that allowed her to come right up to me and suggest we ride out together on a Sunday afternoon. By rights, you see, she should have had her mother mention it to my older sister, who would have then mentioned it to my mother or some such. For me, at least, it seemed promising. And it stirred something deep and strong I'd almost forgot how to feel.

We still had a buggy then, but a wheel was broken and had been since I'd been home. Somehow I never got around to working on it during that week. When Sunday morning came, I set about trying to get it put back together. Maw took the wagon to church, and Thomas sat in his chair by the barn and kept me company while I worked. I had got in the habit of talking to him as if we were actually carrying on a conversation. So far as I could tell, it didn't do much for him one way or another, but it comforted me some.

The rim of the wheel was bent, and one spoke was broken, so I had to fire up the forge and try to straighten the rim, asking Thomas's advice as I went along. After four or five hours of work, I had patched the rim and had made a passable spoke. Then when I was fixing to put the wheel back on the buggy, I finally noticed why nobody had bothered to try to do the job before. The bearing on the end of the axle had cracked when the wheel had hit whatever it was that'd broke it. I had a patched-together wheel and nowhere to put it! I had worked all morning for nothing!

When I finally stopped swearing, I noticed that Thomas was half smiling, although he wasn't really looking straight at me.

"Oh ho!" I said. "So you finally heard something you liked, did you? Well if that's what you want, we can both give up, 'cause Maw would skin the pair of us if she heard a word of that—and on a Sunday morning. Still, if you were to decide to swear, she'd probably be glad to hear even that."

With that, an idea popped into my head. Somehow working on the wheel and swearing (which probably go together for most men) had started something for him. I put some more coals on the forge and stood Thomas up. "Here," I said. "You turn this fan, and let's see if we can get an iron hot." I put his hand on the crank and started turning. To my surprise, he kept on turning while I found a horseshoe and shoved it down into the coals. When it was the right shade of red, I pulled it out and began to work it on the anvil. At the sound of the hammer, Thomas looked at the anvil and stopped turning.

"Reckon you want to have a go?" I asked him, never daring to believe he might actually say or do something.

When he reached out his hand for the hammer, I jumped and felt the hair rise on my neck as if I had seen a ghost. I let him take the hammer and held the shoe on the anvil, waiting and looking for some spark in his eyes, but there was nothing. Then I followed his eyes and noticed that the shoe on the anvil had got cold. As quick as I could, I put it back in the coals and turned the crank to send air blowing up through the forge. Again I waited until the iron was ready to be worked, and then I put it back on the anvil. Thomas bounced the hammer on the anvil to get his rhythm going as if he did that every day, and he commenced to work the horseshoe as I turned it. Then he stopped again when the iron began to cool.

I wanted to keep talking to him—felt like I had to keep talking to him—but my throat was closing with a sob. "Think—think!" I told myself. "Do something else! Don't let him put the hammer down."

I plunked the horseshoe in the water tub and croaked out, "Thomas, that one's done." Then, looking around the forge like a crazy man, I saw a broken gate hinge, picked it up in the tongs, and jammed the broken end into the coals, scattering live coals on the dirt floor. Again I turned the crank, and after a minute, I put the hinge on the anvil. "See can you can nip the end off that and punch us another nail hole, Big Brother."

Without another word from me, he pounded the broken part off on the cutter bar and flattened the squared-off end. After one more heating, I centered the hinge so he could punch the hole.

We worked for an hour until he was panting. At first frantic, as if any break might ruin the magic, and then more calm and quiet, I found one blacksmith job after another to do, talking all the time. He was listening to me, and even better, when we put the work on the anvil, he knew exactly what to do. Once he even looked right at me and nodded when I asked him a question. He was thinking!

When Maw finally pulled up in the wagon, I deliberately did not go out to unhitch it. She could hear Thomas's hammer, so after a minute, she pushed through the door to the forge, fussing as she came. "If you can't go to church, the least you can do is come and unhitch the mule for—" And then she caught sight of me motioning with my head to Thomas and him, sweating from head to toe, bending the red-hot shaft of a hoe over the rounded end of the anvil with soft, careful little blows.

"Just needed to finish that, Maw," I said, and then I took the tongs from Thomas's left hand and dipped the hoe in the water. Then I set it in a row with all the other work he'd finished and said, "By God, he's quiet, Maw, but he sure ain't forgot how to smith."

For once in her life, Maw was without words. She never even corrected me for taking the Lord's name in vain on a Sunday. She was that flabbergasted!

It was a slow process for months and years after that. Some days he had a bad day for no reason we could figure, and it would look as if he might be going backward again. We learned not to push him when that happened. Still, he was plenty steady enough to keep us going.

It's hard to imagine how almost out of our minds with happiness we'd get when Thomas did the smallest thing. Somebody just walking up on us would have thought we were all touched. We were grown-up, adult people, niggers and whites, standing around grinning like mules eating briars because a thirty-year-old man was cutting his own meat at the table or feeding the chickens without being told!

I'm not saying that Thomas has ever got completely right. He never will be. But he started on that day to be with us again.

We still get surprises. Last Christmas, all in secret, he made a doll prettier than anything you could buy in a store for our youngest granddaughter, and he wrote her a Christmas card with her name on it in a beautiful hand. Up to that point, he hadn't voluntarily taken up a pen in all the years since he'd come from the war.

I called for Amelia in the wagon that Sunday afternoon. She looked a little funny at me when I drove up, but she picked up her skirt and stepped on a wheel spoke, and I reached down, took her by the hand, and pulled her up onto the seat beside me.

"Amelia," I said. "I do apologize for calling on a lady in a farm wagon. I had figured on having a proper buggy by this evening, but the broke wheel had other ideas. It was not in a mood to be set right."

"Well, I have been put off by things and people smarter than a buggy wheel, and I suspect some not quite so smart. I guess I can endure even this humiliation." And she took my arm and grinned.

"On the other hand," I said, "it's an ill wind that blows nobody good, and I think we were blown a whole heap of good over that confounded wheel."

She looked at my face to see if I was teasing, but I think my voice had already given me away. She said, "And that would be?"

"That would be Thomas's beginning to wake up. Amelia, he even talked to me! He said a word right out loud. And we worked together in the smithy for two or three hours..." My voice seized up again, and I had to stop.

"Oh, Gabe!" she said. "Oh, Gabe, did he *really* talk?" She picked up my hand and squeezed it till it almost hurt.

"Didn't say much, but it was to the point. I declare, Amelia, I like to swooned. I ain't told Maw yet, but it was my swearing set him off. I found out I couldn't repair the wheel, and I just let out a stream of foul words would turn the air blue—and on a Sunday morning. When I looked over at him, he was just a-grinning."

"Well, if we're going to be keeping company, Mr. Corley, I'll have you know there'll be no more of that." But she was half smiling when she said it.

"I was raised right. At least Maw tried. But if I'd thought I could make Thomas light up like that, I'd a started a long time ago."

"And I would have encouraged you to try it." She gave my hand another squeeze. "Oh, Gabe, I'm so happy for you all. Especially for your poor mother. I don't know how she's survived all this."

"Yep, it has aged her for sure. But when she saw Thomas with that hammer in his hand, just going along like it was ten years ago, she looked that much younger herself. Matter of fact, I think I lost a year or two myself."

"Well, young man, lets take a ride over toward the churchyard, and you can tell me all about it on the way. If my father looks out and sees us holding hands in the front yard, we'll have to go and sit in the parlor with him."

When I finally ran down talking, I thought to ask about her family and give her a chance. I pulled the wagon up under the trees in the churchyard, and little bit by little bit, we began to get into the serious business of courting. Being as how we were both a little older than most courting couples starting off, and we were more or less broke in by what we'd been through, it wasn't as hard as it might have been. When we got back to her parents' house again, I promised to have the buggy fixed before another week.

She said, "Maybe you'd better ask if I fancy riding in it with you before you go to all that trouble."

I said, "I truly hope you will." And I meant it.

She brushed my cheek with a kiss and said, "Don't bother getting down, Gabe. I can find my way to the door. I'm obliged to you for the ride...and for your company, come to think of it, buggy or no."

CHAPTER ELEVEN

The next Sunday I sent Maw off to church in the wagon with Thomas sitting by her side. I rode off in the buggy alone to take Amelia to church with me. It was duly noted by every man, woman, and child in the building that Amelia Sperry had come in on my arm—and a good three-quarters of them had to turn and say something to a neighbor on the pew. By three o'clock that afternoon, there probably wasn't a person in the county who didn't know. For the most part, we been riding to church together ever since.

We weren't in any great sweat to get married right off. Courting suited us just fine, and we enjoyed it for the better part of two years. We didn't have money or our own place to live then, but that wasn't mainly what held us back. The years we'd spent away from each other had been full of things going on inside us and around us—things neither one of us knew about the other. It took some time to feel around and to see how we'd changed and what we each one had to learn. Since neither one of us seemed to need to try other partners just for the sake of trying, it was comfortable taking all the time we wanted. It also turned out to be a good thing. I had to learn again how headstrong Amelia could be, and she had to do some getting used to my moods, which I couldn't always control. I still can't.

The touching and holding part was good from the very beginning, except, of course, that I was a little anxious to move faster than Amelia was inclined to let me. There weren't a lot of chances in those days to be alone, even though we were grown-ups in our twenties and old for marriage by some standards. When we did have a chance to kiss and cuddle awhile, I'd get to thinking I wanted more and start trying to unhook or unbutton something.

Once when we were riding home alone from church on a Wednesday night, we stopped to admire the moon. It was early winter, and she was wearing a wool coat. I had undone one or two coat buttons, enough to slide a hand inside the coat and then under her blouse.

She kissed me and said, "That's a cold hand, Mr. Corley."

"I 'spect it is," I said. "Would you mind if I warmed it a bit more?"

"My momma would say I ought to slap your face, get down, and walk home, Gabe. But the truth is, I don't mind a bit, which is why I think you'd better let me hold *both* your hands."

"Who's gonna know if you don't? We're both grown-ups, ain't we?"

"We are grown-ups, Gabe. And that's the trouble. I like being touched about as much as you do, and it would surprise you"—she stopped and pulled away, studying my face in the moonlight—"or maybe it wouldn't surprise you. Either way, fact is that I might want to get on with it as much as you do. But since you missed out on courting all those years in the army, maybe I'd better explain some things.

"First off, my daddy knows pretty much exactly when we left church and how long it takes to drive to our front door. My momma knows how long it takes to unbutton this dress I'm wearing and to get me out of what's under it. Now, under the rules, they'll allow us ten, maybe even twenty minutes of leeway, but not much more. After that, there's going to be serious question asking."

"You mean to tell me that almost-married folks in their late twenties got to answer to parents like thirteen-year-olds?"

"That's exactly what I mean, Gabe! But that doesn't worry me near as much as what would be said in the community. Somebody would look out a window and see us driving by at the wrong time with my bonnet at the wrong angle. And the next morning, every tongue in this end of the county would be wagging to beat the band.

"I don't think of myself as a proud woman, Gabe, but I'm a sight too proud for that!"

"Whew," I said. "And I thought a canister shot was bad!"

As much as I wanted and needed her that way, though, I think it's true to say that I got caught up with her mind and spirit just as much. She was smart and quick—smarter than me (and most other people) in some ways; but I have to say that Amelia is the most fair-minded woman I've ever known. She's never used her sharp wit to try to lord something over me. Sometimes it made her impatient with folks who couldn't keep up with her, and I confess that she could be right sarcastic at those times. But she never would take advantage of the people she loves.

On the other hand, she has always refused to argue "like a woman" by giving in to a man or flattering him. She didn't even do that with her own paw, much less with her brothers or me. I came to love that part of her and to be proud of it, even when it made me furious.

Everybody in my own family had learned to read, and none of us was stupid, but there was something exciting about Amelia's curiosity I'd never run into before. She'd borrow books from wherever she could and then read them all the way through, and then she'd want to talk about ideas. She'd push me to think about some idea and then make me defend it, so I'd end up surprising myself. Sometimes she'd even get started on the Bible and make me feel a little uneasy about asking questions nobody could answer. It's like once her mind got going on something, she'd worry it like a bulldog.

The bad part of that was that she could most always read *me* too. Trying to lie to her was a lost cause right from the beginning.

By the spring of '69, it was pretty plain to both of us that it was time to be married and living on our own. Everybody in both families talked about it, but it was Amelia who sat down and figured out a plan that would actually work. Her family's land butted right up against the edge of town, which was where she wanted to live.

"I love your family and your farm," she said, "but I want to be out of sight of either family. I don't want anybody looking out the window to see when I hang out washing or walk down the road."

Not a week after that, we had a little set-down talk with Amelia's Paw. I had stayed over at their house for Sunday dinner, and before Mr. Sperry could get away to take a nap over his book, Amelia caught ahold of him.

"Papa, Gabriel and I would like to talk to you for a minute. Do you mind?"

"I reckon not," he said. "It sounds serious."

"Oh, Papa, it's not that serious. But Gabriel and I do have a little business proposition for you."

"Oh, business," he said. "Can we talk business on the Sabbath?"

"Well, sir," I said. "It ain't exactly that kind of business, but then again, I reckon it is. Since Amelia and I are promised, we were thinking we'd like to begin making plans for our own house. Amelia allows she doesn't want to live all the way out at our place. She'd like to be a little closer to town."

"Yes, Papa," she put in. "And I was talking with Gabriel about maybe building a little house for us close to your woodlot by the town limits. Oh, Papa, if we had even as much as an acre, we could set up housekeeping and have plenty of room for a garden and everything we need. If you could deed it to us, we'd promise to raise your grandchildren on it. Could you just think about it?"

"Oh," he said. "And we're all the way up to grandchildren, are we?" I could tell he was trying to sound serious as death, but Mrs. Sperry was peeking around the kitchen door, nodding her head at him, and he was having trouble not smiling. "I suppose if we have to consider the welfare of grandchildren, I can't really refuse, can I? Meily, I think that's a good idea." Then to his wife he said, "Momma, what do you say? Can we spare an acre to get these two started?" And of course, "Momma" had to hold her apron to her eyes and smile and nod. "Then I guess it's settled. We're an acre poorer, but we're promised grandchildren." He held out his hand for a solemn handshake with me and kissed Amelia. "Now can I get on with my nap?"

As soon as the property was officially ours, we started in building. We didn't have two dollars to rub together, but I had timber to trade for finished lumber and windows and such. Thomas, Amelia's brother, and I could do all the rough carpentry. We worked most afternoons until dark, and if the farmwork was light, Thomas and I could work all day on Saturdays.

Still, it did seem to drag on. It took us about six months of working pretty steady when it wasn't pouring rain, and I got more impatient the closer we got to finishing. It was only when our own four rooms were finished, tight and square and neat, that Amelia would agree to set a wedding date. We spoke to Reverend McGill after church one Sunday to no one's surprise.

"Been wondering when you two would finally set a date," he said. "We've all been happy to think you'd be starting a family. Why don't you come by the manse before supper tonight, and we'll do a little talking?"

Since Reverend McGill almost never did just "a little" talking, we calculated when the end of his Sunday nap time would be and arrived at the manse about four. He was a little sleepy even so, and it took a cup of Mrs. McGill's strong tea to get him going. He wanted to talk about the church's ideas about marriage, how the relationship between husband and wife was like "Christ and the church," and "loving your wife as you love your own body."

You'd think people who'd been listening to that at every wedding for the last twenty-five years would've understood the basics, but we just nodded and answered "yes, sir" at the right times.

Reverend McGill seemed pleased to be doing his duty of making sure we were not dangerously ignorant or heretical. Amelia was unusually restrained, and I reckoned that she didn't want to make it any longer than it absolutely had to be.

There was a whole different kind of talking came after we had left the manse and were on our way to Amelia's house in the buggy. With a little interruption for a cold supper, we went on for the next three or four hours—I don't remember exactly how long. The substance of it—at least the part I remember—went like this:

"Gabe"—she was holding my eyes with hers tender-like, but as serious as I'd ever seen her—"I want you to understand that I love you better than anybody else ever could. Never mind the New Testament. I love you as if we were one person already. By this time, there's no doubt left in my mind that you and I chose the best people we could ever choose to be our partners. I think I'd marry you no matter what, but I want to be certain that you understand things the way I do. Am I scaring you?"

"I don't reckon you are. Making me feel a little melty inside, I guess, but not scaring me. Should I be scared?"

"No, no, no. That's not what I mean at all. It's just that sometimes I get the feeling you aren't there—or at least, not *all* there—when we're together. Sometimes I know you're with me, but other times, when we're talking about serious things, you seem to go away somewhere, and I can't find you anymore. It worries me to think that you're holding reservations about our being together, and you're afraid—or at least not willing—to talk about them. What I want to say is, no matter how upsetting you think they might be, I'd rather you talk about them. I'm a lot less afraid of knowing you have reservations—and I'm not saying you do—than of not knowing what they are. Does that make sense?"

"Generally speaking, Amelia, everything you say makes *some* sense. You're a little ahead of me sometimes, but you most times make sense. I reckon you may know something about me that I ain't found out about in just the same way yet."

"I'll give you an example, Gabe. Last Sunday evening, we were sitting on the front porch—you remember? We were talking back and forth, and it felt so warm and good—like we were holding each other even though we weren't even touching. Then you said something, and I said, 'You know, Gabe, you're the only person I ever even thought about loving. It's like I was just born to be attracted to you and nobody else.' And all of a sudden, like closing a door, you were gone. You were staring out across the field as if you were seeing something I couldn't see. I got quiet because it scared me a little, and you didn't even look back at me for two or three minutes. Do you remember that?"

I did remember, and it panicked me for a minute to think Amelia might have been reading my mind. "Hmmm," I said. "I *think* I remember. I could have just been wore out; we'd worked on the house for as long as there was light. I could have just nodded. Can't say for sure."

"No, it wasn't sleep, Gabe. You *went* somewhere else! It doesn't matter. I promise! You can talk to me about whatever it was. Or if it was something from the war you don't want to talk about, just tell me. I swear I won't insist on talking about things that make you sad or afraid! I just need to know if that's what it is."

I was having trouble staying in the conversation then. In a way, I wanted to go back to that soft, warm place in the Virginia hayloft, but I loved Amelia too much to be unfaithful to her that way twice in a row—leastways not in front of her. Going back would have been like a drunkard reaching for the jug when he'd promised his family he'd never take another drink. Without my ever meaning to do it, I'd let the daydreams of Agnes become a second crutch, and they had took over. They would come without my sending for them. When Amelia had said, "The only person I ever even thought about loving," I'd said to myself, "But you're not the only one *I* ever thought about!" And then I'd been gone, drifting along down that comfortable old river.

"I reckon it was the war, Amelia," I half lied. "Most of it was bad, and I guess I need to tell you I still wake up with nightmares sometimes." I stopped to think for a few seconds. "But there were times after I was wounded that were hard beyond being hard.

"I don't want to talk on about it. It's over and done with; but things come back on me sometimes without any warning.

"I'll try to do better about talking to you. I'll try not to get down the way I was then if you'll try not to let it bother you."

"Your maw already told me about the nightmares, darling." Her eyes were soft and close to tears then. "I guess she didn't want me to be scared half to death the first night of my marriage. But I need to know that if you leave like that when I'm trying to be close, it's not because of me. It doesn't mean you don't want to let me in or that I'm being too forward or too something. That really frightens me, Gabe, because I mean to give you all of me there is to give. I can't do it any other way. I just need to know, is it safe for me to do that?"

That, I knew I could answer, and I did. "Amelia Sperry, I swear I will make it safe for you. There's no way for me to deserve you, but by God, I do want all of you."

"There's no need to swear, my love. I think I know everything I need to know. And just so there's no mistake about it, it's never been a case of deserving on my part or yours. You don't know me as well as you will, but I'm sure there will be lots of times I won't deserve you. I'll settle for our loving each other the best way we know how."

There was a formal wedding service a few weeks later for our families and for Reverend McGill. Amelia and I began sleeping together after the service, but we had already said our vows the night of that conversation in her parents' front parlor.

CHAPTER TWELVE

It's entertaining just being in love, especially during that first part when you're thinking about your partner all the time and waiting to be with her again. It had been years since I'd felt anything like that, but I'll declare that Amelia was enough to make me think I had never got the full benefit. She was not experienced in the actual coupling part itself, but that didn't seem to bother her or me. She turned out to be as bold and as curious with our bodies as she was in her mind. In fact, I think her mind was the better part of it.

Not that her body wasn't enough to make a man sweat. She was not slender—"round" would have been a better word for her, round all over—but at least until after our first two babies, she was as firm as could be. Her dark hair and fair skin made her a sight to behold and, even better, to feel against my own skin.

For that first year I could hardly wait to be alone with her. I'd come in from the field so tired I thought I couldn't walk up the steps. Then she'd flounce by in her nightdress or stop and kiss me real slow on the back of the neck, and I'd get so excited I could hardly even wait for us to drag each other to the bed—and there were times we didn't make it that far.

We'd wake up in the morning hungry for each other, and I'd have to pull myself away from her when she was still lying bare in the bed and leave for the fields without breakfast. I'm sure it showed when I rode up on Uncle Foot with my face still flushed, because he took to remarking on it.

"Lawd God, Mr. Gabe," he'd say. "A man yo age, and still carrying on in broad daylight! You goin' ta make yo'self so poor you'll blow away when de breeze come." I found that I couldn't be cross with him, and I had no intention of denying it.

We was lucky to have a full year like that—a year of our own playtime before Amelia started our first child. (Though I'll have to say the reason it took a year wasn't because we didn't give it plenty of chances.) By then we were twenty-seven years old, and in those days that was late for a first child. Amelia had said she was anxious to start before she got "too old," so neither of us was sorry when she missed a couple of months and then began to get a little broad in the hips. I think she hinted to her sister-in-law before she told me outright. I had seen them whispering together, her sister-in-law cutting her eyes at me and smirking, but I had already suspected it. She didn't come out with it until I found her leaning over the slop bucket one morning, looking pale and miserable. I rode off to work that particular morning with another kind of glow.

I worked as hard that year as I ever have before or since. In spite of the fact that we still lived hand to mouth, life was better for me than it had been in a long time—maybe ever. Julius had moved back to our place with his wife, and we helped him work over an old cabin close to the woodlot. He was my partner in our timber cutting. We had a team of oxen then and were selling to the railroad and to a local sawyer. In some of the cleared land, we planted corn to sell, and there was a fellow who ran a stillhouse up the creek and would buy as much as we had extra. He wanted to pay me in whiskey, but in those days I was thinking about the baby coming, and I insisted on cash money.

At the same time, Amelia had begun to do some baking for the woman who ran a boardinghouse in town so we could have a little more cash for the house. Carrying the child didn't seem to bother her at all after she got over being sick in the mornings; and after I got over feeling strange about it, making love was better than it ever had been. Watching her belly grow and her breasts swell up, I was like a child with new toys.

When we'd sit in church, there was a kind of peacefulness about Amelia, like to say, "This is where we was supposed to get to. Me a mother, you an upstanding husband, people nodding respectful-like, and the other women clucking over and asking, 'How're you feeling, honey?'" She'd spread out and ruffle her feathers like a hen setting in the sun all content.

Maw and Thomas seemed to be doing fine without me living there with them. I was by the house every day, and I sometimes ate the noon meal there to keep from having to ride all the way back home. Thomas helped Uncle Foot and his children in the fields and occasionally did a little blacksmithing for the neighbors. Nobody had money in those days, but they'd barter eggs or vegetables for the smithing, and they seemed happy to not have to take time with it themselves.

Thomas started out a better hand than I was at the forge, and he got better and better as he went along. Down the years, he got to where he was experimenting with making ornamental ironwork for his own amusement, and eventually he did begin to sell gates and window screens and things like that for the fancy houses in town. Odd as it seems, thinking back on how he began to come out of his "sleep," he did some of his best work with carriages and buggies. He could do the fine work with wheel rims and springs and such almost as if he'd been born knowing how to do it.

To be fair, I ought to say that while I was beginning to get back on my feet and feel like a proper man again, it was a bad time to be living in the South, and especially in South Carolina. Carpetbaggers were still everywhere, and it was hard to protect ourselves from them because there were still Federal troops stationed there. The legislature was mostly run by darkies, and there was even one on the state supreme court. I don't know that they done a whole lot worse than our white politicians would have, but it rankled folks so bad that they were almost crazy with it. It made for an ugly feeling that I didn't know how to handle.

It seemed to me that there were people in the town, some of them war veterans like me, who made a full-time occupation of standing around complaining. You couldn't go in the store or do any kind of business without getting into a conversation about carpetbaggers and niggers. The level of hate was about poisonous to breathe. I could mostly get along with it, and I tried not to get myself upset and to nod and mutter so they'd think I agreed with them, but sometimes it was hard not to say how tired I got of it.

Some of their grievances were real, of course. The Federals had done things like make it more expensive to send things by rail into the South than to anywhere else in the country. It was a tax on us who'd done "wrong" by their lights, but of course, it hurt everybody who lived there, women, children, and darkies—the lot of us. We were being punished, and that part rankled me too, but at the same time, I partly understood it. I had trouble, though, working up a full head of hate for the poor darkies. It seemed to me that they hadn't done anything to start the war and that they were sharing the same hard times we were. So far as I could tell—and I was with them every day—the niggers I knew were mostly as accommodating as they'd even been. Aunt Rannie, for God's sake, was sewing things for our baby when her own children hardly had shirts on their backs! But there was no use trying to talk that way to the people who had decided to make a business out of hating the darkies. Best to go about your own business and try not to be bothered.

One of the fellows that seemed to spend a lot of time in town just talking was Vance Hunnicutt. I'd known Vance and his family since school days. They were what upstanding white folks called "shiftless," which meant that they lived on poor land and didn't seem to care much about bettering themselves. They'd plant a crop and then let the grass and weeds take it rather than putting in the work to make it produce something. In bad times they'd hire out to other farmers, but people always said you had to watch 'em careful because they'd do a lot of leaning on their hoe. There were some folks said they'd steal. About the only thing they seemed to produce without fail was too many ragged, runny-nosed chaps; that's the way I'd known Vance growing up.

He was a year or so older than I was, so he'd volunteered for the army before I had. He'd come home missing his left arm, and as near as I could figure, he thought that gave him leave to do nothing at all. I'd see him, still wearing the garrison cap from his army uniform, hanging around on the front porch of the store in town, chewing and spitting and ragging on any darky that happened by. Once or twice we'd talked awhile about the war and the battles we both knew about, but we never had been friends, and it wasn't easy talking to him for very long.

I don't want to sound like I didn't honor Vance for what he'd done and for what he'd put up with. We'd all been in the same army for the same reasons. For all I knew, he was a good soldier, and he suffered the same as any of the rest of us who got shot up.

But it didn't lend much shine to the Ku Klux Klan that it was Vance Hunnicutt who invited me to join. I had already heard about the Klan. I did admire General Forrest, who they claim had started it. As a general he was probably the best cavalryman, pound for pound, ever born. From what I heard, there was no Confederate cavalry—nor Union either, for that matter—who fought harder or smarter than General Forrest's.

I also understood why folks would want to band together to protect themselves against the carpetbaggers and scalawags; but as much as I admired the general, I couldn't work up much enthusiasm for the people like Vance who I saw joining up around our town. So when he asked me for about the third time to come to a meeting, I had to get it straight with him.

"Vance," I said. "I just ain't much of a one to join things. I got more than I can do without going off to meetings at night, and I don't much cotton to fancy robes and things."

"I reckon," he said, "you'd just rather let the niggers take over once and for all, then. I tell you, Gabe, they're going to be running the country 'fore long, and you and me's going to be stepping off the sidewalk for 'em. You fancy some nigger bitch having your wife over to clean her house? Well you'd better get used to the idea, 'cause that's where it's heading. And the only way to stop it is for you and me to stand up and be men. There's one thing they understand, and that's a knock in the head with a stick a-kindling."

I nodded and looked away for a minute to kind of get myself settled down. Then I looked Vance in the eye and said, "Vance, if it ever comes to that, I reckon I'll stand up for my family or for any other white folks—*if* it ever comes to that. But I don't think it's going to. I work darkies every day, and ain't nobody yet thought about making me step off the sidewalk for 'em. As far as I can see, they're thinking about the same things I am, which are feeding a family and keeping a roof over our heads. I don't see how abusing the help is going to improve my chances of doing any of them things. Now, I'm obliged to you for inviting me, but I just ain't interested. If you'll excuse me, I need to get on with what I was doing."

Since it looked like he didn't intend to move, I stepped around him and started on to where I was going. As I brushed past him, he touched his cap and said "lootenant" as if it were a swear word. And that's the way he greeted me every time we met up after that. You might say it did not contribute to a feeling of warm comradeship between us.

CHAPTER THIRTEEN

As Amelia got further and further along, I found that I was spending more time thinking on her and our little house. It was all I could do to keep from riding all the way back home at dinnertime, even though it would have taken an hour or more out of the workday. It didn't help that the women were up to something with her just about every day. I'd come home and find the house full of 'em; they'd be sewing or cutting up old flour sacks and talking about baby things to beat the band. Maw retrieved the old cradle she'd used with all of us from my sister's house, brought it over, and set in the corner of our bedroom. Amelia, who was smaller than most, was carrying the baby way out in front of her, which caused all the women to nod their heads like wise women and agree that it was surely going to be a boy.

When the baby had moved down to where it was getting ready to be born, Maw took over my place in the bedroom with Amelia and made me a pallet in the living room. Amelia saw I was a little set back by all the strangeness of this, and she went out of her way to pay attention to me. She'd always had a tender heart, so she wanted to take care of the strays even when she had enough on her own mind. I guess I must have been looking pretty much like a stray toward the end there.

When she began to have her pains, I sat with her on the bed and held her hand and tried to occupy her mind by talking about things like names for the baby and when we'd build another room. But when her water broke, Maw sent me packing into the yard and told me to find something else to do. Her labor was real long that first time, and it made me sick to my stomach to hear her crying so, but Maw wouldn't let me go for the doctor. She said she'd know if there was anything serious wrong that she and Aunt Rannie couldn't handle.

I reckon she must have been right, because when our little Gabriel Lee was born, he was a picture-perfect boy. Amelia looked more peaked than I had ever imagined she could, but she had the proudest, happiest look I'd ever seen on a human face. And for all the smell of milk and baby vomit and diapers, I could lie down beside my wife again, which seemed almost as important to me as being a father.

His whole name is Gabriel Lee Corley, and we decided to call him Lee. There was some talk of making him "Little Gabriel" or "Junior," but he wasn't a "Junior," and I didn't fancy having another person stuck with the name of an angel. Maw was happy we had used her chosen name again, but she seemed real content with Lee. He was her third grandchild, and he was the first one to carry the family name, Corley. Being a boy, he would keep it, and if he lived and married, he would carry it on.

He was born in October, which gave him a fair chance of surviving the summer sickness that took so many new babies in them days. All things considered, it was a good outcome for the whole lot of us, even though I saw right off that I would never be first fiddle again in my own house.

For the first two or three months, it seemed like there was always somebody else living in the house with us. Maw was there for two solid weeks, and then Aunt Rannie took to spending most of the days at our place. I was glad for the help while Amelia got her strength back, even though I missed having our house, and Amelia, to myself. But by Christmastime, things were beginning to look more like I'd been used to.

At first I didn't want to hold the baby except when I was sitting down for fear I'd trip on my bad leg or drop him or something. He was so tiny, and I felt clumsy with him. But as he grew and actually began to know my face, I felt better about holding him, so I was able be of some help to Amelia. When he had got to the point of putting his hand on my face and "talking" to me, it was hard for anybody to take him away from me if I was in the house.

Maw went around telling people I was a fool about the baby, which I guess was right. Amelia acted matter of fact, but I could tell that it pleased her to see me loving him so. She was better from the first about sharing me with Lee than I'd ever been about sharing her. And she could tell when I was sulking, sometimes almost before I could.

It was late at night, and Mother Sperry had decided to stay over again, even though I'd offered to take her home at least twice. I knew Amelia was tired, so I tried to lie quiet and let her go on to sleep.

"Gabe," she said, "I know it's hard sometimes. I mean, hard on you with all the women being here and making over Lee and all."

"I reckon it's hard on both of us. But I know they mean well. They're trying to help."

"And they are helpful, Gabe. But it must seem to you that we never have any time alone together."

"Well, we don't, now do we?"

"I know, I know," she whispered, running her hand soft up and down my arm. "I'm sorry for that. You know I miss it as much as you do. But I just don't know what to do about it. I can't tell Momma or your maw to go home. If they thought we were ungrateful or they weren't welcome, it would just break their hearts.

"I saw Momma come and take Lee out of your arms this evening without even asking. And I saw you go out to weed in the garden. It made me so sad I wanted to run after you. And Momma never noticed a thing."

"Well, I'm sorta like you. I don't know what to do either. I guess the only thing to do is get used to it. Maw said I was spoiled growing up, being the youngest and all. Reckon I'll have to get unspoiled."

Amelia was quiet for a while, and I thought she might be drifting off to sleep. Then she said, "I never spoiled you, Gabe. But I want to. And I'll find a way." Then she kissed me—one of those wonderful, long, soft kisses of hers that could go almost anywhere. And I believed her.

One of the things I'd wondered about when Amelia had first got pregnant was how Thomas would take to a nephew. His "waking up," as we called it, was still going slow, and it was off and on. There were days when he would talk some—or at least answer questions—and other days when he'd be almost like he was at first. It was like he was fighting his way through a thicket to get home, and some days he'd get tired of fighting and just set down.

Since there was nothing we could do to change it, we all decided we'd just leave him be when he needed that and make hay when it looked like we could. Maw would read to him some at night. When he went to church with her, he would sing the hymn tunes he liked whether he used all the words or not. When Amelia and I were around him, we'd always talk as if he was in the conversation whether he made out like he heard us or not. If him and me were working together on a good day, he'd respond to everything I said and even make suggestions, although not always with words.

The first time we got out with Lee to go over to Maw's house for Sunday dinner, Amelia made a point of going straight to Thomas.

She introduced him to Lee, holding the baby close up to his face, and Thomas grinned and reached out to touch him. Lee seemed to study his uncle for a minute, and then he grinned back. Amelia said, "Would you like to hold him, Thomas?"

And Thomas, still grinning, said, "Yup."

Amelia showed him how to support the baby's head, and just like it was an everyday thing, she handed her firstborn over to him. Thomas took Lee as soft as you please, holding him just like Amelia had said, leaned back in his rocker, and began to rock ever so gentle.

Although Thomas seems to love all his nieces and nephews, from that day to this one, him and Lee have been best friends. Lee grew up around this strange, mostly silent person and just figured that that was the way he was supposed to be. There were times when he was colicky or just contrary as a baby, and Amelia would put him in Thomas's arms, and he'd get quiet. Later, when Lee was a little chap, he could toddle over to Thomas, grab a finger, and lead him anywhere he wanted to go.

During all Lee's growing-up years, if the family was doing something and Thomas wasn't in the room, Lee wouldn't let us go on until he'd gone and fetched him. There's somewhere in the Bible where it talks about "a little child leading them." Lee turned out to be one of the people who led Thomas further out of his thicket.

When Lee was about a year old—I recollect he was walking good and saying some words—we were driving back from town late one Saturday evening. Lee had fallen asleep in the back of the buggy. Amelia leaned over against my shoulder and said, "Gabriel, I need to ask you a question."

Her using my whole name set me to thinking right off. When we were on good terms, she mostly called me "darling," and when we were fussing, it was "Gabe." But "Gabriel" meant something serious.

"I reckon you can always ask," I said, trying to make it lighter.

"Well, it's like this," she started. "It worries me to see us always so strapped for cash money. Here we are, married for going on three years, and we're still borrowing you mother's buggy, which is about half gone anyway. And then there's the farm. You and Julius are still dragging out those big old logs with a chain, and it's awful hard on you—not to mention the fact that you've just about killed the oxen. We need mighty near everything, and there's just never any money."

I didn't know where the conversation was headed, but it made me a little hot to hear her saying I wasn't a good provider. I said, "We have as much as anybody else, Amelia. Nobody I know has any cash money. We got a good house, and we eat good. Times will get better someday. We just got to be patient."

"But what if they don't get better, Gabe? What if we just wear ourselves out and still have nothing to leave to our children? Nothing to live on when we get old?"

"I don't know what you're going on about, Amelia. I'm doing as much as I can do—more than most people. And we're doing all right."

"Gabe, I know you're working hard. And you're smart into the bargain. Between the logging and the new land you're plowing, you're a wonderful manager. But I'd like to help."

There was silence for a minute. That was giving me a bad feeling inside, and I had to try hard not to just cut her off. "Well," I said. "I reckon you could learn to plow."

"No, Gabe," she went on, "I'm serious. I talked to Mrs. Gibbs at the boardinghouse today. The trains are stopping in the middle of the day now, and she has more than she can do alone. She likes my baking, and she wants me to come and work for her. She's even thinking about building on to the dining room and serving two tables at dinner. It would mean we could have some spare cash, buy things for the farm, and live a little better. I want to do it, Gabe. I really want to."

She was quiet, and I knew I was supposed to say something, but my mind was going in all directions at once. My first thought was to shout out what I was thinking, which was, "No, you ain't going off to be anybody's hired woman! No! My wife ain't working!" But I was able to keep myself from doing that. Even so, my voice was rising when I answered her.

"And while you're keeping house for someone else, who'll take care of our son and our house?'

"Gabe, it's only in the morning till the end of dinner. I could be home again by two o'clock. Aunt Rannie and Phoebe love to take care of Lee, and I'd make enough money to give them something every week. The boarders and folks from the train are paying twenty-five cents just to eat dinner! I could earn four or five dollars a week. Think what that would buy us."

I still wasn't trusting my mouth too much, and about that time, Lee woke up and began to fuss. Amelia reached around and pulled him up on her lap, and we both stopped talking for a while.

I got a bad habit of sulking when I get in a fight, especially a fight with a woman, and I 'spect Amelia seen a sulk coming on. So she said, quieter then, "Gabe, I know you don't like it, but we're living in hard times. You don't have to answer yes or no. Just think about it, and we'll talk some more later."

The fact is, I never could much argue with Amelia for any length of time. For one thing, I loved her mighty near to distraction, and I hated the coldness I felt when we were fussing. Hated it like poison! For another thing, I knew she was at least as smart as me, and a sight smarter about most things. She didn't try to jolly me out of a sulk the way I've seen some people do. She just seemed to know by instinct that it made things worse for me. When I'd had time to think for a day or two on the business of her going to work, I brought it up myself.

"Meily, I been thinking about what you said about helping Mrs. Gibbs at the boardinghouse. I'm sorry I got my back up so quick. I reckon I was only seeing it from my side."

She turned around from the sink where she was washing some greens and dried her hands on her apron. "Darling, I know you didn't mean any harm. It's a hard thing to think about, I guess. Do you want to talk about it now?"

"I don't really want to, but I reckon we got to. I know you'd figured it all out before you brought it up. Just kinda let me in on the details as you see 'em."

"Well, the boardinghouse serves three meals a day every day but Sunday. On Sundays there's just the folks who are actually staying there, not any people from the train, so Mrs. Gibbs can handle that with the two girls who work for her. I'd work Monday, Wednesday, Friday, and Saturday. Aunt Rannie or Phoebe would help me get breakfast on for all of us, and then I'd leave Lee with one of them and go off to work at about eight. I'd help finish up breakfast at the boardinghouse and then start baking two days' worth of bread and cakes and pies for them. After helping with the dinner meal, I would come back home at about three in the afternoon and have some time to do things I need to do here.

"I suspect Mrs. Gibbs wants some help with the bookkeeping and shopping too. She looks pretty worn down these days. Just having another pair of hands she can trust is what she wants. I know I can do this, and Gabe, it would feel so good to think I was contributing something to our house."

"Amelia, you *are* our house to me. You and Lee."

"I know that, Gabriel. I know that. And you and Lee are our house to me too." She came to me and put her damp hand on the side of my face. Then, looking up into my eyes, she said, "But I worry about you working yourself into the ground and still having nothing. This'll maybe give us a chance to see a little daylight. Please, can't we just try it awhile and see how it works?"

"You know I can't say no to you. But I don't want you wearing yourself down. I married the prettiest woman in Laurens County, and I'd like it to stay that way."

"Thank you, Gabe, for not saying no and for believing I'm pretty. I don't know or care much about 'pretty,' but if you really think I am, that's the only thing that matters. And I promise I won't get worn down, and I won't neglect you and Lee. You'll see. I might even look better." And she reached up and kissed me. We were still standing like that when Lee came through the door and tried to push in between us, so we picked him up together and squeezed him until he giggled.

That night Amelia made a point of seeing that we'd be alone in the house, and Lee got put to bed before it was dark good. Then she filled the tub and bathed the both of us together (on a weeknight!), and we made love somewhere between tender and ferocious until I was about wore out. But I still didn't want to stop. Gracious!

I'll say this for Amelia Sperry: when she wants to welcome a man home, he'd have to be an idiot, dead, or one or t'other not to hurry up and get there.

Amelia worked at that boardinghouse year in and year out for almost twenty years. She worked there through four children, if you count Lee, even taking the babies with her when she was nursing. Within a year, Mrs. Gibbs had turned over all the bookkeeping and banking and most of the buying to Amelia. Amelia learned to buy the staples in bulk right off the train so they didn't have to pay the store's commission. She saw to adding on to the dining room and the three new rooms on the second story.

By the time Mrs. Gibbs got too old to stand on her feet anymore, they were working four girls in the kitchen alone, and there was another waiting tables and cleaning the rooms. Her own children never exactly cottoned to the idea, but Mrs. Gibbs started saying early on that when she died, the boardinghouse would go to Amelia, and it did.

Over the years, Amelia's salary bought things, including more land, for the farm and for our little logging business, and it built new rooms on our house too. Finally we even hired a man to tend the gardening part of the farm and the animals—we were selling that much butter and vegetables and meat and such to the boardinghouse.

Our two middle children were girls, and although Amelia said she didn't want them working there, the older one, Katherine, did spend a lot of time with her and was a big help. Our younger daughter, Agnes, tended to pet me a lot, and I never complained. I reckoned we had one apiece, which seemed to suit both Amelia and me just fine.

CHAPTER FOURTEEN

I suppose I should have seen it coming, but I didn't. I never took the Klan business seriously until it was almost too late. In some ways, I guess it was partly my fault. We went on selling corn to the fellow run the stillhouse, and eventually Julius and I got to taking the little flask of his whiskey he'd offer when we'd drop off a load of corn. At first I'd take it home and put it on the shelf for making medicine and whatnot, but Julius seemed to have a taste for it. He'd usually save it for a Saturday night after work, but as time went by, he took to nipping on it as soon as he got ahold of it. It didn't bother me. I wouldn't let him get drunk enough to hurt himself or me at work. If he came in drunk on a Monday morning, I'd make him lie out until the middle of the day.

The trouble, when it came, didn't come from work. It came from what the whiskey did to Julius's mouth. For a darky, he'd always been right smart with me. We'd known each other almost since we were born, and I never took offense because none was meant. But when he had taken a little whiskey, Julius could be right uppity with almost anybody, nigger or white.

I wasn't there, so I can't say what really happened, but as it was told to me, Julius crossed paths with Vance Hunnicutt's mother early one Sunday morning. Mrs. Hunnicutt had never been a person of delicate temperament, and I reckon she swore at Julius and told him to get his black ass out of the road. When he was sober, Julius had enough sense to not fool with the likes of the Hunnicutts, but he wasn't sober. As she told it, Julius swore right back at Mrs. Hunnicutt and embroidered his speech a little bit with some words about "white trash."

That must have been what Vance had been waiting for, because it wasn't more than a day or so later that things began to get right complicated. Our youngest boy, William, was about three, so Lee must have been about sixteen. Everybody was getting ready for bed one night when there came a pounding on the back door like somebody wanted to beat it down. When I opened the door, Julius's boy like to fell into the kitchen.

"Mister Gabe, you got to come quick! Them nightriders is taken Daddy. They gone kill him, Mister Gabe. Please, sir. Please come!"

"Now calm down, son. Where'd they take him?"

"They drag him off behind a horse toward the crick ford. They say if we come out the cabin, they gone shoot us too."

"How many were there?"

"I don't know, sir. I was about too scared to look at 'em. Maybe ten—maybe more."

"All right, boy. Now you get back home and take care of your maw. And tell her I'm coming. You hear?" And he was gone, his bare feet pounding across the yard and down the road.

I stood still, blood sounding in my ears and my mind working like it would when we were moving into a battle during the war. "Think quick, Gabe," I thought. "Don't make any mistakes!" Then I shouted to Lee.

"Lee, you and Katherine saddle my horse and one for you. Run. Hurry! And get your rifle. I'll be out there in a minute."

"Stop right there!" said Amelia. "You're not taking that boy out of this house. And I don't want you going either."

"Amelia, I ain't got time to argue. We're talking about a man's life here. Lee ain't going to get hurt. I promise. He's not going to be in any danger—he's just got to be my backup. Do you want him to grow up knowing he could have stopped a murder and didn't do it? He's got to come."

It took me about three minutes to load my revolver, and I slipped powder and shot already wrapped in paper into my pocket. Amelia stood there all white faced, watching me and holding Agnes but saying nothing. When I started out the door, she began again.

"Gabe—" But I didn't let her finish.

"We'll be back," I said. "Just leave the lamp on, and we'll be back."

I made sure Lee had loaded his rifle and had extra ammunition, and we took off riding hard toward the creek. As we rode I shouted instructions to him and made him say them back to me. "I'm counting on you, Son. Do exactly what I'm telling you—nothing more and nothing less. And whatever you do, if anything should happen to me, you get on that horse and hightail it back to your maw. That's your first job—to take care of your maw and the little uns. Are you clear on that?"

And he shouted back, "Yes, sir."

When I could see the light of their torches, we stopped, and I put Lee in position where I wanted him. I whispered the instructions one more time, and he whispered them back to me. Then I turned the horse and rode right down the slope and into their circle.

Julius had been hung up by his wrists to the bottom limb of a big oak. I imagine they meant to leave his body there at the ford where anybody crossing would have to see it. Ten or twelve men in Klan robes and masks stood in a circle, one of them playing with a bullwhip, cracking it around Julius's head and taking some pleasure in ragging him. When I rode into the light, the man with the whip stopped and faced me.

"Welcome, Lootenant Corley," he said. "You finally decided we're good enough for you to associate with? You figure to join us in teaching this nigger some manners?"

"Evening, Vance. I'm sure you and your friends are good enough for associating with just about anybody in this neighborhood. What was it you was figuring to do?"

"I done already told you what I'm fixing to do, Lootenant. I'm fixing to take the hide off this here nigger, and if he's still alive after that, we're planning to hang him up for the crows."

Surely they must have seen that I was wearing a sidearm, but nobody appeared to notice it until I drew it and cocked it. "Now, Vance, I'm sorry if your maw got her feelings hurt. I do apologize, 'cause nobody ought to be sassing anybody's mother. That's a fact. But it's also a fact that your maw would be even more hurt if you was to turn up dead. So what you're fixing to do is cut Julius down from that tree and go about your own business. That particular nigger happens to be one of mine, and he's got a full day's work to do tomorrow."

"Well, listen to mister high-and-mighty Corley. Lootenant, I don't take orders from you. Never did and never will. And if you don't think I'm a-going to hide this here nigger, you just watch me." And he drew the whip back over his shoulder and started to swing it.

I put a bullet in the ground then, about three or four inches from his right foot. In the dead silence that followed the shot, I pulled the hammer back again so they could hear the sound. He stopped his motion and looked toward the other men. "One of you want to kill this son of a bitch so I can get on with what I come to do?" he said. But his voice had lost some of its edge.

"Well now," I said. "I reckon if everybody was to pull together, you might kill me. But you all know damn well I'd take Vance and at least one or two of you before you could do that. And you know I will if I have to. But it ain't as if I was by myself." Without taking my eyes off Vance, I took my hat off with my left hand and slowly lowered it to my side. When the hat touched my horse's side, a rifle shot sounded from the dark up the creek bank, and the bullet actually tugged at the high peak of one of the Klansmen's hats. Their heads jerked up toward the sound, and several of them took a step backward.

"Don't nobody move just yet," I said. "We need to make a decision. What you reckon, Vance? Is whupping a nigger worth dying for? If so, you go right ahead, 'cause there's going to be some dying here tonight if you do. And if anybody tonight, or any other time, comes on my property again in one of them bedsheets, there's going to be even more dying. This is my nigger, and I'll manage him and all the others live on my land. You got no right to touch him or anything or anybody that belongs to me. I didn't fight Yankees for four years and get my goddamn leg shot off to come home and kowtow to the likes of you. So"—and there I raised the pistol and aimed it at Vance's head—"you got about thirty seconds to make up your mind, Vance. 'Cause if that whip ain't on the ground in that time, you're a dead man." I meant every word of it, and I think that sounded in my voice.

Vance stood for a few seconds and then threw the whip onto the ground. "All right, Lootenant," he said. But there was a slight tremor in his voice, and it wasn't anger. "All right, have it your way tonight. But there'll be other times. I know where to find you."

"And," I said, "I hope you'll do that."

Then, still pointing the pistol, I walked my horse to the tree and cut the cords holding Julius's wrists, and together we walked out of the circle of torchlight.

None of us slept much that night. I doubt if Julius and his family slept in their cabin for a good many nights after. If the Klan had decided to come for us and burn the house or whatever, we probably couldn't have stopped them. I still don't know why they didn't—maybe it was shame or the realizing that we could make it costly for some of them, or maybe it was simply the fact that most of them weren't willing to harry a veteran or take on a white man's family. I knew who most of them were, and more than half were not veterans themselves. Some were no-accounts like Vance, and some were upstanding citizens, including at least one preacher. They were all so mad they didn't know what to do or who to blame.

I was mad at some of the same things they were, but I wanted them to stay away from me and leave my people alone. I had no idea whether the whole group would decide they had to do something, but I felt pretty sure that there would be another day of reckoning down the line. I kept an eye over my shoulder for a long time. But I made up my mind that I wouldn't let myself be afraid.

It took Amelia a while to decide just how she felt about my taking her son off into the night without her leave. I didn't often go against her wishes in front of the children that way, especially in something that had to do with them. I know for certain she didn't like the feel of it. But she must have reasoned it out in her mind that there were some things worth risking even your own son for.

Until she was able to finish with that, our conversations were mostly business, and there was no touching at all. I didn't try to hurry her getting over it. She came back to me when she was finally ready.

I won't say Julius stopped drinking altogether as a result of his scare. He drank until he died, but that night couldn't help but change him. All the cocksure wildness I had seen and kind of admired just seemed to drain right out of him. He kept to himself more than he had in the past and took to asking my family to bring things from town when he needed them. He still worked hard, and we still got along, but there was a kind of silent meanness took ahold of him. It was like he necessarily wanted to, but he just couldn't help feeling all white people were somehow as sorry as the Klan.

Uncle Foot and Aunt Rannie were scared about out of their wits and wouldn't go anywhere but home and church and work for years, so I guess in some way, the Klan won after all. I hated that and would brood on it some. Probably still do.

CHAPTER FIFTEEN

I guess if I'm going to be honest, sooner or later I got to tell about some things I'd as leave not mention. I said that whiskey didn't amount to much for me, and it didn't to begin with. For years I'd take that little flask from the stillhouse and give it away or save it for medicine or Christmas punch. In those days everybody had whiskey in the house to make up a spring tonic or whatever, but I just never fancied it.

Then, in the late winter of the year William turned five, we all went through a real bad patch. There was some kind of lung fever going around, and the children brought it home from school. Pretty soon we were all down with it, except Amelia. We took turns nursing the children until I came down with it. I got a pretty high fever, and it would just about burn me up until I would go out of my head and get to raving. The doctor told Amelia to give me a shot of whiskey when that happened, and it did seem to break the fever for a while so I could rest.

When I finally came out of it, I was weak for a long time. Spring was late that year, and it was rainy. The children were home from school. Agnes in particular didn't seem to be getting her strength back, which worried me right considerable. I wanted Amelia to stay home and take care of us, and I near about insisted on it, but she wasn't willing to leave her precious boardinghouse, so I was stuck with sick chaps and Aunt Rannie in a dark, cold house.

I hated being sick. Lying in bed, I'd get to thinking about the worst days of being in the hospital during the war, and I'd get in a black mood so bad that I couldn't even work up any interest in food. And when I lay in bed at night, sleep just wouldn't come. Amelia could see something was wrong, but it appeared to me she wasn't willing to do much about it, and I said as much. Looking back I can see that that was foolish thinking, but at the time it fit with whatever was going on in my mind.

I began to blame her for the way I was feeling, for everything going so wrong, and especially for Agnes's being sick. The long and short of it was that I began to take a nip of whiskey along during the day. In my state of mind it made sense to say, "Well, it helped dull the fever, so maybe it'll dull all this melancholy feeling." It didn't, of course, but it made me sleepy, and I'd pass the day easier. Then when I couldn't sleep at night, I'd take another nip.

I drank up all there was in the house, and as soon as I was able to get out again, I made a trip to the stillhouse and came home with a whole jug, which I then stored out in the corncrib. It was the beginning of the time when that jug never went dry—the time when, like as not, you'd find a flask somewhere in my saddlebag or even in my pocket. That jug came to be like the story about the fellow caught a wildcat with his bare hands: it was a sight easier to catch than it was to let go of.

It's strange how things seem to pile up on you. When Lee was about eighteen, he took to a notion that he wanted to go off to college. We'd known folks who'd done that—mostly town people and families with lawyers or doctors or preachers in them—but nobody in our family ever had. I was opposed to it, first off because I was selfish. Lee had become my right hand. I guess he had as much mischief as any other boy in him, but fact was, he had turned out to be smart as a whip and a good hand to work. He never gave us any trouble to speak of. In fact, by the time he was fourteen or fifteen, I trusted him more than I did most adults. It was nothing for me to send him off with the darkies or the hired help and expect him to work himself and them like a grown man. And he'd do it.

But it wasn't just that I depended on him: I loved him from the minute he was born. He'd come into the world at a happy time when I'd felt whole again for the first time in a lot of years. He'd also come into the world looking like his maw. Some men might've resented folks saying, "He favors Amelia, don't he?" but I liked hearing it. All that being true, I was inclined to say "no" to the idea of sending him off to South Carolina College and to end the discussion right there.

But, as usual, Amelia saw things in a different light.

"Gabe, I know you don't want to lose Lee. I don't either. But we got to think about what's best for him. We've both worked real hard to see that our children wouldn't want for anything. I'm wondering if this might be the one thing Lee will want most in his life. I suppose we can keep him at home with us—for a while. But sooner or later, he's going to go away whatever we say. If college is what'll make his life good for him, we need to think about it real hard."

"I *been* thinking hard. I think it would cost almost as much to keep him down there in Columbia as it would cost to keep the other five of us here. Do you reckon it would mean we'd be bound to send the girls and William off when they decide they want to go somewhere?"

"I'd be surprised if any of them want to—or even could. You know Lee is by far the best scholar in our little two-by-four school. Mr. Harden says Lee's been doing more than half the teaching for the last three or four years now. I just think he deserves a chance.

It might be a stretch for us, but that's why we've been working so hard. Please, Gabe, let's try it for at least a year. He can see if he really likes it and if he's an apt college student. If not, we can bring him home."

And so it went, back and forth for most of the spring months until finally I found myself arguing with myself even when I was alone. And I was losing! In May we asked Mr. Harden to write his old professors at the college, and around the end of the school term, Lee and Amelia rode down there on the train to talk and look around. When the cotton had been ginned in September, Lee went back alone, and except for school holidays, he was gone from then on.

Generally speaking, the fall of the year when the weather turns cool is the best time for me. I love the feel of it and the smell of it in the air and the woods. But that year it seemed like all I could think about was death. I was grieving hard for Lee, missing him every day when I got up to work, and I wasn't willing to be comforted. Little Agnes had turned fourteen, and suddenly she was following her big sister to taffy pulls and was helping at the boardinghouse, at least partly so the two of them could be near the other young'uns who lived in town. When they were home they were off in some corner giggling about who had looked at who with Amelia egging them on.

It sounds dreadful silly to say I was hurt and jealous of fifteen-year old boys, but it didn't feel silly at the time. It felt like I was having things snatched away from me again. It felt like I was hauling myself hand over hand up a long rope to where I could breathe easy at last, and then I'd just be pushed back down to the bottom again.

A year and a half into my affair with that whiskey jug, it was beginning to look like my only dependable friend.

It's almost comical looking back—how I always had a reason why whiskey wasn't a problem for me. To begin with, I decided that all I had to do was keep myself on short rations, and I couldn't get in trouble. I'd fill a little flask before I rode off to work and tell myself that any grown man could drink that much during the day and not hurt himself. But then when it was mostly empty at noon, I'd ride all the way back home, pretending I'd left something or other. I'd lose an hour's work and still drink more than my ration.

As much as I was willing to fool myself, I wasn't willing to lose all that work time, so I got ahold of a quart bottle and made a place in my saddlebag for that. When that didn't seem like enough to be safe, I took to just hiding a second jug wherever I was working. It's a wonder Julius and I didn't kill ourselves, or each other, during those days, but somehow we learned to make allowances. We'd do most of the dangerous work—felling trees and the like—in the early morning before noon. Then we'd do things like limbing trees or sawing after the noon meal (if we ate any), figuring we'd be less likely to drop a tree on ourselves.

Of course, neither one of us would have said we drank more than ordinary, so whatever we did was "ordinary." Other people had to have noticed I was drinking, especially the people run the sawmill or the store folks in town. But people in those days minded their own business and said nothing to us. Amelia did notice that I'd be dragging when I came in from work and not eat much supper, but I put it off on getting older or working harder without Lee's help.

The girls weren't paying much attention to me anyway, so I didn't pay much attention to them. One of the ways I convinced myself that my drinking was "ordinary" was that I never missed a day of work unless I was hurt or sick. And as strange as it sounds, I wasn't hurt or sick very much.

What Amelia *did* notice was that I took to spending more and more time away from home by myself. It was hunting season, and I'd go off into the woods for two or three days at a time. Even at my worst, I could still shoot straight in the mornings before I was liquored up, and I usually brought home meat.

On Sundays I'd mostly sleep, and Amelia and the children would just go off to church without me. Maw took to ragging me some about church, but nobody seemed to be that serious about the whole situation. When I was home during the day, I was mostly spending time in the barn or somewhere else around the place so I could drink and not be disturbed.

I can't believe Maw was really the first one to notice, but she was the first one to try to pin me down. I was setting on the front porch at Maw's house with her and Thomas on a Sunday afternoon. We were rocking and talking, and I was figuring on how soon I could get away and get back to the jug.

Maw said, "Son, it seems to me you got liquor on your breath, and it's three o'clock on a Sunday. It kinda worries me. Fact is, I been worried for some little time now."

"Maw, it ain't nothing to concern yourself about. I got a little toothache and held some whiskey on it to draw the pain."

"But you've been drinking. I smell it on you in the middle of the day."

"Maw, I tell you it ain't nothing to worry about. If I take a drop now and then, I got my own reasons. A man works as hard as I do has got a right to a little tonic without folks commenting on it."

"You know I don't mean any harm, Son. There ain't no cause to get riled up. People who love you got a right to fuss over you sometimes."

"Well right or no right, I don't take kindly to being looked after. And I don't have to set and listen to it." I stood up and stomped my peg leg on the porch harder than I needed to.

In his flat, calm voice, Thomas said, "You don't want to listen 'cause you know she's right, Gabe. Truth be told, you're drinking every day, and you're more than half-drunk when you start home in the evening. It's a wonder you and that fool nigger ain't killed each other by now—and it'd be a shame to leave them beautiful chaps, not to mention Amelia."

He made that whole long speech without changing the speed of his rocking or raising his voice. Those were the first and last words he ever spoke about it.

"Well," I said, "I hate to interrupt you all's managing of *my* life and *my* family, but I got better things to do. What I drink and when I drink is my business. If you don't like it, I guess I won't impose my society on you any longer."

When I reached the bottom of the porch steps, Maw started again. "Gabe, I wish you wouldn't..." But her voice trailed off. I jammed my hat on my head and never turned around.

When I got home that evening, it was almost dark, but after I put up the horse, I didn't go straight inside. For an hour or two, I sat by the barn with my pipe and the bottle. When William came looking for me, I had a hard time getting on my feet, and he stood there looking, all at loose ends, wondering whether he should try to help. When I was halfway to the house, I realized I still had the bottle in my hand, and I just dropped it in the yard. It was then that I looked up and saw Amelia standing on the front steps, watching. She stood a minute longer and then just turned around and walked back into the house.

I knew it was coming, so I tried to stay up late enough that she would already be asleep when I got in bed. It never worked. When I finally managed to get undressed and under the covers, she said, "Gabe, I hope you're sober enough to understand what I'm saying. I don't have any idea what to say. I never in my wildest dreams dreamed anything this confusing to me. I know I can't make you stop drinking, and I know I'll never stop loving you. But I got to ask you this: if you're going to be a drunkard, don't do it around the children. It humiliates them, and it hurts them, and they don't know any better than I do how to behave around it. I wish with all my heart you'd stop and be your old self"—and she touched me softly—"but if you won't or can't, I have to ask you to stay away from the children."

I tried to think of something to say. What do you say to a weeping wife who's loved you better than you've ever had reason to hope for, who would probably die for you, but who doesn't want you around her children? In any event my thinking apparatus wasn't working by then, so I got up in the dark and went out in my nightshirt onto the cold front porch. I sat in a chair and cried most of the night, half hoping Amelia would come out and say something that would sound hopeful, but when daylight came, she hadn't said another word. And of course, I needed a drink to get started for the day.

Sometimes when I try to remember that winter, I just have to wonder how I've lost so much of it. I swear I can remember more from some school days fifty years ago than I can about the last winter I was drinking. I know I was sleeping hither and yon because Amelia was serious about not having me back in the house, and I was too mad and too humiliated to try to force my way in. I'd sleep in the barn if it was mild or sometimes at Julius's cabin in front of the fireplace if it was cold.

I still worked most days, but I was getting less and less done because I was beginning to be sick. I think Maw and Thomas came to fetch me home to Maw's house a time or two, but I wouldn't stay more than a night because they put such a crimp in my drinking. Toward spring, I think they about gave up on me too.

On Christmas day, Lee was home from Columbia, and Maw helped me get cleaned up some for dinner at her house; it was so dreadful sad being there, what with the girls afraid to speak to me, me ashamed to look at Lee, and Amelia looking like she'd cry any minute, that I finally just wandered off and never went back.

CHAPTER SIXTEEN

There were two things that finally stopped me from killing myself altogether with drink. The first one was that I ran out of money. When we'd sold the last of the corn, the fellow at the stillhouse was willing to carry me on credit for a month or two, but as good a customer as I'd been, he couldn't afford to do that forever.

Our word had always been good with the stores in town, but Maw and Amelia had asked the general store not to sell spirits to me anymore, and I was too proud to beg. The man owned the tavern was willing to take a chance on me for a while, but I 'spect he was about to cut me off too when something else happened. That was the second thing.

One night I slept under the little lean-to at the back of the tavern where they stored the empty barrels and such. The sun woke me up, and I was setting up and trying not to puke on myself when I saw two fellows walking down the alley toward me. I pulled myself up the best I could and shoved my hands under my belt to stop them shaking. I think I was at the point where I would have begged for money—I needed a drink that bad.

There is a Season

But as I was getting ready to say something, I suddenly saw it was Vance Hunnicutt and one of his young'uns, a boy about twelve or thirteen with almost-white hair and washed-out blue eyes like his Pa. Vance stopped across the alley and looked me up and down, slow and careful, enjoying every second of it. I did my best to stop a dry heave, but I couldn't quite make it.

"Son," he said to the boy, "take a good, long look. This here's our town sot. He's just an ordinary drunkard, but you can call him 'Lootenant Drunk' 'cause, you see, he wasn't no private foot soldier like your daddy. Oh no, he was a high-and-mighty officer, so you got to address him as 'Lootenant Drunk.' Ain't that right, Lootenant? And not only is he a sot, but he's also a nigger lover who turns on his own kind. I 'spect he's sleeping here in the alley because some nigger bitch kicked him out last night. That right, Lootenant?"

The boy was grinning a slow grin that made him look almost puzzled. He seemed to be trying to figure out whether this was just some kind of fun grown-ups had or whether something serious was about to happen. He looked from me to his paw to see if he was expected to say something, and then he licked his lips and decided to stay quiet.

"All right, Vance," I said. "You had your fun. Now go on about your business. You got no call to be going on in front of your boy this way."

"I don't, Lootenant Drunk? Oh, I think I do. I think this is better than school learning for him. He needs to know what a nigger-loving drunk looks like. He needs to know the difference between a real man and a turncoat." He seemed to be considering his eloquence for a minute, and then he went on, "Yes, siree, that's what you are, Lootenant. A turncoat. You done gone over to the enemy. If we was still in the army, they'd shoot you, like as not."

Then, turning to the boy, he said, "Well you seen all you need to see? Good, we can't stand here all day. But I do want you to know how to say 'good morning' to a turncoat." And then he hawked and spit on my pants leg. "Go ahead, Son. Say good morning to the turncoat, nigger-loving Lootenant Drunk."

I moved so fast I surprised myself. As bad off as I was, I outweighed Vance by at least forty pounds, and I drove into him as hard as I could, pinning him against the opposite wall of the alley. The breath went out of him with a huffing sound. Then I staggered back a half step and threw a clumsy punch into his head with my left hand. Vance stepped to his left, his leg buckling a little, but he didn't go down. Then he jammed his hand into his pocket and came out with a knife. When I began to throw another punch, he ducked, circling to his right, and raked the point down my arm. I stopped and looked at my left arm. My sleeve had been cut, and my arm was already dripping blood from just above my elbow almost to my wrist.

In spite of the pulse pounding in my head, I was still groggy and not sure what to do. Vance was circling then, his teeth bared in what might have been a grin, except that it wasn't quite.

"Well, look at Lootenant Drunk," he said. "You ain't so high and mighty without your horse and your pistol. Let's see how you fight down here on the ground." And he jabbed the knife at me, forcing me to stagger back again. Then Vance was beginning to enjoy himself. He bent over low, holding the knife in front of his face in his one hand and waving it slow in little circles so it looked like a coiled snake moving its head.

He took a quick half step, and I jerked my hand out of the way just in time, and the knife cut into my right side at the ribs. The pain was sharp, and I could feel warm blood, but I couldn't tell how deep the cut was. Then I seemed to hear Sergeant Cureton's voice from all them years ago saying, "Use your leg, Gabe. You can kick further than you can reach, and there's a whole lot less to bleed on your boot heel than on your hand."

The pain and the feel of blood running down my side had woke me up enough that I began to calculate. It occurred to me that Vance would always have to come from the same side since he only had the one hand. He was crouched low with his legs spread far apart. If I could avoid getting stabbed too bad again, maybe I could use my feet. He swung again, but I managed to jump back.

When he jabbed again, the knife cut across my belly, but then I had a plan, and I was concentrating as hard as I could. I swung my hickory peg leg up between his legs and right into his crotch with all the strength I had. It lifted him clear off his feet, and he fell back into the alley on his back, gasping, and then rolled into a ball. I scooped his knife from the dirt and fell with my knee in his side. With my left hand, I grabbed his hair and jerked his head back, at the same time putting the knife to his throat. I think I truly wanted to kill him and might have, just the way you'd stick a pig, if it hadn't been for his boy.

"Stop!" he screamed in my ear "Don't! Don't hurt my pa! Please don't hurt my pa!" His voice began to break in a sob.

I could hear footsteps running down the alley then, and another voice said, "Gabe, what's going on?" And then, the voice said, "Easy, Gabe. Easy! You don't want to kill him. He's trifling, but he ain't worth swinging for." It was the voice of Mr. Easton, the man from the general store.

For a while I couldn't quite bring myself to let go. I reckon I wanted Vance to get the idea that I had his life in my hands real well fixed in his mind. I waited until his breathing began to level out a little so I knew he was listening. Then, with the sharp edge of the knife just drawing blood from his throat, I made a little speech.

"Vance, goddamn it, you got to stop this. We lost the goddamn war. We lost it, Vance. It wasn't our fault. Good men died on both sides, but there were just too many of them, and we couldn't win.

It wasn't our fault, but we lost. Whipping niggers and even killing me won't change that. You got to find something else to do besides trying to figure out who to hate. Next time—if there is a next time—I'll finish this. You mind me?" And Vance, the whites of his eyes showing, nodded his head.

I took the knife away from his throat, folded it, and tossed it to the boy. I reached for the wall behind me to support myself, stood up, and stepped back from him. Then I fell out.

When I woke up, I was lying on a table. I seemed to be hurting most everywhere a body could hurt. I heard Dr. Ashe's voice saying, "See, Amelia, I told you he'd wake up and spoil it for me. If he'd stayed out another twenty minutes, I could have finished all the sewing, but now he'll be raising Cain. Gabe, it's Virgil Ashe. You got to hold real still until I finish seeing how bad your belly is cut. You understand?"

"I understand," I said, and I let it go at that.

Then from somewhere to my right, Amelia's voiced asked, "Gabe, what happened?"

I tried to turn to see her, but Dr. Ashe said real sharp, "Gabe, hold still!"

"Amelia," I said, "are you here?"

"I'm here."

"I reckon what happened is that Vance Hunnicutt wanted to show off for his boy. You know I never had much sense about getting into the wrong fights, even when I had any sense. It appears that this was the wrong one"

Dr. Ashe grunted like he wanted to agree but didn't say anything. Then he took a deep breath and spoke to his nurse. "Well, you can't say you haven't seen a lucky one, Lucy. He missed dying in a field hospital to come home and miss dying in an alley by about one inch. You need to be sure there's pressure on that cut in his side when you do the bandage.

There is a Season

"And for God's sake, Gabe, don't be sitting up by yourself until these stitches in your belly have healed. And keep clean. Don't be sleeping in alleys and sheds if you want to live. Otherwise, Amelia can go ahead and order your tombstone."

I stayed at Dr. Ashe's house that night and the next while he oversaw his handiwork. I don't know why I was surprised to learn that he knew all about me being a drunk, but I was. He gave me a little glass of whiskey along during the day when he saw I was about to go into the shaking fits, but he also made me eat something. It was like bribing a child with candy to do something he don't fancy doing.

When Amelia came with the wagon to fetch me home, Ashe talked to her in front of me like I wasn't there.

"Amelia, you got to know Gabe is still coming off the liquor. I know you hate it, and I don't blame you. You've got good reason. But you've got to dose him with it like medicine every three or four hours. If you don't, he could go into fits and even die. After another day or so, you can reduce the dose and then quit. Keep the bandages clean and change them every other day like I showed you. I'll come by the house whenever I'm coming that way. If he doesn't die from the liquor, and his stomach wound doesn't putrefy, he should make it."

He stopped for a minute and looked like he was considering whether he ought to lecture me or just give up. Then he said, "Gabe, you're a tough old jackass. By rights, you should be dead. If you ever get back on the liquor, you'll die, and pretty quickly. I suppose what you do with your own life is your own business; but in my opinion, you ought to give a thought to Amelia and the children."

He stopped again. Then he said, "Gabe, we've known each other a long time. Mrs. Corley was my Sunday-school teacher, and I've always thought highly of your family. Hell, I used to think highly of you. But if you ever get drunk and cut up again like this, find yourself another doctor. Don't call me."

Then, without waiting for me to say anything, he turned around and walked back up the steps and into his office. When I stole a glance at Amelia, she was red with humiliation and biting her lip to keep from crying.

It wasn't what I'd call a warm homecoming. Amelia had hired Uncle Foot's youngest boy to come and stay at the house to help look after me. She explained to him how he was to get me up and down and how he couldn't leave me alone until I was able to move around by myself. She'd made up Lee's bed for me, and the boy, Eli, was going to sleep on the floor beside me.

When I was settled in, the girls came to the door and said "hello, Papa," almost like they were scared of me. There were no kisses or hugs. William was even more standoffish. He took every chance he had to be out of the house, and the most I ever got out of him for months was "yes, sir" or "no, sir." I could hear folks in the other rooms going on like they always did, talking, laughing, and arguing, but when they were around me, it was like they were at a funeral, and I was the corpse. Except in William's case, it was more like the corpse had overstayed its welcome and had gone to stinking.

For the first week or so, it didn't much matter to me how other folks acted. I was occupied with keeping myself alive. The doctor was right about the little drams of whiskey keeping the fits down, but that's about all they did. I woke up every morning with my hands shaking like I was palsied. There were whole days during the time before the fight that I couldn't recall anymore. A time or two I was right up to the point of begging Eli to go find the jug for me, but then I'd remember that look on Amelia's face. I'd roll over toward the wall and just lie there, sweating and shaking.

Then, by and by, the days began to get a little better every day. I was finding I could keep food down, and I was even hungry sometimes. The knife wounds were healing and getting on from the aching stage to the itching stage.

About a week after he'd finally pulled out all his sewing thread, Dr. Ashe stopped by for the last time. My shakes were gone, and I'd begun to put on a little weight. I was able to roll over and get out of bed by myself, so I'd taken to setting on the front porch. Virgil Ashe found me setting there in the rocking chair and stepped up onto the porch. He looked at the scars, which were still red welts, and poked at my stomach to see if he could make it hurt. Then he stepped back and nodded.

"Gabe, you're doing fine. I declare, you do amaze me. You must be made out of buggy springs and shoe leather!"

"I had good care, Virgil, and I'm much obliged."

"Well you're welcome, Gabe. Listen, I've been wanting to tell you I'm sorry I spoke that way in front of Amelia. A doctor sees so many things he can't do anything about, and it's just frustrating to see someone killing himself more or less voluntarily. I guess it was my frustration speaking. Anyway, I'm sorry, and I want you to know I'll always be willing to treat you or your family. I hope you'll understand."

"You got no call to apologize, Virgil. Like you said, we've known each other for a long time, and I understand you couldn't any more turn your back on somebody than you could fly. You were mad, and you had cause to be mad. I'll always be grateful to you."

"Uh-huh. Well tell me the truth, then. Have you been tempted to go back to the jug?"

"Only about eight or ten times a day. But I reckon it's getting a little better now, slow but sure. If I can get well enough to work so's I can keep my mind from running on, I'll be all right."

"Give it another two weeks before you do anything heavy, Gabe. Feed the chickens or weed the garden a little until you can feel your strength coming back. Then move kinda cautiously for a while. You lost a lot of blood, and you weren't in good shape to begin with. I'm really surprised you weren't jaundiced. You must have a liver like a boiler plate."

"Was that what you meant when you allowed I'd die if I was to go back to drinking?"

"That's a big part of it, but you can't always tell what'll break down first. Some people's stomachs give out and start bleeding. Other people get a wet brain and go kind of simple. Eventually it affects everything. Your problem is that you're already partway there. If you ever start drinking again, it'll go fast."

"Not even a sip of the Christmas punch, then?"

"I 'spect you know the answer to that, Gabe. You've already proved to me—and to yourself—that you can't stop with a sip. If you're smart, you'll never get near it again in any form. If I were you, I wouldn't even take medicine made with alcohol unless it's a matter of life and death. The risk is just too high.

"One more thing and I'll leave you alone: I know that darky you work with—

Julius, is it?—I know he drinks every day. If you go back to working with him, I'm afraid you'll be a goner. If you're around it—the smell of it and seeing him able to drink when he wants—you'll be back into it within a week. You'll tell yourself, 'Well I'll only have the one taste,' but within a few days, you'll be drinking the same way you were when you got cut up. There's just no way around it, Gabe. You have to make your peace with that and start over."

"I had already given some thought to that myself. It galls me to think that something got the better of me that way, and I can't lick it. It's a weak man can't make up his own mind and act on it, Virgil. A weak man."

"You may think of it that way if you want to. I'm a practical man myself, and I have to get along with what I can see. I guess you could fool around with trying to show that you're not a weak man, but my own belief is that it would take a foolish man—a damn foolish man—to gamble on losing his family and his life and on having his children remember him as a drunkard and be likely to hate him for it. If you take that bet to satisfy your own vanity about being strong, it appears to me you're gambling with other people's lives."

"Well now, for a doctor, you do know how to turn a phrase."

He smiled as he turned to walk down the porch steps. "Funny you'd accuse me of that, Gabe. I'd say you're the word spinner. You take care, now. Give my regards to Amelia."

He was right about my feeling all wrung out. When I began to be able to get around again with my cane, I tried a little heat at the hoe, and in just a few minutes, I had to sit down. It was a good month after I got up before I was able to even begin doing a day's work, and then I was slow. Julius came by from time to time, but I put him off, saying I wasn't up to snuff quite yet.

CHAPTER SEVENTEEN

At last that wouldn't wash any longer, and I just had to say outright that I wouldn't be working with him anymore. I didn't try to say why, but he could see I wasn't drinking, and he likely knew. In the meantime, I commenced working half days with Thomas and the darkies, getting the gardens and the row crops in. Julius wanted to have one of the other boys work at the logging, and I let him take one of the field hands, a big, strong boy a good ten years younger than Julius. I owed him that much. What finally happened was I began to suspect that he and the fellow at the sawmill were not keeping a good account of what he was cutting. Seemed like when I counted the fresh stumps, there'd be half as many as the number of logs we were getting paid for. The other boy wouldn't say anything, and I couldn't blame him. It was my business, not his. I hated it worse than poison, but by harvesting time, I just had to tell Julius I didn't want him cutting timber anymore at all. I told him he was welcome to work with his paw and the others, but he wouldn't have any of that.

There is a Season

After that I didn't keep close track of him. Amelia wanted me to collect rent on the cabin, but I couldn't bring myself to do that. He had young'uns, some almost grown and some little chaps. I couldn't put them out. I heard he went and worked at the sawmill for a while, but he had slid pretty far by then himself, and they wouldn't keep him long. He lived on the place until he died, and I didn't ever see him or his family in real need. It seemed to me that Julius was like the mirror of what I could have been—and almost was—if something hadn't interrupted.

Some people would call the "something" God, and I don't suppose I'd argue with that. I don't think or talk in God language much, but I ain't opposed to it. I do know this: I wouldn't ever have stopped by myself, and going on the way I was, I'd have been dead long before Julius. Probably not many preachers would think to credit God for having some peckerwood like Vance cut me half to death, but I do know that Amelia and Maw had been praying hard for me to be saved from the liquor, and I know the cutting is what finally did it.

Julius's widow lives here still, and some of his children do too.

We remember things from our own peculiar points of view, of course, but life runs along whether we're watching or not. Maw was getting older, losing her eyesight, and having trouble getting around. It got to where Amelia and the girls were doing Sunday dinner, even though we all still called it "going to Grandma's for dinner." Maw would set in a chair and kind of oversee, but it pained me to see that she was going downhill. She and Thomas were thick as thieves, and I worried about what would happen to him when Maw died.

Lee finished South Carolina College and came home to read law with an attorney over in Laurens. I had grown to depend on him, and I'd never quite got over missing him around the place. I'd find myself saying, "If Lee was here we could…"

After a long time, Amelia and I started sleeping in the same bed again. Finding each other again after my trip into the jug was harder than I'd hoped it would be. I think we both wanted to be back where we'd started, but try as we might, that never did happen. It ain't like crying over spilt milk—it's just that after all the hurting, things between us healed over different, like a broken arm or leg that never works as good as it was. We still loved each other. In fact, the loving has gotten better in some ways every year since. Still, the broken places will ache, and when the moods are on me, I grieve a little harder because of them.

We were lying in bed talking one night when Amelia brought up the subject of Lee.

"I wish you wouldn't take on over Lee so much, especially in front of William," she said. "We all miss him, but that's just something that happens when children grow up. They move on because we brought them up to move on."

"I never saw myself as taking on. I'm only saying what's true. He made my life a lot easier the same way you've done."

"But William is still here, and he's not Lee. He's a different person, and he's still your son. In fact, if you'd look at him for himself and not compare him to Lee, you'd find he's a lot like his daddy. When he finishes getting his growth, he's going to be the spitting image of you. He even sounds like you."

"Hmmm, I s'pose. I think what seems strange is he saw the worst of my drinking. I'm afraid he's not been able to let it go—to forgive me."

"Gabe, I think you've not been able to forgive yourself. Yes, William is different. Lee grew up from the time he was born knowing he was the apple of your eye. William has some years in his growing up when he didn't know anything about you—didn't know how you felt about him because you didn't know. It'll take some time, but he wants you to love him too."

"I'd give anything in the world if I could go back and have them years over again, Amelia. But I can't. So what must I do?"

"I don't know that there's anything in particular you need to do, Gabe. Just see him. Take him into your life as if he were Lee. There are some things he can't or won't do the same as Lee, but there are some other things he'll do better—or at least different. He really wants you to know he's there."

And, of course, she was right. Without trying to make a fuss of any kind, I commenced to take note of William. On working days when he was out of school, I began to make a point of asking him to work with me. I found out right away that he already knew the field hands better than I did. When there was a question of who ought to be chopping cotton on a particular day or who should be cultivating the corn or tobacco, William would generally know. So I took to asking his opinion. It turns out he had watched Lee and Uncle Foot running the farm during the years I'd been drinking, and at thirteen he knew almost as much about most things as I did.

We began setting on the front porch together after supper and on Sundays, either talking about things—most often the farm, but not always—or just rocking.

During that fall, when the harvesting was done and hunting season came around, I made a point of not going in the woods unless William was out of school and could go along with me. I even held out enough money to order him the rifle he'd been looking at in the catalog, a better one than Lee or I had. I couldn't honestly argue like we needed it, and it was the kind of thing Amelia would have usually raised an eyebrow over, but she never so much as peeped.

Sometimes when Lee came back, the three of us would ride over and pick up Thomas so the four menfolks could go off and fish together. Probably the boys never give much thought to them times now, but they're some of the best memories I have. I wish there was a heap more like them.

CHAPTER EIGHTEEN

It was Amelia first mentioned the veterans' encampment in Virginia. She was reading the newspaper and saw a story about Confederate veterans holding a reunion. For a lot of years I hadn't much wanted to remember the war, but then, going on fifty-five years of age, I reckon I was becoming sentimental about things. Amelia read the story aloud to me one evening after supper. That night before we went to sleep, she brought it up again.

"Darling, I noticed you got kind of quiet a while ago when I read about the Confederate encampment. I wonder if that's the kind of thing you'd ever want to do."

"I never gave it much thought, Meily. It's a long way off, and I'd have to ride the train and stay in a hotel. It'd cost half a year's income."

"Oh, it wouldn't cost any such thing! You'd only have to be gone a few days. I think it might be good for you to see old friends."

"If there's any of them still alive."

"All the more reason to go now, Gabe, and not wait until they're all dead or too old to travel. Besides, I think it's important to remember. It was a great war, and you all did great things. It deserves to be honored."

"I never felt much honored. It honored me just to get home alive."

"Well, I won't nag you about it. But I do think you ought to consider it. We have some money in the bank. It won't hurt a thing for you to get away from here for a while, so just think about it."

I pulled her over to me and kissed her neck and nuzzled her for a spell. Then I spread out to sleep. But I noticed that in spite of feeling warm and drowsy, the idea of the trip kicked up a little excitement in my chest.

It was a strange notion, me taking money out of the bank to go off on a trip by myself for no good reason. I had a hard time getting my mind completely around it, so I just worked it over for a few days without talking about it. As the time passed, that little excitement began to grow until I found myself saying, "Well, why shouldn't I? It ain't like I do it every year. It'll just be this once, and I'll get it out of my system."

When I spoke to Thomas about him going with me—if I decided to go—he just shook his head and said, "Nope. Ain't interested." I had figured on that. We mostly never talked about the war, but occasionally when we were working together, Thomas or I would use some army word. I never came to know what'd happened to him, and I don't particularly care. Like him, I got more memories than I want. It would have made it a little easier if we'd been going together, and yet in another way, I liked the idea of being by myself.

Maw drug my old uniform out from where she'd kept it. She and Amelia and the two girls made a considerable fuss over patching and sewing it so it'd look decent. The borrowed lieutenant's bars were put on a new shirt. I'd never owned an officer's blouse, and when Amelia offered to make one, I said no. I allowed as how I'd go back the way I'd come home as much as possible.

They all came down to put me on the train, me feeling foolish in my Sunday clothes and carrying Maw's old carpetbag and a dinner basket with enough food for a harvesting.

I had not set foot on a train since I'd first joined the army. When I had about settled into the seat, we stopped at Gold Hill, where I had enlisted, and my head was suddenly about flooded with the memories of that day. I raised the window, closed my eyes, and smelled the breeze, and for just a part of a second, I was that same rawboned country boy riding off to war. I thought of William again and felt the tears coming until I opened my eyes and made myself look out the window at the fields going past.

I don't reckon it would have been possible for me not to remember Agnes Pinckney when I was remembering so much about the war years. It started on the train as I saw other men my age getting on; some of them were wearing all or part of a uniform. We'd howdy and swap stories until we had one car just about full of veterans. As we changed trains and headed toward Petersburg, where the reunion was, more and more folks from all over the Carolinas and Virginia began getting on. By that time I was one of the "old-timers" on the train, and we began making it our business to welcome folks who looked like our crowd.

"Where you from?" we'd ask. Or, "What unit were you with?" And then we'd settle into talking about everything, not just the war. Somehow it was different talking to folks who'd been the same places and done the same things we had. Even if you'd never seen them before, it was like having a brother who'd grown up in the same house. We could go from remembering a particular battle to describing our wives and children without missing a lick.

Mostly we never had to explain anything. When somebody got to yarning about taking winter coats off of dead Yankee bodies or about being so scared that he dug with his bare hands during an artillery barrage, other people would just nod and give a little smile like, "Yes, Brother, I'm just like you." And we knew there was a whole heap more we could have said, every one of us, that didn't need talking about. We just knew. And it came on me as a great surprise that it was such a great comfort.

I already had a rough idea of the map, so I knew we'd pass somewhere close to the Pinckney farm. What I didn't know was whether the particular rail line I was on would be the same one that passed through their town. When the train stopped and I saw the name of the town on the station house, it was all I could do to not stand up and walk toward the door. But I managed to not make any kind of show of myself, and I marked the two or three men who got on. The others had been calling to them out the window, and one of them found a seat in the front of our car.

When things had settled down again, I stood up to stretch and just happened to find myself in the aisle next to him. "Say," I said, as quiet and calm as I could manage. "I think I recognized the name of your town."

"That right?" he answered. "You probably did. There was right considerable fighting around here."

"Yes, I was here and there myself. I lost this," I said, hitting the wooden peg with my cane, "somewhere around here. And I was in a field hospital on a plantation. Let me see—what was that name? Pinckney, I think. Is there a Pinckney plantation back there?"

"There is," he said. "Old Colonel Pinckney died five or ten years ago, and his widow and son run the place now. There wasn't no hospital there when I got back home from the war, but I hear tell there had been one there. Not far from the big house."

"Hmmm," I said. "I'd kinda like to go out there and just poke around. See if there's anything I remember. I was such a fool that I joined up again after I left the hospital. Some of us just learn slow, I guess."

"Ain't nothing to be ashamed of. I'd be right proud if I was you," he said. Then we swapped names, and he shook my hand. "If we're on the same train when we come back this way, I'd be proud to ride you out to the Pinckney place. But if we ain't, you can always hire a buggy at the livery stable in town. If you need a bed for the night, you can stop at our place."

"I'm obliged to you. If I happen to decide to stop off, I might just take you up on that offer. How often does the southbound train stop?"

"There's one some days and two others. But don't give it no thought. If you have to wait over, we'd be glad to have you."

We talked awhile longer and yarned a little about the fights we'd been in before I made it on back to my seat. But by that time, my mind was made up. As soon as we got off the train at Petersburg, I went straight to the window and changed my ticket so I could stop over.

The reunion was like nothing else I've ever done before or since. The hotels and boardinghouses in Petersburg was plumb full to overflowing, and there were folks sleeping in tents on what we called the "parade ground." I was lucky and found a place I could share at a hotel, sleeping on a cot in a room that was already full.

Everybody had at least part of a uniform that they could still fit into, but in general, it was an army of fat, bald old men. Still, we mustered every morning, more or less by states and units, and heard speeches and lectures from them who'd written histories of the war. We ate our meals together and talked, sometimes almost through the night. We'd argue about what was the worst or best thing we remembered. It didn't seem a bit peculiar to see some gray-headed fellow telling a story to five or ten others who were nodding and trying to wipe tears without being noticed. And, like I said before, it didn't matter. Even if we wouldn't have chosen to keep company with each other anyplace else, we were all brothers at that reunion.

When the time came to head back to the trains and the bugler played "retreat," we all saluted and cried some more, knowing we'd never see each other again and that there'd never be another time just like this for us.

I waited through the morning for my train, and I like to worried the poor station manager to death, trying to make sure it was the train that stopped at the Pinckneys' town. When we finally got to the station there and I could get off, I'd been standing at the door almost since the last stop—I was that eager. I went straight to the livery stable and rented a buggy. I got good directions to the farm, and as soon as I was out of sight, I whipped the horse into a trot.

Then as I was going along down the road, it dawned on me that as hot as I was to see Agnes again, she might not want to see me at all. Maybe there had been a scandal, and she was living as an outcast. Maybe she had grown to hate me over the years. Maybe she wouldn't even know who I was.

I stopped under a shade tree to think about that for a spell. If I just turned the buggy around and went back into town, I could get on the next train, and nobody would ever have to know I'd been there.

Finally I knew I'd never rest easy until I had at least tried, so I climbed back in the buggy, and fifteen minutes later, I was driving through the gate. When I knocked on the front door, a darky girl I'd never seen answered the door and allowed as how Mrs. Pinckney was at home and asked if I'd please wait on the porch. I found my heart was beginning to pound, and my breath was coming short.

And then she was there, opening the door and looking up at me. For a minute we just stood there, and then she said, "My word, Gabriel Corley, it's really you, isn't it?" She came and stood on her tiptoes to kiss my cheek, and the smell of her skin was so familiar that her last kiss could have been the day before. It was all I could do to not pull her to me and kiss her proper.

I'd had times when I couldn't remember real well what she looked like, but I knew as soon as she opened the door that I would have recognized her anywhere. She was a little thicker around her middle, and her hair had some gray in it, but as I saw her, she was still as beautiful as the first day I'd laid eyes on her. In that one minute I felt what it was to be a nineteen-year-old boy again, hurt and sad and so much in love I could hardly stand it.

"I'm right flattered you knew me," I said. "I've had considerable wear since we last met."

"Gabriel, are you trying to say you wouldn't have recognized me?" she said in that old teasing tone.

"Agnes, I'd recognize you now or twenty years from now if I should happen to still be alive. As far as I can see, you haven't changed a bit."

"Well, a bit, I think." And she smiled again. "For goodness' sake, let's don't stand here on the porch looking foolish. Come in, and tell me all about yourself. I'll bet you've been to the reunion in Petersburg."

"Exactly where I've been."

"Ever since I first read about it, I've been having daydreams that you'd stop by. I'm so glad I was right."

"So you still think about me now and again."

"Oh, Gabriel, there is seldom a day when I don't think about you."

"I got no right to feel this way, but I can't help saying that pleases me, Agnes. It pleases me a whole heap. And Grady, is he still with you?"

"He is, Gabriel. You'll certainly have to see each other before you leave. He would never forgive me if I let you get away." She stopped and called down the hall for the girl who had answered the door. "Rachael, would you ask the cook to make us some lemonade and also find Mr. Robert and Grady and have them come to the front parlor."

Then turning back to me, she said, "You've got to start at the beginning and tell me all about yourself. I'll bet you're married and have a dozen children!"

"Well, not a dozen, but four good ones. And one of them is named Agnes."

"Agnes! Really?" A look came across her face that was somewhere between surprise and something else—maybe alarm. Her hand flew up, and she tilted her head to one side and pushed a strand of hair back into place. "You named a child after me? Was that...did you have to persuade your wife?"

"Not much. She and Maw pretty much named Gabriel Lee by themselves, and Katherine was named for Amelia's aunt. By the time Agnes came, I just said it was a name I'd always fancied, and she agreed."

"Amelia—that's your wife?" I nodded. "Amelia didn't ask where you'd heard the name?"

"Not as I recollect. Folks'll go through a whole heap of names when there's a baby on the way."

"Yes, of course, but if it were me, I'd think...I don't know. Maybe I'm imagining things. But it doesn't matter. I'm very flattered... and very touched." She paused and touched the corner of her eye with the back of her hand. "Oh, Gabe, I will love thinking about your child carrying my name!"

"Well, there wasn't any way to ask you beforehand. I'm pleased it meets with your approval."

She was smiling then with her whole face, but especially with her eyes. She tucked her feet under the chair the way I remembered seeing her do the very first time we'd sat in this parlor together, and she commenced to rock ever so gentle. And then she began asking questions. She quizzed me about the ages of the children and what they looked like and what they were doing. She asked some about Amelia and about my mother and told me that her own mother was still alive.

As we were just beginning to get ourselves reacquainted, I heard men's voices coming down the hall. One of them, I knew right off, was Grady's, and the other, a white man's voice with the same Virginia way of talking that Agnes had. By the time they were in the door, I had stood up.

When Grady saw me, he stopped dead still and just stared. Then he said, his voice all husky and falling, "Marse Gabriel, is it really you? I never thought to see you again in this life. Lawd God, it does my heart good!"

I wanted to hug him, but the other man was behind him, and I was afraid they'd all think me peculiar.

"Well, Grady," I said. "It pleases me right considerable to see you as well. I notice you're getting a little gray around the edges, same as me. Are you well?"

"Tolerable well, Mr. Gabriel. The Lawd's been good to me."

Then Agnes stepped forward and caught the sleeve of the young man to pull him toward me, and I saw his face clear for the first time. I must have looked like I was fixing to have a spell, because Grady took a half step toward me. The man could have been my William, except that his hair was lighter, and he looked a little older!

"Mr. Corley," Agnes said real quick. "I'd like you to meet my son, Robert Pinckney the third. Bobby, this is Sergeant Corley, who was stationed at the field hospital during the war and actually fought to protect our house. You've heard me speak of him to your father."

"Sergeant Corley," he said, and he reached out to shake my hand. "I do recall Mother and Father speaking of you. Mother would tell the story about how terrified she was and how you and some others protected the house. I'm so pleased to actually meet you."

"Well, I'm pleased to meet you too," I said. "We did have a little set-to with some deserters right out behind the house. And Grady here was the hero of that engagement."

"Father mentioned that too," the boy said. "We've been lucky to have Grady, especially since Father died."

"Yes, I can imagine," I said, smiling at Grady. And then, since nobody else seemed to know exactly what to say, I asked, "Have you had a good year?'

"This one has been good," Robert said. "Wouldn't you say so, Grady?" Grady nodded. "The tobacco looks good, and we're told that leaf prices will hold up. We may actually have some cash money left over if it sells well."

I turned to Agnes. "As a father myself, Mrs. Pinckney, I have to say that you and the colonel have a lot to be proud of."

"Yes," she said, "Bobby's father was enormously proud of him, and of course, I have spoiled him outrageously." She patted Bobby's arm and looked up at him with a proud smile. Then she turned to the two men and said, "You two go on now and let me catch up with Mr. Corley. I was just hearing about his family. Bobby, if I can persuade him to stay on for dinner, you can hear war stories then. And Grady, I'm sure the two of you will want to talk for a little."

When we were sitting down again and the girl had fetched the lemonade, Agnes said, "I'm sorry, Gabriel. I should have warned you rather than springing it on you unawares. We've always talked about how much Bobby looks like Robert—we did that from the day he was born. I gather from your expression that he must resemble someone else as well."

"He could swap places with my younger son, William, and you'd never know there'd been a switch. It like to startled me out of my wits when I looked up and saw him."

"Yes, Grady and I both noticed that. It pleases me to know that all those times I told him he looks like his father were not really lies. I see now that he does."

I was still fighting to take ahold of all this in my mind. I took a deep breath and tried to steady my voice. "Agnes, you're saying that Bobby is *my* son."

"Of course," she said. "He's *our* son, Gabriel. Yours and mine. I have to tell you also that Robert knew, and he was very proud of Bobby. I know he would have liked to have his own children, but I don't think we ever would have. Along with everything else you gave me, you gave us the gift of Bobby as well.

"As you can probably tell, I dote on him. Probably too much. He has been my strong right hand ever since Robert died. He's as good a child as any mother could possibly want."

"I just can't take it in, Agnes. I don't…all these years, and I never knew! I reckon it's a good thing I didn't know. I mighty near died from missing you for a couple of years. If I'd known, I'm afraid I might have just come back, and Lord, wouldn't that have been a mess?"

"I thought about trying to get word to you, but I knew that would be foolish. If you survived that horrid war, you had your own life to live. And see, you have lived your own life, haven't you? Did you get my answer to your letter?"

"I got it and carried it around until the paper turned to dust. It's what kept me alive during the rest of the war. I believe I see now why you mentioned going to Richmond to see your husband."

"It was such a strange mix of feelings, Gabriel." Her voice dropped almost to a whisper, and she looked past me out the window. "You can't imagine how hard it was for me. It hurts me to even remember that awful, awful time."

She shook her head and took a long breath that came out in little sobs. For a while she held a handkerchief to her mouth, and it was so quiet that, along with her little sniffs, I could hear the clock in the hall ticking.

Then she went on. "I was still deeply in love with you and half-mad with worry about you. I knew I was carrying your child. If I couldn't have you, I wanted that baby more than anything in the world. Yet at the same time, I still had—will *always* have—a great love and respect for Robert. To be pulled two ways like that is the worst feeling in the world."

"I'm truly sorry for that, Agnes."

She held up her hand as if to quiet me. "It's not for you to be sorry, Gabriel. We both made choices, and under the same circumstances, I would make them again. But I do want you to understand my part of the story. After you left, I wheedled my way onto a train to Richmond, mostly, I think, on the strength of being Robert's wife. When I got there I sat down and talked to Robert. I told him everything. I told him I'd do anything he wanted, except give up the baby.

"He was terribly hurt, of course—terribly! He actually wept. That was the hardest part of the whole situation, having to sit and watch him cry, not knowing whether he would let me try to comfort him or whether I could even reach out and touch him.

"In the end, when he did decide to forgive me, he did it in a very Robert-Pinckney way; that is, in a very considered, deliberate way and without any recriminations."

My chest was hurting in an odd way, and when I tried to talk, it came out in a kind of croak. "I'm sorry for him too, Agnes. I reckon I was hurting so much myself that I didn't have room in my mind to think about how much I might've hurt others."

"It's funny, but Robert never actually spoke of you but once. When I told him about…us, he asked if you were a decent man, and if I'd been…involved…voluntarily."

"And you said?"

"I told the truth on both counts. That seemed to be enough for him. In some odd way, I think he saw me as a war casualty. I also believe that my being very young when we married helped him to forgive me.

"Whatever he was thinking, he never even considered any course of action except keeping the child and claiming him as our own.

By the time Bobby was born, Robert was already devoted to him—utterly devoted. As long as Robert lived, they were inseparable."

"And everybody thinks he looks as much like Robert as you let on?"

"There might've been some people who had suspicions, but I really believe the Pinckney family sees him as Robert's blood. Which, so far as I am concerned, makes him Robert's blood."

She stopped for a minute and looked at me in a solemn way. "I wonder, will this make it hard for you in any way, Gabe? Are you going to…I don't know…hate me?"

"It does give me some more to think about, now doesn't it? But hate you? I don't rightly see how I could hate you without hating myself. I reckon I might have cause to hate myself, having a child I've never helped to rear. But I loved you—love you—so much. And as it turns out, Bobby is doing what I most wanted to do at the time, which is to take care of you."

It was a passing strange afternoon. We'd talk a mile a minute for a while, interrupting each other and running on from one thing to another. And then there'd come a great silence, and we'd look at each other and smile, almost shy-like. Then off we'd go again, remembering and asking questions and telling things that had happened in the twenty-something years we'd been apart. She was still as warmhearted and easy to talk to as I had remembered. And the same way it used to when we were young, the sun dropped away twice as fast as I had expected it to. It seemed to me we could have talked for days.

We had a cold supper together with Bobby, and true to his mother's promise, I told some of the war stories that weren't too hurtful to me. I tried to remember the kind of things that would make him laugh, but of course, he wanted to know about the battles, which were hard to remember.

Still, I was glad I could talk to him that one time, especially with Agnes smiling at both of us like she was about proud enough to pop. By then it was beginning to hurt me some to look in Bobby's eyes. I reckon it was guilt, or maybe I was grieving that I would never see my own flesh and blood again. Whatever it was, I was finding it hard to swallow. And I was thinking how good a drink would taste.

After supper, Grady and I had a drive around the farm in the hired buggy, and I had a chance to thank him again for all he had been to me and mine. If I hadn't done anything else, that would have made the trip worthwhile for me. When we pulled up at the big house and Grady was about to step down, I reached out and shook his hand.

"Grady," I said, "I reckon you know how much you did for me. I think having you here near about saved my life."

"Go on, Marse Gabriel," he said, looking down. "No such thing. You a strong man. Always was. All's I done was give you a hand up, same as you woulda done for another man. I was proud to know you."

I had to smile at that, thinking how I'd looked the first time he'd seen me. "I know that, Grady. I know that. And that's what makes me so grateful. I got to get on, Grady."

"Yassuh."

"I won't likely see you again in this life, but if I should make it, I'll look for you on the other side. In the meantime, look after them."

"Yassuh, I will do that. I will look after 'em. We look after each other. And you take care of yo'self."

I drove off just before sunset, looking back over my shoulder for as long as I could see Agnes and Robert standing on the front porch and Grady at the bottom step.

I had enough money for a hotel room, and I reckon I could have tried to find the fellow said I could stay at his house, but I didn't feel like I could bear talking to another human being for a while. I just sat on the station platform with my case and dozed off and on through the night. By eleven the next morning, the train had carried me over the North Carolina line, and I was on the way home again.

The children were waiting at the train station, and Agnes ran ahead of the other two. She hugged my neck real hard and said, "Oh, Papa, we were worried about you! We met the train yesterday, and the other veterans got here, but not you. One of them remembered seeing you at the station in Petersburg, but they didn't know where you might be."

"Oh," I said. "I'm afraid your old papa's going lame in the brain. I got to yarning with another fellow from Captain Rose's troop and never even saw my train leave the station. By the time I put him on his train, I'd missed my own. I spent the night setting in the station, and then the train that brought me to Columbia stopped at every pigsty in three states. I'm about wore down to a nub." And that is the way the story still gets told to this day.

Amelia was late at the boardinghouse that evening, and by the time she got home, I had bathed and shaved and lain down to rest. She woke me up with a soft kiss. "I was worried about you! The children said you missed your train. Maybe we shouldn't let you go off alone anymore."

"Darling, I'm not sure I want to go off anymore at all. I'm about wore out, but I'm glad I went."

"Was it really good for you, Gabe? I was worried it would make you sad."

"It did. It made me sad and happy, sometimes at one and the same time. It makes me wonder too if all those things truly did happen to me. If I didn't have a hickory leg, I could almost believe it was a story in a book. It all seems so faraway and strange now. I don't want to do it again, but I'm truly glad I went. Did you miss me?"

"I did miss you." She kissed me again. And then she gave a little giggle. "And I've got a list of things for you to do all saved up!"

I groaned and tried to roll away from her, but she held me. Then she nuzzled my neck and got up to go and help the girls with supper.

PROVIDENCE

Her mind returns to the present: it's 8:30 p.m. on a Sunday, and she's in a strange pew in a different church. She checks carefully to be sure her face and posture reflect a rapt attention to her husband's sermon. She is aware from long experience that people in the congregation watch her to see how she's responding. Indeed, she's an important part of the preacher's connection to his congregation, and especially to the women.

As she surfaces, she's not surprised to hear that he's relating his version of a minor disagreement between them from some months ago, and she thinks, "Glad the kids don't have to hear this one!"

Leaning both elbows on the pulpit, he looks down at the congregation and takes them into his confidence. "Now some of you know my wife, and for those who don't...how shall I put this? Let me just say this: she is not inclined to give up without expressing her opinion. And as is often the case, especially where the kids are concerned, I came to see that she was probably right. I may not be the smartest man in the world, but you don't stay married for twenty years without knowing when to shut up. And I did!"

There is a murmur of quiet laughter in the congregation as husbands and wives exchange glances. Here and there a wife gives her mate a good-natured elbow by way of emphasis. Although she didn't know he would share the anecdote, she's not surprised he did. Especially when he preaches away from his own congregation, he's likely to include a throwaway line or two designed to make contact with the congregation on a personal level.

The various parts of the preacher's sermons are so familiar to her that she can generally follow them without conscious effort. When she surfaces for a second time, she can guess that fifteen or twenty minutes have passed since he finished his introduction. She nodded thoughtfully at the appropriate places, clued in by the preacher's voice talking about "significant insights." It's a handy survival technique she developed over many years of accompanying her husband on spiritual-enrichment weekends such as this one.

In the center of the fifth pew from the front in Willow Oak Church, she finds her chin cupped lightly in her right hand and her gaze riveted on her husband's face.

The preacher's powerful baritone completely fills the ears of the faithful and echoes from the far corners of the balcony so that when he stops, the silence itself seems to ring. He finishes the story of the pitiful orphan boy he once met in Puerto Rico.

"A child horribly disfigured by burns and abandoned by family, and yet he still sang in his clear, pure voice a hymn of praise to Jesus." It is one of his best stories, and he tells it well.

Then, with his head turned ever so slightly to one side and two fingers just touching the corner of his left eye, he speaks with a hint of a break in his voice, which is now low and throbbing with emotion. "And I"—he pauses and seems to search for words, his right hand touching the heavy silver cross that hangs over his heart—"I, scarcely able to even comprehend the depth of such faith, knew I was in the presence of Jesus. The Jesus who said, 'Unless you become as a little child, you shall not enter the kingdom.' Oh, friends, if we could just put away our sophistication and forget our graduate degrees."

His voice begins to rise again, each sentence a calculated step in its ascending volume. "If we could just forget our fancy clothes! If we could just leave our vain attempts to make the gospel meet *our* worldly standards! Just accept Jesus as that little boy does! Then Jesus *would* come into our hearts tonight. That is my prayer for each one of us. Promise me! *Promise* me that you'll try! Oh, it's so important."

Once again his voice drops almost to a whisper, almost to a sob, and he says, pausing a full five seconds between each word, "Just...promise...me...you'll...try." He then continues more quickly. Say it now in your heart with me." He bows his head. "Jesus, come into my heart."

At the sanctuary door, the preacher greets the faithful with a warm handshake and a modest smile, his wife standing on his right a half step behind him. Tall, blond, and almost boyish, he makes an impressive figure in his clergy vestments. His pulpit gown is trimmed in red velvet with three broad stripes on the sleeves signifying his honorary doctorate. The gown and its trappings, including the academic hood he wears tonight, were purchased by the women of his home church to celebrate his tenth anniversary with them. They are, for him, as much a part of his church persona as the pulpit bible. And yet this apparent formality is almost completely offset by his friendliness and cheer as he greets old friends.

On the way back to their hotel, the preacher shares the backseat of the limo with his wife. She is small and much quieter than he, though not at all mousey. She is the perfect minister's wife, smart and self-effacing, never competing for the limelight, but pleasantly spunky. When the preacher makes humorous references to her assertiveness, as he has done tonight, the congregation can chuckle aloud and feel the touch of his common humanity with them. Now, faraway from his home parish, he turns to her for reassurance.

"How do you think it went?" he asks.

"OK, I guess. How did it seem to you?"

"Hard to tell in an evening service. People are tired, even drowsy if they've had a couple of drinks. They seemed to be with me, though."

"From all the comments I heard, I think you were a hit. Of course, you still have fans in this part of the state from the years we were in Des Moines." If he hears the irony in her use of "fans," he gives no indication of it.

"Yes," he says. "I suppose so. And I guess I *should* have improved since I've been at a larger church and preaching for a television audience."

"Ummm," she says noncommittally.

The preacher is silent again, turning inward to review his performance as he will do several times before sleep comes tonight.

He's surprisingly introverted for a man who's one of the denomination's most celebrated pulpiteers. The work of meeting people and trying to focus his interest on them is a constant strain. Sometimes if a meeting or a dinner party is long, he'll actually perspire with the continuous effort of socializing.

By contrast, he welcomes his time in the pulpit, where he is alone and in control. Standing in the circle of carved walnut, the great bible open before him and his head ten feet above the parishioners', he feels the comfort of isolation and mastery.

It is a hard-won mastery. He had first to conquer that innate shyness, although he never completely lost it. Then, over the years, he's had to acquire and polish his repertoire of gestures and mannerisms. But his principal asset has always been that marvelous voice, a tool almost without parallel among the preachers he knows. Even though he's never practiced the art of homiletics well enough to please the seminary faculty, no one could *ever* help remarking on the gorgeous, rich tone of his voice—or on its volume.

There is a Season

All taken together, his awkwardness with people, his very modest ability to fashion sermon outlines, and his gift of an operatic voice determined the way his preaching style developed.

Some time in the middle of his senior year in seminary, he became fully aware of both his peculiar gifts and the gaps in his abilities. He wondered what could he do to make the best of this odd package. He knew that he had a good memory. Experience had taught him that a simple, repetitive sermon with repeated references to the scripture text could be memorized. He also discovered that congregations were very impressed with ministers who could preach without notes. And finally, he learned that everyone attends to stories, especially sentimental ones, whether they relate to the subject at hand or not.

He knew that if he applied his skill at varying his voice tones and volumes to a memorized text, he could simulate the best qualities of a professional actor. He could become Charlton Heston reciting the book of Exodus for the cameras. He could become Ronald Reagan hitting his marks and addressing the nation like a benevolent grandfather who sometimes had to be stern with naughty liberals.

Especially for the larger audience that shies away from excessive thought content, he was spellbinding. Others in his congregations learned over time to seek out another place of worship or to attend Sunday school and skip the sermons. But the crowds of the spellbound were always much larger; and wherever he went, a certain percentage of the women in his congregations were secretly in love with him.

Once he reached the height of his development, he was tailor made for the large, wealthy congregation that now paid to televise his services.

And now he was trapped.

In terms of progress through the ecclesiastical ranks, he had succeeded beyond his wildest dreams. He and his family lived at a standard that would be hard to give up. The new luxury car each year, the house in the mountains, the private schools for his children, the complimentary club memberships—all these had become familiar and comfortable to him, like an old pair of shoes. But he was acutely aware that he had only the one trick. He lived in constant fear that someone would say, "Look, the emperor has no clothes!" and the whole structure would come tumbling down.

A part of his discomfort was the fact that he actually did so little. The church cheerfully hired staff to support him: there were three associates to visit and do pastoral care, an educator and her assistant to run the thriving Sunday school, and a business manager to take care of the expanding staff and buildings. At meetings of the official board, he had only to give the opening prayer and pass out the agenda. The twenty-four men and women on the board were the kind of people who ran corporations and medical practices and college faculties during the week. There was no challenge in the business of the board that was likely to tax their abilities. Except for weddings and funerals, his time was his own.

Not that he presumed. He was in his study by 9:30 sharp, five days each week. He provided nominal supervision to the staff. He had many hours to spend on constructing sermons, and he was allowed to work without any interruption short of a major death in the congregation.

All of this made a certain kind of sense. Upper-middle-class Christians do not want a minister who hovers, and certainly not one who challenges them with radical piety. A "powerful preacher" who leaves them alone is exactly what they ordered. What terrified him was that people seemed to believe that he was some kind of holy man.

It was the veneration from people who should have known better that he carried like a great weight between his shoulders.

There is a Season

As they pass the hotel desk, the clerk calls them by name. "Good evening, Dr. Clement, Mrs. Clement. Have a good crowd tonight?"

"Better than I deserve, I'm sure. But yes, it was a very nice crowd. Willow Oak is a lovely congregation," he answers.

"It must be!" the clerk says, thinking to himself that they pay a lovely price for that suite he's staying in. Then he adds, "Anything you need this evening?"

"No," the preacher says. "We're fine."

In the suite, he hangs up the gown and heads immediately for the shower. After the service, they stayed for a punch-and-cookies reception in the church fellowship hall. He is soaked with perspiration and bone tired. When he emerges from the bathroom, she is propped up in bed with her book. She slides from her side and goes to brush her teeth as he climbs wearily under the sheet. She lingers a little longer than necessary, hoping that he will start drowsing, but when she returns, he's waiting for her, and he reaches a hand around her waist before she's able to pick up her book again. She turns to him and gives him a peck on the forehead as he slides a hand under her gown.

"Ummm, nice," he says.

She pushes away a little, trying to look in his face. "You sure?" she asks with a smile. She keeps her voice cool and slightly humorous as if she were discussing options with one of their children. It is her signal for expressing permissiveness without enthusiasm. "You've got that men's breakfast early in the morning. Will you need to get up early to go over your presentation?"

"I've got that one by heart," he says. "I don't need to rehearse."

"And I think I've got this one by heart," she thinks. "Always wants it when he's tired." But she says, "I never could resist a romantic come-on." Once again, he misses the gentle irony in her voice.

The next morning he's gone before she climbs out of bed. She enjoys a longer-than-usual shower and indulges herself with a big breakfast in the hotel coffee shop. It's a rare pleasure for her to have a quiet morning without children or a husband to intrude on her thinking.

She's been doing a lot of thinking in the last six months. Both children are in high school and doing well. The son's not brilliant, but he's competent, and she's made sure he'll be well prepared for college. The daughter, eighteen months younger than her brother, is already a year ahead of him academically. She'll be able to do whatever she wants.

Child-rearing is the one area of her life with which she is generally satisfied. In the last several years, that satisfaction has taken on another significance. She very much wants the children to be solid enough to handle her leaving the marriage. She knows it will set them back. If nothing else, the outrage of their grandparents and the sympathy of her friends will be unnerving.

"But," she argues to herself, "neither one of them is stupid or fragile. They both sense by now that I'm reaching the end of my rope. Might've known it before I did! Still, I'm sorry for them."

"And him?" the quibbling voice inside of her asks. "You're not sorry for the man you promised to love, honor, and obey?"

She pauses with the coffee cup in both hands, pressing the warmth to her lips. "Yes, I am sorry for him. Have been for years. But it has nothing to do with being married to him. If I go, he'll be at loose ends for about six months, and then some cute, young divorcée will snap him up, and the church will give him a sympathy raise. I'm sorry for him, but I'm more sorry for myself having to live with him. If I don't get away soon, I'll turn into a nasty, neurotic bitch. Hell, I may already be one. It's bad enough getting old; I don't have to be the kind of old woman who makes everybody around me miserable.

"What makes me really sorry for myself is that I've almost lost any religious faith I had, and that's one of the reasons I married him! Now I'm not sure of anything. I may never be able to walk into a church building again."

She waits until the seat belt light goes out and the flight attendants begin taking drink orders, and then she says, "When school is out, I think I might take Gloria and visit with Mom awhile. We haven't had a good visit in a long time. You and Jake can batch it for a while. How does that sound?"

He raises one eyebrow to let her know he's surprised. "Sounds OK, I guess. How long would you stay?"

"Gloria has to be back for her summer job by June tenth. We'll get back before then. You all could handle it for a couple weeks without any trouble, couldn't you?"

Actually, she knows Jake will love having free days in the house alone. Since the preacher himself seldom comes home during the day, it will be a minor inconvenience for him.

"Well, we'll miss you guys, of course. But I think we can handle it. I sort of dread having people find out, though; the women will want to fuss over me."

"Let Betty run interference for you," she says, naming his long-time secretary. "She can figure out any supper schedule you want, and just tell the rest of them you're not available. That way you can pick and choose the ones you know you'll enjoy. Actually, she can do it better than I could. I'll stock the freezer for you guys, and Jake can certainly shop when he needs to."

When the coast is finally clear, the preacher's wife falls into her favorite chair in the den and dials Cynthia's number. She doesn't need to look it up; she has talked to her old college roommate at least once a week ever since they graduated.

"Cyn, it's me! How's tricks?"

"Marty! Where the hell have you been? You just get back?"

"Yeah, you never listen, or you'd remember that we had to stay over for the men's power breakfast this morning. I could have called, but I thought I'd wait to get comfortable."

"Men's power breakfast!" Cynthia snorts. "Now, ain't *that* a kick in the ass? So, how'd the tall-steeple preaching go?"

"'Bout the same, I guess. We had 'em rolling in the aisles. I will say this: they get their money's worth. They scheduled him about eight hours a day, and I had to be with him for four or five of those."

"Oh, the price of fame and adulation, Martha dear. Did you have to help him shovel the money into the bags too?"

"Give it a rest, Cynthia! I can be smartass by myself. Right now I need someone to speak softly and scratch behind my ears."

"I know, sweetie. I only rattle your chain because I love you. Seriously, what's going on right now?"

"From the outside, nothing at all. But that's what I need to talk about. I'm coming up to Mom's house in about a week. Can you get a day or two off, and we'll drink wine and talk? I need it bad."

"Your therapist awaits, Marty. I've been wanting to see you for months now. Just tell me when you're coming in."

The trip begins much as she expected it would. In spite of the fact that she and Gloria agreed the night before on a time to get away, Gloria is slow and whiney. When she finally starts moving, she can't find the clothes she wants to pack, most of which are in the dirty-clothes hamper. Marty can feel impatience rising in her almost like panic. When she hears her own voice, she's using her "fishwife tone."

"Gloria, for pity's sake, will you come *on*? You *promised* you'd be ready to go before nine. We'll hit the Atlanta traffic right at lunch hour if we don't leave in the next ten minutes."

"Give me a *break*, Mom!" The voice coming down the stairwell is as strident as her own. "This is supposed to be my vacation. We've got all day, haven't we?"

Marty is on the verge of an angry reply, but she checks herself. Her rush has nothing to do with Gloria. She has no business dumping the anxiety on her daughter. She trots up the stairs and stands in the door of Gloria's room.

"I'm sorry," she says. "You're right. We do have all day. Can I help with anything?"

"No! You can't! Just leave me alone for a few minutes." Then, as Marty turns, her daughter's voice softens. "Well, you can see if the stuff in the dryer is done."

"OK, I'll check."

Marty makes herself take deep breaths as she folds her daughter's clothes using the top of the dryer for a counter. She pads back up the stairs and puts the clothes on the unmade bed with Gloria's suitcase.

"I'm gonna grab some more coffee," she says. "I'll be on the front porch."

For the first hour of the drive, Gloria hugs her pillow and dozes, leaning against the door, her feet drawn up on the seat just touching Marty's hip. Then she sits up, yawns, and stretches, pulling the band off her blond ponytail and turning the rearview mirror to comb her hair.

"I'm hungry," she says. "Can we stop and get a biscuit?"

"Yeah," Marty replies. "I'm about ready for a break myself."

When they're back in the car, Gloria launches into a conversation about her favorite cousin, a girl one year older than she, the child of Marty's brother. Both of Marty's siblings, her brother and sister, live in the same neighborhood with their mother, the neighborhood in which they grew up. Spending time with the cousins is Gloria's main reason for wanting to visit with Gran.

Her mouth full of biscuit and orange juice, Gloria says, "Alice has been talking about her jock boyfriend again. I think she's trying to make me jealous. She wants me to date his friend so we can go out together."

"Well, I suppose it's just possible that Alice's boyfriend can be a football player and a nice person at the same time. Maybe his friend will be fun."

"Yeah, but I don't want to start dating somebody who lives four hours away. Even if I like him, it can't go anywhere."

"Does it have to *go* somewhere? Can't it be a date for the sake of double-dating with your cousin?"

"That's kind of an odd concept, Mom. Besides, what if I really like him a whole lot, and then we can't see each other? We'll write letters until we both get tired of it, and it'll be a royal pain trying to decide who'll call it off. It's like dating somebody at summer camp."

"I guess it could turn out that way," Marty says. "But I thought dating was for getting to experience other people. You know, different people. Can't you enjoy just dating without having to have a grand passion for him?"

"Spoken like a true parent, Mom. Did you really date people just to *experience* them, as you call it?"

"God, it's been so long I can't even remember, darling. I dated lots of people in college, but that's different, I guess."

Gloria stuffs the last of the biscuit into her mouth and chews thoughtfully for a while. When she gulps the orange juice and wipes the corner of her mouth with the heel of her hand, Marty barely resists saying something about manners. She senses that it's not the right time to sound like a "true parent" again.

Gloria says, "So after you dated all those different people, what made you decide on Dad?"

"What made me decide on your dad? Good question. Let me see. He was sweet and sorta innocent. He wasn't pushy the way some boys are. Of course, we met at the church fellowship on campus; we had *that* in common. He'd already decided to go to seminary, so when we began to get serious, I believe I thought I'd enjoy being a minister's wife. Is that enough?"

"Don't ask me! You're the one who decided. Or I guess you and Dad together decided. It's hard for me to even picture you with somebody else. I don't know why I asked."

"It's a reasonable question. You'll be making a decision a few years from now—
   that is, if you get married."

"*If* I decide to get married? You mean you think I might not get any offers?"

Marty smiles at the thought of her beautiful child not getting any offers. She reaches over to touch Gloria's hair. "Sweetie, you'll get *lots* of offer. As many as you want. I was just thinking that people your age have more choices than we did in my day. I don't know. Maybe you'll decide to be the president of General Motors and not even have a husband. Things are changing so fast that there may not *be* marriage by the time you finish school."

"Yeah, right! There'll *always* be marriage, Mom. If nothing else, we gotta do something with the kids. Besides, I'm taking that marriage and family life course in summer school. I can't waste a whole course."

"I'm glad you're taking the course, but that's probably not the best reason to get married."

They both giggle. Then Gloria sits up straight and holds up a finger. "Oh!" she says. "That reminds me. One of the units in the syllabus is something called 'recontracting,' and we're supposed to ask our parents if they'd do a marriage-satisfaction survey. You don't have to do it, but I'd get credit for the assignment."

"Recontracting?" Marty says. Her heart takes a strange leap.

"Yeah, you know. I think it's like labor unions asking for a new contract. You recontract every so often, and then it's a different marriage, or else it all goes to hell. Pardon my French."

"Your French is pardoned, but don't do that around Gran." Gloria makes a face that says, "Mother, I'm not *that* stupid!"

Marty goes on. "So what are we supposed to do with this survey thingy?"

"You're not *supposed* to do anything, but if you want to help your poor daughter's school career, you can volunteer to do the survey about 'factors that lead to satisfaction in marriage.' Since my parents have the perfect marriage, I assume you'll know all the right answers."

"Sweetie, I don't think anybody is quite perfect if they're honest."

"No? I'm curious. Everybody at church says you have the perfect marriage. What would you get low grades on? Or I guess I should ask, what would your marriage get low grades on? No wait—don't tell me! I know! Dad never goes to our after-school events. He always has night meetings and stuff. I've heard you fuss at him about it. Right?"

"That *might* be one of mine, but I'm sure your father would have some of his own. I'm just saying no relationship is perfect."

Gloria looks out the window, focusing on something in the countryside, and then she turns back to Marty. "Mom," she says. "Have you ever thought about divorce?"

Marty's heart does that alarming jump again, and she can feel her pulse beginning to pound. "Divorce? Why would you ask that? We've got you guys to look after. We both love you very much."

"Yeah, I *know* that, but people with children get divorced all the time. Half my friends' parents are divorced. I just wondered if it had ever occurred to *you*."

Marty takes a deep breath and tries to make her voice sound natural. "Everybody has bad times, but we've never talked about divorce."

"No, Mom, I didn't ask if you've ever *talked* about it with Dad. I asked if *you* have ever thought about it. I was just wondering why people stay married and what makes them start thinking about divorce."

For just an instant, Marty finds herself unable to focus her thoughts. Then, in a flash of panic she thinks, "The little stinker! She was leading me to that question!" She says, "I can't speak for people in general. It's complex. I think we get married because we're infatuated, and we have this idea that we'll live happily ever after. Then we make adjustments and face reality, and we decide to either stay married or to get divorced. It wouldn't be the same for any two couples."

"Well, I *know* that! But..."

"But have *I* ever thought about it?"

"Yeah. But you don't have to answer if you don't want to," Gloria adds quickly. "It's really none of my business."

"I think it's as much your business as anybody else's, and I'm really not stalling. But I need to know if there's any reason why you're asking now. Is it curiosity about the survey, or did it just occur to you in the conversation?"

Gloria squirms around in the seat belt and folds her left leg under her so that she's facing her mother. She reaches to put a hand on Marty's arm in a strangely adult-to-adult gesture. "Mom, I don't want to weird you out or anything, but there is something. Even Jake has noticed, and you know him; he doesn't see much of anything."

Marty's heart is thumping, and for a moment she's afraid she might be getting faint. She knew there would be a conversation like this at some point, but she was sure it would be later rather than sooner.

"It's not that you're doing anything so different," Gloria goes on. "It's just like you're not *with* us anymore. Dad comes home from a meeting at church, and you're in bed with the lights out at ten o'clock. Then he mopes around and asks us if you're OK. You sorta talk in monosyllables in that cheery voice like everything's A-OK, but half the time, you're somewhere else."

Gloria stops and lets her hand slide from her mother's arm. Suddenly she looks afraid.

"Oh, sweetie," Marty says. "I'm sorry I let it go until it made you uncomfortable. I should have sat down and talked to you, but I guess I wasn't sure myself. I didn't want to lay things on you before I talked to your Dad. I'm *still* not sure about anything."

She stops and reaches for the lukewarm coffee. At the same time, Gloria turns the radio volume down to zero, and suddenly the silence is very intense. Marty takes a deep breath and plunges ahead. "But since you were braver than I was about it, you deserve a straight answer. You'll have to promise to keep it between us for now. I need to talk to Jake and your dad myself. Can you promise?"

Gloria nods. Her eyes are beginning to become wet, and a strand of hair has fallen on the side of her face. Looking at her, Marty's heart suddenly aches, and the tears begin in her own eyes.

"It's nobody's fault," Marty says. "It's certainly not your dad's fault. But somehow we've just gone in different directions. Or maybe he's gone in the same direction, and I haven't been able to go with him. Whatever it is, I can't seem to stay focused on being married anymore. And it's driving me crazy—almost literally. Sometimes I think I'm losing my mind."

"Could it be the hormone stuff, Mom? You're the right age, aren't you?"

"I don't know, darling. I'm almost the right age, but it doesn't feel like hormones. It feels like...it doesn't feel like anything I've felt before, but it's been coming for a long time."

For a minute or two, they're both occupied with tissues and sniffles, and then Marty grins crookedly and says, "Guess I ruined your vacation, huh? Bad timing!"

"No, Mom. Not your fault. I've been trying to find a way to talk to you. In a way, it feels better. At least we're talking about it. It's not just sitting there, waiting to grab me."

Marty reaches for her daughter's hand and holds it hard. Gloria leans over and rests her forehead on their clasped hands, and for several miles, they are silent.

Then Gloria sits up and reaches for a dry tissue. "You're going to talk to Aunt Cynthia, aren't you?" It's more statement than question.

Marty nods. "Cyn is not exactly objective," she says. "But she is an outsider, and she's very bright. At least it's safe to talk to her, and she can help me look at alternatives. I really, *really* need that right now."

When they pull into Gran's driveway, Alice and Gran are rocking on the front porch. Alice comes down the front steps, and Gloria gets out to meet her. "Cud'n!" Alice shouts, opening her arms. Gloria replies, "Cud'n!" In the last year or so, this has become their own private version of a redneck greeting. Alice runs around the car to get a quick hug from Marty, and then the two girls disappear. As her mother reaches for a more sedate embrace, she examines Marty's face carefully.

"Hi, darling! Are you OK?"

"Fine!" Marty replies. "A little tired. You know how hard it is to get Gloria up and going. And I've got the usual allergies—nose and eyes running."

"Oh, sorry!" her mother says. "Alice wants to spend the night. I told her I'd check it out with you first."

"Well, we'll probably regret it, but I'd say yes. This is Gloria's private vacation, and her cousin is a big part of it. They're old enough to handle themselves."

"Good! They're both such beautiful children. I've gotten to where I enjoy having Alice around. I wouldn't mind if she stayed with me all the time."

"You get lonely, Mom?" Marty asks.

"Sometimes. But more often, I'm just bored. Having a child around keeps me in contact. It's funny. I used to think I was tired of cooking when you kids were still living here, but now I love fixing dinner for Alice."

Marty smiles. "I'll try to remember that the next time I'm in a grocery store swearing!" She gives her mother's hand a quick squeeze and kisses her on the temple.

Marty and Cynthia are wearing T-shirts and shorts. They sprawl in lawn chairs on Cynthia's little patio. The bricks of the patio are old and worn but somehow friendly. Among the shrubbery, a gardenia bush is just beginning to bloom, its scent flowing around them in the breeze. Marty turns her chair so that the afternoon sun is square on her back, wiggles her shoulders in the warmth, and then stretches her feet and hands in front of her. "Oh, God, Cyn, this feels sooo good! It feels like I've been swimming under water, and I can finally come up and breathe!"

Cynthia smiles and nods slowly. Then she takes a sip of wine and holds the glass up in a salute. "It's been a long time between drinks," she says.

When Marty finally breaks the silence again, her voice is low and somber. "Cyn, I'm gonna have to go. I wanted to wait until the kids were both away"—tears begin to roll down her face, and she pauses to wipe both cheeks—"but I just can't make it." She blows her nose on a napkin and picks up her wine glass again. "If I don't get out, I'm afraid I'll go bonkers and make a scene in church or something. On the way up here, I found out that Gloria and even Jake know something's wrong." She laughs and wipes her nose again. "She thought I was menopausal and crazed by hormones!"

"Smart girl!" Cynthia says. "It was a good guess."

"She is smart. You can't really hide anything from the people you live with. I just didn't have the guts to talk about it. Gloria says that even Ray knows something is wrong. He's asked the kids about it."

"Then you've *gotta* do something," Cynthia says. "The longer you wait, the more they'll make up their own stories about it. The truth is gonna be awful enough for them, but the made-up stuff will scare the shit out of 'em!"

"I know. I finally had to spill it to Gloria. She's taking a marriage course in summer school, and she used that to get *me* to talk!

Can you imagine her figuring out how to get her dysfunctional mother to deal with something?"

"Yes, I can. And give yourself a pat on the back. She learned that somewhere. It sure as hell wasn't from the preacher man."

"I guess. Sometimes I worry that I've made her *too* much like me. When we fight I hear my own words coming out of her mouth. I'm afraid that when it sinks in, she'll hate me." Marty is crying again. "Oh, Cyn, if Gloria and Jake leave me, I won't be able to stand it! I think I'd kill myself."

"Give them some credit, Marty. Don't you think they love you as much as you love them? You'd give *them* the benefit of the doubt no matter what they did. And they know it."

Marty is shaking with sobs, and her speech is coming in gasps. "But they're teenagers, Cyn! Their life is horrible enough without my...my fouling it up!"

"You were a teenager too, but you got over it. Are you saying they can't cope as well as you did? Do you think it would make it easier if you gritted your teeth and tried to be a good wifey? If they've *already* seen you getting crazy, think what you'd be like in another year!"

They are quiet, and Marty's sobbing gradually gets softer. She heaves a sigh and rolls her eyes upward. "I don't know," she says. "It's just that there's no good way out. It's like choosing whether you'd rather be shot or hanged. I just wish I could be different."

Cynthia nods. "There *is* no good way out. But there's a bad way and a *less* bad way. You do have that much choice."

It happens in the year AD 20—"twenty years after the divorce" in Marty and Cynthia's code. Retirement from the school system is still five years away for Marty. But Marty likes her job—always has. And the schools like her. The first two years were rough for her: she moved, went back to school for her certificate, found a job, and got the kids launched—and any one of those tasks alone would have stretched her.

The next years got better as the situation became "normalized," and her relationships with everybody gradually settled. As she suspected would be the case, her mother had the hardest time with the whole thing and would repeat endlessly her complaint of, "But you had everything! Why couldn't you have worked it out?"

To Marty's vast relief, the children went on being themselves, and she feels today closer to them than ever. To no one's surprise, they also cared tenderly for each other and for their father.

Ray, on the other hand, did not bounce back as she was sure he would. Within five years of their divorce, he left his dream church to work for a much smaller congregation. And it was not until he moved again to his "twilight-years" church that he was found by a widow his own age who cheerfully undertook his care and feeding. That had weighed on Marty. In her moments of self-blame, she worried that he would die alone and she would take an extra load of guilt to her own grave. It pleases her that he seems to be well matched, and she has told him so.

Cynthia, her lifeline through it all, gently coached her when the time came to move back into the "dating game." (How she hated that term!) And now, she's finally settled with a partner, a fellow teacher who has no more an idea of remarriage than she does. Marty is beginning to feel the stability and contentment she has worked for.

The year is AD 20, and the occasion is a parent conference. This meeting is not with a young mother but with a grandmother almost her own age who's parenting a fourth-grade grandson. The child is struggling, as both she and the grandmother know, but Marty feels instinctively that he will make it. She told the grandmother this, and she also felt it was essential to say how much the woman had meant for her grandson's progress.

Now, as the conference winds down, both women are feeling the bond of a common purpose. In the afternoon's warmth in the classroom, in the glow of a newfound kinship, the grandmother takes a risk.

"Clement is an unusual name," she says. "I wonder if by any chance you're related to the minister, Dr. Raymond Clement?"

Marty considers briefly whether she should take the easy way out and simply say "no." But she answers, "Actually, I'm his ex-wife. We have grandchildren about the age of yours."

"Yes," she says. "I've followed his career, so I knew he'd been married and divorced. Would you like to know why I've kept track of him?"

"If you'd like to tell me," Marty says.

"The fact is, I think he saved my life. Is that melodramatic or what?" She grins shyly. "Oh, I guess you never know what *might* have happened, but I felt at the time that he did. He came to preach at our church in Iowa for one of those 'spiritual-enrichment weekends.' I'm sure he did it all the time in those days, so you'd have no way of remembering it." Marty nods and smiles.

"Anyway," the grandmother goes on, "I was a mess right then. My husband had just left me with two children. My self-esteem was in the toilet, and I was broke. I was thinking real seriously about dropping the kids at my mother's house and killing myself. Had exactly how I'd do it all figured out.

"I'm sure a part of it was a desire for revenge on him. But whatever it was, I was making plans.

"Then, on an impulse, I went to a Sunday-evening service, and your husband—your ex-husband—was preaching. It's amazing after all these years, but I remember the exact story that grabbed me. He told a story about a little boy he'd seen in Puerto Rico. A child in such a horrible fix that I couldn't help comparing his situation to my own kids'. And I said to myself, 'Well damn, Myra, you're in a hell of a mess, but compared to that kid, your children are living in the lap of luxury. If there really are people like that, and *they* can be grateful for life, I don't guess you've got any business throwing it away.'

"And I went home that night and hugged my children for a long time, and I started to climb out of the hole."

"Isn't it strange how some little thing like that...or I guess it's not so little, considering...But isn't it strange how something can have that kind of effect?"

Marty smiles. "It is strange," she says. "And, I guess, kind of wonderful." They are both quiet for a moment, and Marty watches the dust motes in the shaft of the late-afternoon sun. Then she goes on. "It occurs to me that you could almost say the purpose of Ray's being there was to speak to you—and maybe to nobody else *but* you. And maybe the purpose of *your* being there was to stay alive until today, taking care of your grandson. Does that seem too farfetched to you?"

"Well, I suppose it would be farfetched," Myra says, "if it weren't for the fact that I *am* here taking care of him." Then, as an afterthought she adds, "And, of course, you're here taking care of him too."

YOU ARE THE MAN
—2 SAMUEL 12:7

The general browsed through the set of orders Sergeant Heatherly had just deposited on his desk: "Pursuant to… Captain Uri Radomsky is hereby ordered to report to…during which time Captain Radomsky will be temporarily assigned to… temporary additional duty…Signed Brigadier General David L. Ray." Across the top of each page, the word "SECRET" was stamped in red ink. Every letter was perfect. He scrawled his signature and dropped the papers in his confidential out-box.

"So, Heatherly," the general said. "Yes or no. Is Radomsky a Russki spy?"

"Negative, General! Second-generation Russian immigrants are more loyal and patriotic than we are."

"Maybe more than you, Heatherly, but not more than me. I've always had my doubts about you anyway."

"You know best, General; but I'm even more patriotic than second-generation Russians. And they usually make really fine soldiers."

"Probably right, Sergeant. Probably right. Now get back to work."

"Sir."

"Well, as we say around here," the general thought, "'Heatherly don't make mistakes.' Just my luck to get a four-eyed secretary, and one probably light in the combat boots, but I gotta admit he's efficient as hell. On the other hand, I can't complain. I *better not* complain. 'Cause God knows, I have had it another way!"

General David L. Ray leaned far back in his chair, his hands locked behind his head, and spent some minutes enjoying a warm series of memories from his younger days as a senior officer. "The best?" he asked himself. "Hard to name just one. But Jonesy undoubtedly had the best boobs in the army, *and* she wasn't a bad secretary. Can't beat that combination! Most importantly, she didn't raise hell when I copped the odd feel. I should have outgrown all that by now. If she—if she *and* several others, come to think of it—had chosen to be complaining bitches, I probably wouldn't have gotten the star. Hell, I might not have even kept the uniform! Hard to believe it's gone that far."

It was not a new reverie for the general. It was fairly common, two or three drinks into happy hour at the officers' club, for him to return to these familiar grounds with his friends.

"Hell," somebody might start. "It's not enough we took risks we didn't have to take. Some good friends got their asses shot off."

"Then, when we weren't getting ourselves shot at, we slaved in some godforsaken post in friggin' Mudville."

"Yeah, without our families."

"Without our families, living in some splinter village of a BOQ with the roaches fighting the friggin' rats!"

"And then you finally get home, and some little twat seduces you, and they wanna take *your* commission!"

"Commission? Hell, today they'd put your ass in the stockade."

"Well, gentlemen. Face it. We're supposed to man up when it's combat time and then turn into pussies when we finally get back home."

Still, in spite of the tired, old refrain, the officers at the senior end of the bar seldom got into trouble anymore. Either they had become more skilled at playing the odds—at choosing women in the lower ranks who were likely to be willing to allow "favors" for the sake of advancement or for some other enticement (usually tragically misplaced romanticism)—or the senior officers had finally gotten old enough to go straight. Sometimes, they'd been scared straight by their wives!

Surely, General Ray, who'd been married thirty-two years to his lovely wife, Deidre, knew all that as well as anyone. So why had he just signed a set of orders sending his neighbor in the married officers' housing neighborhood to temporary duty with a special-forces detachment in the horn of Africa?

In a way, General Ray's lovely wife, Deidre, was herself indirectly to blame. Faced with the perennial question of what to get a general for Christmas, Deidre had resorted to research. First she'd gone through the magazines in the rack that sat beside her husband's recliner. Aside from sports and gun magazines, the predominant theme that emerged was power tools. To her surprise, she realized there were whole catalogs featuring nothing but power tools of every conceivable shape, size, purpose, and power configuration. Next she launched a subtle fact-finding campaign involving random questions during relaxed weekend breakfasts and suppers that followed a particularly happy happy hour. Finally, she even enlisted the help of their youngest daughter (Ray's favorite) in pumping the general for information. Would he really be likely to enjoy his own workshop featuring an assortment of tools arrayed on a state-of-the-art workbench?

As usual, Deidre was right on target. But she was not about to stop with the job half-done. On a Monday morning when the general was hard at work, she dropped by the office of the base facilities officer. She wondered if a facilities crew could possibly arrange to install a workbench and tools along the back wall of the general's capacious garage if she, the general's wife, paid for all the equipment and supplies. And oh, by the way, she would say, might facilities have a carpenter who could cut a good-sized window over the bench and hang a work light as well?

And wouldn't you know it, the facilities officer was only too happy to accommodate her in every particular, and he even added some fancy fill-ups that only he could have imagined, such as insulation and a baseboard heater.

So it happened that the general's daughter no longer had garage space for her car (what a betrayal!); and the general began spending free time in a luxurious shop complete with comfortable chairs and an excellent television—and a window.

It was there on a winter evening, while the general was using his power grinder with a soft copper–wire brush to remove some rust spots from an old favorite shotgun, that he happened to look up and see the bedroom light come on next door. And he discovered in that instant that Mrs. Betty Radomsky was a full-blown exhibitionist. And stunningly attractive! Yes, the same Mrs. Radomsky who was married at the time to Captain Uri Radomsky of the Army Special Forces. Furthermore, on subsequent evenings (and afternoons and mornings), he realized that Mrs. Radomsky, from her screened porch, could see him whenever he walked from his own back porch into his new shop, but she could not be observed from any window except the shop window; he realized that this information clearly guided her behavior.

Now if you are a reader of liberal sentiments and are willing to leave questions of good taste and freedom to mature adults, it would seem that this situation might be viewed as technically ideal. We have two persons, one a fifty-something man of the world, still virile and healthy, and the other a twenty-three-year old attractive nymphet fully aware of her physical charms and anxious to share them with the wider world. These are two chronological adults, both of whom are willing and capable of bringing pleasure to each other with no apparent harm to the wider world.

And, fortuitously, the general had the power to remove the only immediate impediment to sharing that pleasure to their heart's content.

On the other hand, being not only liberal but also intelligent, you can see immediately that no Eden is without its serpent: in this case, they were dealing with the serpent who whispers into two sets of ears almost simultaneously, "This is wonderful, but could we not make it still better?" And what child of original sin has ever been able to resist the urge to take the merely wonderful and gamble on making it still better? In any event, resisting urges was, at that point, far from the top of David and Betty's hierarchy of values.

Meanwhile, life among the other denizens of Fort Wiley continued more or less as it always does. Officers and their families came and went in accordance with the needs of the service. An important engine of support and good order for the married officers' spouses continued to be the organization and management of the post officers' wives club.

In theory, this "club" was a voluntary association. In reality, all officers who hoped for a relatively smooth tour of duty (never mind advancement and a chance for a regular army appointment!) knew that there was nothing voluntary about it. When the chairwoman called a meeting, any wife not in active labor or otherwise unavailable showed up at the meeting properly arrayed. At this time in history, that chairwoman was Mrs. Colonel Nat Henderson, first name Jane.

Colonel Henderson was the base executive officer, a hard-bitten, old cavalry officer who had repeatedly earned rank in combat. The book on him was that he probably would never be promoted to general; he was somewhat lacking in couth, and he was the first to acknowledge as much. What he wanted out of life was an honorable, unblemished thirty years and a good retirement. Being so minded, he had a very low tolerance for any hint of loose discipline. In fact, General Ray was himself a little intimidated by the old man; but in his role as base commander, David thoroughly enjoyed having somebody who could knock heads when knocking was called for.

And Nat Henderson was so adept at dropping the hammer that he almost never had to do it.

Mrs. Nat Henderson, Jane, had pretty much the same calming effect on the officers' wives she shepherded. Her graying head of red hair benefited from regular chemical enhancement, which gave her the nickname, among the other wives, of "Big Red." She, of course, knew that, even though no one would have dared to utter the words in her presence.

Even so, Big Red had seen enough of the tragic side of army life to be a genuine mother figure to the younger women, and especially to those going through a hard time. Long tours in combat zones meant lonely, anxious times for wives of any age, but especially for younger women with small children; Big Red went out of her way to be kind and nurturing to them. When the worst happened, it was Big Red who was there to hold and comfort the survivors. They knew they could seek her out.

She also knew from experience how damaging to morale a wayward wife could be. She was not above explaining this damage in detail, in public, when the occasion arose.

Since the Colonel and Jane Henderson lived just around the corner in married officers' housing, the general and Betty Radomsky were, from the very first, careful to cover their tracks—tracks that often led through the Radomskys' backyard and onto her screened porch. Also from the very first, they both confessed to being genuinely pleased that their exertions seemed to have resulted in a surprising level of vigor and competence on the general's part. As if they needed any more encouragement!

At the time of the general's first cross border incursion, Mrs. Radomsky's husband was barely into his second week of deployment. His letters were to arrive at infrequent intervals since he and his detachment were a very long way from any army post office—and a long way from *any* sign of civilized society! They were also involved in work that required the utmost attention to their surroundings, which were almost as hostile as the people who lived there. Indeed, waking up alive and with all their body parts intact every morning was by no means to be taken for granted. And, like all true special-ops soldiers, they loved it.

In a different story, the mention of "his second week" might have been simply a passing detail. Unfortunately for Betty and David, it would turn out to be distressingly relevant—and sooner rather than later.

No one was surprised when Big Red showed up at Betty's door one Wednesday afternoon. She often made informal calls to express support for women whose husbands were then actively in harm's way and to be sure the young wives planned to show up at the wives' club social on Thursday afternoon. Betty, who was no fool, took her meaning. In fact, the lecture before the refreshments was aimed at sharpening life skills specifically for the army wives in their role as primary support for the nation's guardians of peace and security.

Betty also had occasion to comment on that same lecture to the base commander himself later in the evening while he was busily engaged in trying to bring his pulse and respiration back down to somewhere near normal. Betty's impression of the lecture was that it seemed a bit biased toward pampering soldiers, as if they were more important than normal people. And the general, then leaning on an elbow to better observe her exquisite facial features, was inclined to agree with her views.

"Uh," he grunted. And then he said, "The top brass wants us to keep you girls on your toes. Help maintain the officers' peace and contentment."

"So," she answered. "How'm I doing?"

Nat was just slipping into the comfortable zone between giving minimal attention to the tube and actually allowing himself to nap. Peaches, the miniature poodle, was nestled under his left arm, already asleep. He was aware of Jane, who was seated on the sofa at the edge of his peripheral vision to his left. Although a stranger would not have seen or heard anything at all from her direction, Nat could intuit that she was not settled.

"All right, Momma," he said. "Spit it out."

"Spit what out? I didn't say anything."

"But you wanted to. So let's hear it."

"Well it's work related, so I didn't want to bother you."

"Your not wanting to bother me bothers me."

"Oh, it's not all that important, but I was just thinking about poor Betty Radomsky."

"And what's so poor about her?"

"It's nothing I can put my finger on, but I'm worried. I ran into her outside the GYN clinic yesterday, and we talked for a minute. I just—I don't know. I just got the impression that she was worried. You know, about her husband and all."

"And you were never worried when *I* was in the field?"

"Oh, of course I was, Nat. But she's so young, and those special-op boys get into all kinds of dangerous stuff."

"Hopefully it's dangerous to the bad guys. That's what we pay 'em for."

"Anyway, I just got to wondering; so when I got home, I called Sylvia Crawford—she's Betty's best friend…"

"Jane, I think you're about to tell me more than I want to know. But anyway, who's Sylvia Crawford?"

"You know. She's that warrant officer's wife. The pilot."

"Oh, Crawford. Yeah, I know who he is. Artillery spotter. Getting close to retirement. Like me."

"Yes, well Sylvia is sort of Betty's adopted mother on post. Keeps an eye on her, and they—you know—gossip. Not that it's any of my business, but she says that Betty had to change her birth control—give up the IUD."

"Now I *really* don't want to know, but you're gonna tell me, so why did she have to change, and why in God's name does it matter? Radomsky is in East Africa. Although you didn't hear that from me."

"She had to change because those things have all kinds of hormones in them, and they screw up your cycle and do bad stuff. And it matters because they were ready to start a family."

"Yeah. And I should be concerned with this because…"

"Because it's important to them. And that started me thinking about when he's going to be back in country."

"When did he deploy?"

"Two months yesterday."

Nat slowly shook his head, contemplating the startling precision of his wife's database.

"Two months yesterday," he echoed. "And those special-forces deployments are normally six months in the field and then a month at home. If he's any good at all, she should be knocked up in about five months at the latest."

"Don't be crude, Nat. You know as well as I do that family matters are the most important factor in retention."

"He'll have to make regular army before he thinks about being retained."

"I know that."

Following this exchange were a few moments of quiet. Nat turned back to the screen and transferred Peaches to his other side. She lifted her little head for his caress and then snuggled back down and went back to sleep.

"I was just wondering," Jane continued, "why David chose Captain Radomsky for this assignment in the first place. That master sergeant in his division has twenty-something years and has undoubtedly forgotten more than Captain Radomsky knows."

"Probably Captain Radomsky has some specific skill. Knows how to make bombs out of peanut butter cups and C-4 or some such stuff. And, as you well know, in this army, you make rank by being in dangerous places."

"But he just made captain. He won't be up for promotion for years."

"No time like the present."

"Uh-huh. I guess you're right. But I was just curious."

"Momma, you're always curious. But worrying about promotions is way beyond your pay grade. You probably need to let it go."

That was as directive as Nat ever got, or needed to get, with his wife, so it ended the conversation for the time being. But both of them knew that whatever bee was in Big Red's bonnet would eventually find its way out.

The novelty of enjoying his very own nymphomaniac was not about to grow old for him, but David did fall into a comfortable routine. His youngest daughter was back at the university, and Deidre was often busy in other places during the late afternoon when he got home from the office. He and Betty never used the telephone or e-mail, not only because there were inherent dangers, but also because they simply didn't need them. If the light was on in his shop and the blinds were raised, Betty could see it. And if the light was on in Betty's bedroom, he could see it—as well as a good deal of Betty. It was simply a matter of stepping over the fence and strolling across her back lawn. Deidre did not often disturb the sanctuary of David's shop, preferring instead to call him on his cell when supper was ready. Besides, the fact that there was a certain tang of danger in their routine gave David's activities an extra touch of excitement—something like the danger of combat situations, as he told Betty. Naturally, they both assumed from the beginning that contraception was the woman's business. He did remember mentioning the issue the first time they'd been together, but she'd reassured him that "all that" was covered, and the topic never came up again.

Now Betty, despite her predilection for poor impulse control, was not a heartless person. Far from it. She was genuinely worried about Uri's safety, so she was not playacting when she spoke about her anxiety at the officers' wives club meetings. The older wives were realistic in their responses, and none of them tried to minimize her fear or to persuade her that combat was a piece of cake. Deployment to danger zones, they assured her, is just something unique to service marriage that a wife (or occasionally a husband) has to put up with. Since there's nothing else the mate at home can do, they said, she should simply hold her breath and try to stay busy until it's over.

In fact, the concept of staying busy—along with her quiet pride about attracting the most powerful alpha male in the vicinity—was indeed a distraction for Betty. She came to think of their pleasant times together as "staying occupied" in her own not totally unique way. It was almost as if she were doing an ongoing good deed by entertaining this busy executive and using her God-given talents to relieve some of his tensions and work-related stress. It certainly seemed to bolster his masculinity even as it massaged her own self-image and spoke to her concerns about the fleeting years of her maximum-attraction power. Nothing, as they say, is ever totally wasted.

Nor was Uri Radomsky's deployment wasted. No one can be described as a "natural" in the highly specialized work of special operations. It has to be learned one day at a time, but there are qualities that make the process more likely to be successful. Uri was intelligent and attentive. He was willing to take risks but not foolhardy. He was a fast learner because, like all the good ones do, he understood at a deep level that fast learning was the way to stay alive. And a soldier is only useful while alive.

By his third month in the field, Uri had begun to pick up one or two of the local languages, which meant that he could also pick up information by listening to the local people who assumed that, like most Americans, he didn't know what they were saying. As strange as it seemed to him, it was that eagerness to learn that almost killed him. In the fifth month of his deployment, he was on a mission with several of his native "partners," gathering intelligence about a local warlord. The partners invited Uri to join them in a teahouse, where he encountered one of the dangers that he'd had no way of anticipating. One partner had decided that the warlord was more dangerous to his family than to the Americans and had been turned. The teahouse meeting was an ambush, and the jihadis burst through the back door with AK-47s blazing. Uri was hit twice before he could draw his pistol. He fell, dragging a table over on top of himself, and in a remarkable example of coolness under fire, he made the decision not to attempt to get up. While the others fought for their lives, the guilty partner ran out the front door and beat it back to the American headquarters to report Uri's death.

The soldiers responding in force found Uri in a corner, bleeding but still alive. After they had applied emergency first aid and had gotten him safely into the Humvee, the teahouse was blown to bits, and all the storefronts in the village were machine-gunned. Of course, by that time all the birds had flown.

Uri momentarily woke up lying on a stretcher inside the helicopter. He awoke again on the navy hospital ship after his first emergency surgery. At the time of his second surgery, which was in Landstuhl, his home base in the United States was informed of his injuries. And Betty was flown in to meet him when he arrived at Walter Reed.

There was good news and bad news. The bullet that had shattered the platform of his right tibia had also destroyed too much tissue and too many blood vessels and nerves, and there had been too much time between the teahouse and the hospital ship. His right leg had to be amputated above the knee. The second bullet, the one that had gone through his left shoulder, had made a cleaner wound on the way in and out. There would be many weeks of therapy, but his shoulder would ultimately be functional. Being taught to use the replacement leg was another story that included several more surgeries and called into question Uri's future as a career soldier, although it did not absolutely rule it out.

Curiously, the confusion about Betty's pregnancy did not immediately register with Uri. By the time he was finally back in their house on base, it was becoming obvious that Betty was pregnant. When she told him, he seemed to be dumbfounded at first, and then he responded with a puzzled grin.

"Great news, honey! It's what we've been wanting."

"Yes," she said, dumbfounded in her turn. "Yes, it is what we've wanted."

"Well!" he said. "Well, how are you? I mean, how is the baby? Are we all OK?"

"Oh, you know me!" Betty said. "I'm always healthy as a horse. And the baby is fine too. Already kicking me. Wanna feel it?"

He nodded. "Do we know if it's a boy or a girl?"

"A girl," she said in an agony of suspense. When would the explosion of anger and accusation come?

The stranger-than-fiction answer is that the explosion would *never* come—at least not in the way that Betty had been dreading it would. Over a number of months—and finally years—Betty became convinced that Uri had simply lost a number of months. Not only did he never figure out the miracle of his fatherless baby, but he also never figured out a number of other things that had gone on. His several weeks in Landstuhl had simply been wiped out completely, even though he did have fragmentary memories of the hospital ship. In the same way, he would never have any memory at all of the day of his wounding, even though he recalled writing and receiving letters in the months beforehand.

As Betty reconstructed events, Uri—against his own mental convictions—was *forced* by written accounts, the witnesses of those around him, and the Silver Star presentation speech to accept the periods of time that had been wiped clean from his memory. Neither wishing to completely acknowledge that fact nor able to deny it in public (although he continued to doubt it internally), Uri simply resolved not to fight it. Betty had revealed a pregnancy whose origins he could not recall, but he refused to admit to himself or to anyone else (and especially not to Betty—*never* to Betty!) that everything was not normal as Betty clearly appeared to believe it was. He had read and heard enough about posttraumatic stress syndrome and memory loss that he had to believe also. Anyway, it would have been unthinkable to question the woman he so adored and who so loved him.

As it turned out, Betty's deep sorrow was compounded by severe preeclampsia. The tiny premie struggled in neonatal intensive care like a champion, but in the end she lost. And Betty and Uri were joined in their grief by a fierce bond that would never be lost or forgotten. As one might have expected, it was Big Red who was there to hold Betty in her arms and weep with her through those first sleepless hours.

The Radomskys would eventually go on to successfully parent four of their own strong, healthy offspring. Curiously, she never suffered from preeclampsia again.

Uri ultimately did elect to stay in the army. You may have read about his being the first officer with an artificial leg to return to (parachute) jump school in Columbus, Georgia, and to become the first full-time instructor in special operations. And it was Betty who pinned on all his new rank insignias and ribbons. Like her model, Big Red, Betty aged into the model officer's wife. The two women continue to be in touch.

As for the explosion that had so terrified Betty early on, it did finally occur; but it was one of those muffled explosions so far back under the hill that almost nobody hears it and only a few people nearby see the land shift because of it.

When Uri Radomsky returned at last from the series of hospitals, Big Red seized on the opportunity to encourage the officers' club manager to plan a celebration in honor of Uri. All his honors had been presented in Maryland when he had still been an outpatient receiving physical therapy, so almost no one on the base had been able to shake his hand.

The occasion was a huge barbecue on the patio of the Fort Wiley Officers' club, and in attendance were all the post officers and wives, plus the enlisted men from Uri's former division. To say that alcohol flowed like water there would be a shameless understatement. The food and drinks, the band and the dancing on the patio, and the speeches and toasts all stretched into the early morning. Uri showed off his new carbon-fiber leg; Betty was radiant. She left his side only to observe the most necessary of social graces.

As things were winding down, David, Deidre, Nat, and Jane were all sitting together, watching the young folks and appearing very mellow. Anticipating the drive back to the quarters, the girls visited the rest room together, leaving the two men by themselves. The general and his executive ordered a final round of expensive brandy to cap the evening.

Nat began the conversation. "Well, here's to you, David. You pulled it off!"

"I'd say *we* pulled it off. Mostly our wives and the club manager."

Nat raised his glass. "That's for sure. If they depended on two old farts like us, it'd be a sorry party. But that's not exactly what I was talking about."

"No? What, then?"

"I think you know what I'm talking about, but I want to spell it out so there's no confusion."

David put his drink down and leaned forward, beginning to feel a distinct sense of foreboding. "Yeah? What confusion would that be?"

"Well, let me suggest it, and we'll see if we're on the same frequency. What was that stuff that caused Mrs. Radomsky to lose the baby? Preglempson or something?"

"Nat, you're asking the wrong person about that." He affected a raspy soprano voice and said, "Land's sake, Miss Scarlett. I don't know nothing 'bout birthing no babies." He grinned a slightly tipsy grin.

"No, me neither. But Jane called my attention to this one. Betty Radomsky is one of her favorites in the wives' club, and Jane took it hard."

"Yeah? Too bad."

"It was too bad; but they're young. They'll have another chance. Anyway, I was wondering if you knew that when there's an abnormal birth like that, they save tissue samples."

"Oh, really? Glad to learn something. Why would they do that?"

"Well, the cause of a premature birth—whatever it's called—can be genetic or God knows what else. So they save cord blood and tissue for several years in case they need it for research."

David cleared his throat and looked around to see where their wives might have been. "So is there a reason we got on this particular subject?"

"You bet there is. It's interesting because those DNA samples can also be used to determine who the father is—or at least who he's not. And if the judge advocate general guys got wind of that and started poking around the neighborhood, it could be a bad day for the real father."

"What the hell are you talking about? Obviously her husband is the father."

"Nope. As you and I both know, the months don't add up right. Radomsky doesn't realize it—thank God!—but that baby was conceived two, or maybe three, months before our captain came home. And if you remember, he came home in no shape to help his lovely wife with conceiving for another six months or so. The doctors know this, and Betty knows it. My interest is in making damn sure Uri Radomsky never finds out."

"How the hell would he find out?"

"Well, in case you hadn't noticed, Betty is drop-dead gorgeous, and there are men who might want to brag about a thing like that. Might want to—*carelessly*, mind you—

make themselves look like a real stud by bragging."

"Well I'd hope the hell not! What kind of SOB would do a thing like that?"

"Who indeed? But if that *were* to happen, I might be tempted to drop a hint to the JAG folks."

"Now wait a damn minute, here," the general said as he stood up none too steadily. "Are you threatening me, Colonel?"

Nat sipped his drink and leaned back in his chair. "Not unless you're open to threats, General. I just remarked that if it *should* happen, I'd know where to find the man, and I'd make sure he never got another promotion ever. That is, *if* he even managed to keep his commission, which I suspect he wouldn't."

The shade of red on David's face had been steadily deepening. Then he spread his feet to steady himself and drained the last of the brandy. His glass still in his hand, he thrust a forefinger in Nat's face. "Now you listen here—" he began, but by then his breath was whistling hard in his nostrils, and he seemed unable to find the rest of the words.

Nat uncrossed his legs, sat up straight, and raised his voice to be sure he was heard over the music. "You probably need to sit down, David, and relax a little. It's not worth having a heart attack over. You know I never make threats, idle or otherwise. I do, from time to time, make a prediction. To the best of my ability." He then looked over his shoulder. "Oh, look! Here come our girls."

Made in the USA
San Bernardino, CA
05 June 2016